To Stacy McNeely, with thanks

G. P. Putnam's Sons
An imprint of Penguin Random House LLC, New York

First published in the United States of America by G. P. Putnam's Sons,
an imprint of Penguin Random House LLC, 2022

Visit us online at penguinrandomhouse.com

Library of Congress Cataloging-in-Publication Data
Names: McMann, Lisa, author. | Title: Map of flames / Lisa McMann.
Description: New York: G. P. Putnam's Sons, [2022] | Series: The forgotten five; 1 | Summary: Five
children who are the offspring of supernatural criminals and who have special abilities of their
own leave their isolated tropical home and head to the city of Estero, where they hope to find their
parents and the treasure they hid years ago.
Identifiers: LCCN 2021036565 (print) | LCCN 2021036566 (ebook) |
ISBN 9780593325407 (hardcover) | ISBN 9780593325414 (epub) | Subjects: CYAC:
Supernatural—Fiction. | Ability—Fiction. | Parents—Fiction. | Buried treasure—Fiction. |
LCGFT: Novels. | Classification: LCC PZ7.M478757 Map 2022 (print) |
LCC PZ7.M478757 (ebook) | DDC [Fic]—dc23
LC record available at https://lccn.loc.gov/2021036565
LC ebook record available at https://lccn.loc.gov/2021036566

Printed in the United States of America

ISBN 9780593325407 (hardcover)
3rd Printing

ISBN 9780593463109 (international edition)

Design by Eileen Savage | Text set in Arno Pro

MAP of FLAMES

LISA McMANN

G. P. PUTNAM'S SONS

under Joseph II. Holy Roman Emperor and enlightened despot at the same time, he set out to strengthen and expand his rights as Imperial Sovereign with the youthful eagerness that characterized him, and with the easy confidence of a true son of the Enlightenment. In this quest he used time-honored means of imperial dynastic politics, as well as modern concepts of sovereignty, which he applied to the antiquated constitutional customs of the Holy Roman Empire. Important ecclesiastical principalities in the Empire were given to Austrian princes, while in Austria numerous convents were suppressed or secularized; diocesan unions were dissolved and reconstructed according to political convenience, without regard for Papal rights; and the sovereign powers of the state were ruthlessly exploited and expanded in dealings with the Church. The severe quarrel which presently broke out between the emperor and the Princes' Estate of the Imperial Diet brought the Ambassadorial Assembly at Regensburg to a halt, and markedly increased the emperor's influence on the imperial tribunals.

The greatest agitation, however, was caused by Joseph's plans to expand the power of the House of Habsburg–Lorraine in Germany by acquiring large parts of the adjacent state of Bavaria. When the main Bavarian line of the Wittelsbachs became extinct, Joseph occupied Bavaria—by virtue of a settlement of succession which in January 1778 his diplomats had secretly concluded with the childless heir, Charles Theodore, Elector Palatine. Should this venture succeed, it would more or less compensate for the loss of Silesia; the German character of the Danube monarchy would be substantially reinforced, and with it, Austria's interest in German affairs; while the dangerously growing dynastic power of the Bavarian and Palatine Wittelsbachs would again be dismembered, placing southern Germany completely in the Habsburg sphere.

Were the new north German power, Prussia, to permit this, she faced the choice of either continuing the existing rivalry with Austria, in which case a renewed struggle for the possession of Silesia would be fought under far less favorable conditions; or, of reaching an understanding with Vienna over a division of power in Germany. The Prussian statesmen of the next generation chose the second of these alternatives; soon after Frederick's death, Prussia sought an accord with Austria. The outcome was the great up-

heaval of 1803: wholesale secularization of ecclesiastical principalities, mostly for the benefit of the two major German powers; and
sizable territorial exchanges to round off their lands and give them
better cohesion. To be sure, such an upheaval required the most
powerful of external shocks: the convulsions of the revolutionary
wars. But Frederick's closest advisors would at least have liked to
begin the great trade: Prince Henry and Count Hertzberg urgently
counseled him not to make useless sacrifices to preserve the sovereignty of Bavaria and other smaller states, advising him instead
to satisfy his own "convenience" by persuading the emperor to
agree to various additions to Prussian territory in Germany and
Poland. Only this, they argued, was becoming to a great modern
power.

Frederick obstinately resisted such temptations, though they were
also held out by Kaunitz and even by Joseph II. The more the
young emperor played havoc with the historic privileges of the
German Estates, the more zealously the Prussian king used his
influence to defend the liberty of the Princes of the Holy Roman
Empire, taking pains to avoid even the mildest suspicion that his
eagerness might be prompted by selfish motives. He presents a
remarkable picture: the man who had violated the peace in 1740,
who cynically despised the ancient glory of the empire as "dust-
covered trash," at the end of his life turns into a selfless champion
of the imperial constitution! It seemed unbelievable, and for a long
time the genuineness of his intentions was doubted in Vienna.
Could it be merely an old man's desire for peace and quiet, his
vexation that traditional values were being overturned, or was it
peevish vanity that begrudged his young rival's success? For some
time Kaunitz and Joseph flattered themselves that they were able to
see through the "unpredictable" moods of the "morose old man":
in the end, seeing that his military ambitions had vanished long
ago, he would surely keep the peace if he were offered some small
compensation. This seemed even more likely since Catherine, his
only ally, was involved in a new conflict with the Ottoman Empire.

But they completely deceived themselves. When diplomatic negotiations failed to yield results, the old man unhesitatingly went to
war once more. In the summer of 1778, allied this time with his

neighbor Saxony, two powerful Prussian armies entered Bohemia. Was it really a quixotic undertaking for the benefit of powerless princelings, as his brother Henry disapprovingly thought? Not at all. Frederick was never motivated by interests other than the most dispassionate reasons of state. He went to war, in fact, not for the obsolete world of the minor realms of old Germany—which he continued to despise thoroughly, no matter how strongly his proclamations championed the Empire—but solely for the purpose of maintaining the equilibrium between the two great German powers. He felt that this balance was secure only so long as Austria's political ventures in Germany were constrained by the traditional, unwieldy forms of the imperial constitution—forms from which he, on the other hand, did his utmost to emancipate himself.

Frederick's policy was logical, and every step was carefully thought out. But it lacked dynamism. It wished only to save the *status quo,* not to achieve new goals; it was not buoyed up by great hopes. Consequently, the Bohemian campaign of 1778 followed a lackluster course. Prince Henry, who was given the most important mission, failed to exploit his brilliant opening successes; misunderstanding arose among the commanders in the field; and after a few months the whole enterprise ended in a Prussian withdrawal, without a major battle having been fought. Prussian leadership seemed to have lost its former aggressive spirit. On the other hand, no excessive efforts were needed to dampen the feebly burning fires of belligerence on the Austrian side. Maria Theresa, whose attitude once again contrasted sharply with that of her son, practically immobilized him with her attempts at mediation. Nor had Joseph been prepared for such a serious outcome to his Bavarian policy. Russia and France, the allies of the two antagonists, pressed for an early peace. Thus this "potato campaign," as it was called by the disappointed Prussian soldiers—the last of the old-style cabinet wars—ended in a compromise brought about by Russian and French mediation. By the terms of the peace treaty of Teschen of 1779, Austria received the district of the Inn, but had to relinquish her claims to the Bavarian succession. On the whole, therefore, the King of Prussia had achieved his purpose.

To be sure, only Russian support had enabled him to succeed. Without concern for national sentiment, Russia was now admitted

to the European guarantors of the German constitution, joining France, which had held that right since 1648. Frederick wanted to secure European-wide support for his conservative policy in Germany once and for all. However, it remained problematical whether the restless and ambitious Catherine could stay faithful to such a self-willed ally. She was disappointed that the king would not back her latest plans for conquests in Turkey, but that here too he pressed for compromise. Joseph cleverly seized upon this new discord, and expanded it into virtual alienation. With the death of his mother in 1780, his diplomacy was liberated from the cumbersome fetters of her conservative opposition, and with greater energy than ever he renewed his attempts to enlarge the powers of his imperial office. At the same time he maneuvered so adroitly in the oriental question that he appeared at once as the savior of Turkey, the friend of Russia, and the ally of France. In 1784, the latest Russo-Turkish dispute was terminated by mediation in which all major European powers took a hand, except Prussia, which stood apart in complete isolation.

The time seemed opportune for Joseph to carry out the Bavarian plans that had foundered in 1779. He developed a scheme of transplanting the Bavarian electoral house to the Austrian Netherlands, which Vienna had long considered to be an inconveniently remote possession; in return, Austria would annex Bavaria, the Upper Palatinate, and the Archbishopric of Salzburg. Despite the obligations she had assumed at Teschen, Catherine was immediately won over to his project. But French opposition soon frustrated it, and it provided Frederick with the opportunity for his last diplomatic coup. His disappointment at the latest escapades of Russian policy was already prompting him to seek new support against Austria. From the early months of 1784 on he tried to extend Prussian leadership to a party of princes which was organizing to oppose Joseph's "encroachments" on the Empire. For some time the king was frustrated or at least hampered by the suspicions of the minor courts. His own ministers also opposed this move, which was entirely foreign to his customary policies. It appeared to them to involve Prussian diplomacy in the endless quarrels and litigations of the princelings, bind it to obsolete claims, and seriously impede its mobility. Only when the emperor's newest schemes of territorial exchange

became known, did Frederick's negotiations gain impetus. The three great electoral seats—Prussia, Saxony, and Hanover—agreed to defend the threatened imperial constitution, if necessary by force of arms, and were gradually joined by fourteen small states.

The formation of this league had the remarkable consequence that Frederick, the great destroyer of the Empire, acquired during the last days of his life the aura of a mighty protector of ancient German traditions. How deep an impression this phenomenon made on the world of the minor German states is shown, for instance, by Goethe—minister of Saxe-Weimar—who described Frederick as the "lodestar around which Germany, Europe, and even the world seemed to revolve." The court at Weimar was especially taken with patriotic schemes to employ the League of Princes for a lasting reform of the Empire's constitution. The reorganization of the Empire under Prussian leadership—would this not be a desirable goal for Germany's future? But it turned out to be merely a soap bubble. Only fear of Austria had driven the minor princes under the wing of the Prussian eagle; they were moved by particularism rather than nationalism. And Prussia too sought only to further her own aims.

Frederick's League of Princes was to provide Prussian policy with the backing that could no longer be found elsewhere in Europe—a situation that was to be repeated several times in subsequent German history. The league was meant to perpetuate outdated constitutional forms in Germany, and prevent the increase of imperial power. It was not the tool of reform but of reaction. By 1790 a shift in Prussian policy had already rendered it meaningless. But even if the league had held together for more than a few years it could never have led to a recovery of Germany. It has no significance in the history of the growth of the German nation; and even in the context of Prussian history is should be interpreted not as an expression of political strength but rather as the symptom of a momentarily unfavorable political position. Still, the league scored a considerable tactical success by putting a stop to the emperor's plans. And it demonstrated the inexhaustible fertility of our hero's political imagination, which even in his last days allowed him to devise new and surprising maneuvers for extricating himself from difficult situations.

Our account of Frederick's life is drawing to a close. In the course of the many conflicts that he had fought to safeguard his life's work he had grown increasingly lonely. His former companions of Sans Souci had died. The spirit of the French Enlightenment as well as that of German literature had grown beyond his reach. The revolutionary ideas toward which France was turning were making him uneasy; in the writings of his old age he fought passionately against Rousseau's view of life and against the materialism of such thinkers as Holbach. As author and philosopher, the old king occupies a peculiarly isolated position in the cultural environment of his time. His life at Sans Souci shows this clearly enough. No new faces appeared who could take the place of the old friends. A few officers, an occasional Italian man of letters—that was the usual company. As in former times, the royal family maintained a respectful distance, far from the circle of intimates. But Frederick did not consider this solitude a burden; he felt oppressed only during the annual weeks of official court activities in Berlin, from Christmas to 23 January. Once he had escaped from these obligations, he found relaxation and intellectual stimulation in his books, his writings, in music, and in the enjoyment of his excellent collections of paintings and prints, among which he often spent hours by himself. He had learned to manage without his former companions. Empty talk was an abomination to him in any case, and he had never had any use for court poets and sycophants. Whatever tenderness and concern he possessed, was now lavished on his greyhounds.

Far beneath the lonely ruler lay the mass of humanity which he had been called on to govern. As time went on, the officers and administrators who served as his instruments found it increasingly painful to bear the harshness of his ways. In the army men grumbled about unjust and even insulting treatment of regiments to which for some reason the king had taken a dislike during the wars. They complained about his capriciousness, stubbornness, and impatience, about his unmercifully sarcastic criticism during inspections, about cuts in officers' allowances in the face of the constantly growing demands of the service, about the difference in pay between the guards and the line, and above all about his refusal to

grant sufficient autonomy to his senior officers, whom he confused and made unsure of themselves by a ceaseless stream of orders and regulations. The civil service felt particularly insulted by the introduction in 1766 of the so-called *Regie,* a special body in charge of indirect taxation, whose more important positions were occupied by French experts. Derisively it was pointed out that the *Regie* by no means matched Frederick's expectations, while alleged misappropriations by native tax officials were never substantiated.

The taxpayer for his part was indignant about the new ruthlessness with which taxes were now collected, about the snooping for coffee, tobacco, and salt in private households by agents of the state monopolies, and about the increased imposts on the necessities of life. But none of this diminished the popularity of the great war hero among the masses. To be sure, men complained and cursed, and not merely in secret, indeed, it was done so openly that foreign visitors were amazed; but not only were the king's orders obeyed, admiration and even enthusiasm were evident whenever he appeared in public. Friedrich von der Marwitz has described the frequently repeated scene of the king's return to the capital from a military review: tired, covered with dust, bent over his horse, an unpretentious figure in a worn uniform—and yet everyone cheered. Long after he had disappeared the crowd continued to stand silently, bareheaded, staring at the spot where he had ridden past. Frederick's response to such scenes was skeptical, to say the least. A year before his death, in a talk with the philosopher, Garve, he used the term "rabble." When Garve objected that the crowd which the previous day had hailed the king on his entry into Breslau could hardly be considered a rabble, he is supposed to have retorted immediately: "put an old monkey on horseback, let him ride through the streets, and the mob will gather just as quickly."

He was not concerned about popularity, about the approval or dislike of the crowd. Long ago he had detached himself from the warmth of human relationships, family or friends without which the rest of us cannot exist. When his last illness came he no longer stood in need of anyone. He died alone, in the arms of an orderly on 17 August 1786.

Soon after his death it became evident that an era of world history had been buried with him.

Index

MAP OF FLAMES

ALSO BY LISA MCMANN

Clarice the Brave

THE UNWANTEDS SERIES
The Unwanteds
Island of Silence
Island of Fire
Island of Legends
Island of Shipwrecks
Island of Graves
Island of Dragons

THE UNWANTEDS QUESTS
Dragon Captives
Dragon Bones
Dragon Ghosts
Dragon Curse
Dragon Fire
Dragon Slayers
Dragon Fury

GOING WILD SERIES
Going Wild
Predator vs. Prey
Clash of Beasts

THE VISIONS TRILOGY
Crash
Bang
Gasp

THE WAKE TRILOGY
Wake
Fade
Gone

OTHER BOOKS
Dead to You
The Trap Door
Cryer's Cross

PART ONE

THE LAST WORDS

Birdie Golden's fingers were still stained with dirt from digging her father's grave. Tears smudged her cheeks.

"When I'm gone," he'd whispered to her, "look through my crate. I've left you . . ." His fingertips had sparked one last time and gone out, leaving them charcoal-tinged and lifeless. His labored breathing had slowed, and he'd closed his eyes.

Left her *what*? Or maybe he'd just . . . you know. Left her. "Dad?" Her chest had tightened. She'd squeezed his hand. "Dad?"

A moment later, his eyes had fluttered. "Find your mother," he'd said with a gasp. "Tell her . . . I did my best." And then he'd died.

Birdie hadn't expected him to say anything like that. Her mind had been churning the words around ever since. Through the digging. The funeral. And the burying. Today's glorious sunshine hadn't penetrated the numbness. Not even the call of the gray whale. Only those words: *Find your mother.*

Birdie would check Dad's crate in the morning. But tonight,

she left their cabin and headed for the fire pit with her ten-year-old brother, Brix, who was bouncing—*not* joyfully—by her side, and her tiny pig trotting behind. Only the five kids remained in the hideout built by their supernatural criminal parents. Forgotten and alone. And they had a lot to talk about.

TRADITION

Tenner Cordoba scraped the last serving of fish from the skillet onto his plate as the other four ate around the tree-stump table. The wind picked up, rustling the thick trees, and the surf pounded the shore at high tide. An animal howled far away. Tenner turned sharply toward the noise, narrowing his eyes.

Puerco, Birdie's pig, stirred uneasily. *Shh*, Birdie said with her mind, and Puerco settled down.

At the far end of the table was Seven Palacio. He was thirteen like Tenner and Birdie and sat camouflaged by shadows and the black parachute-fabric clothes he wore. Next to him, Cabot Stone, eleven-going-on-thirty, ran a hand over her buzz-cut hair and cast a worried glance at Brix to see how he was holding up. He'd stopped crying.

Tenner dropped into the log chair next to Birdie. "Are you doing okay?" he asked her. He looked at his food, then pushed it around with his fork. For once he had little appetite.

"Better," she said. "Thanks." She caught his eye and smiled sadly.

Tenner lowered his gaze. "No problem," he mumbled, then dropped his fork in the dirt and muttered under his breath. After retrieving it and wiping it off, he looked around the table. Everyone was red-eyed and exhausted. It had been the longest day. They'd never buried anyone before.

Louis had told them what to do when the time came, but that hadn't made it any easier. Pushing dirt over his wrapped-up body . . . It had been the hardest thing Tenner had ever done. Birdie and Brix had been sobbing. Seven had leaned on his shovel, his arms shaking, unable to do anything but comfort those two. Cabot had stepped in, her face a mask. She'd dropped the first handful of dirt. Then she'd taken Seven's shovel. Tenner had helped her with the rest of it. He'd cried in the ocean later.

Tenner wanted to go to bed and forget this day. But there was one thing that still needed to happen. A few weeks ago, Tenner had brought Louis some soup and sat next to him to help him eat it. Louis had put down the spoon and taken the boy's hand.

"You can go your own way, Tenner," Louis had said. His hair was only beginning to gray, and it spread wildly on the pillow.

"What do you mean?" Tenner had asked, confused.

"You're not like your parents. You're in charge of your decisions. I believe in you."

"Oh." Tenner's face had burned, but he'd managed a smile. "Thanks, Louis."

"Will you do me a favor?" Louis had closed his eyes and taken a labored breath. His fingers sparked.

Tenner leaned back to avoid injury. "Of course. Anything."

"Continue the tradition. Keep telling the story of the criminals' escape. It's important. Do it after I'm gone."

Tenner had promised.

And now the time had come. "Okay," Tenner said, glancing worriedly at Birdie. He wasn't sure she was ready for this. "I promised your dad we'd do the story after . . . well, you know. So, who's going to start? Birdie or Brix?"

Birdie's face was pained, but she didn't object. The siblings glanced at each other. "Brix should do it," Birdie said. "It's his turn."

Brix sat up. The story had been part of their lives since they were little. All the people in this hideaway had been supernatural, extremely rare compared to the rest of the world. Dad had said it was crucial that the children not only remember but be able to recite their family history. Knowing that, and hearing his father's voice saying it in his head, made Brix's throat close up for a moment. But then he began the way someone always began. "How did our parents get here?"

They all knew the answer but still looked forward to the story of the criminals' failed heist. Or, as Louis referred to it, their successful escape.

From the shadows, Seven spoke. "Fifteen years ago, after decades of being oppressed in Estero, our parents decided to come to their hideout, where they'd be safe. But first they wanted to do one last heist—of the famous Stone Crown on display in President Fuerte's palace. It had belonged to the first ruler of Estero over a thousand years ago, and it was the president's most prized possession. The criminals knew they would never be able to sell it because it was well-known around the world. But they wanted to teach the country, and the president, a lesson about shunning people like them."

He leaned forward and added a log to the fire, his face appearing to be engulfed in flames. "The plan went wrong. They were recognized and chased by police. But they made it to the roof of the hospital where Cabot's mom worked. And then they came here."

"In a helicopter," Tenner added. "Cabot's mom flew."

"They didn't get the crown," said Brix, "but they didn't need it. They'd left their stash of gold and jewels hidden in Estero, for whenever they decided to go back."

Birdie stared at the fire. Some of the parents were there, no doubt. Like her mother.

"My mom flew the helicopter across the bay through the dark night," Cabot said, scooting forward in her seat to tell her favorite part. "The criminals were ready to jump with parachutes, and they tied their belongings in a cargo net attached to parachutes, too. Then my mom programmed the helicopter to fly on its own, out of sight, to run out of fuel and crash into the ocean miles and miles away from here." She sighed. That was the most romantic of all the details. Even though she hadn't witnessed it, it was a prominent image in her mind—eight supernatural thieves jumping out of a helicopter and parachuting to the jungle beach on this narrow slice of land. Cabot was wearing part of one of those parachutes right now, fashioned into baggy trousers.

Her thoughts flickered to her parents, and her enthusiasm for the story waned. Louis Golden's death had her pining for them again.

"They didn't even have to slow the helicopter down," said Seven.

Brix looked up. That was a detail he hadn't noticed before. "Does it matter that they didn't slow the helicopter?" he asked.

"Yes," said Tenner. His thick eyebrows almost met in a stern expression, and he set his uneaten plate of food on the table. "Every part of the story matters."

Birdie pulled her knees up and hugged them. "It was so anybody tracking their flight pattern wouldn't be able to guess where they'd jumped out."

Cabot nodded. Despite her funk, a small, melancholy smile appeared on her face after talking about her mother.

"It's going to be different here without Louis," Tenner said, his voice catching. Louis had been there for him when his own parents hadn't.

Cabot and Brix nodded, eyes wet. Everyone went silent for a long, reverent moment, almost as if they'd planned it in honor of the parent who'd stayed.

After a while, Seven cleared his throat and wiped his face with his sleeve. "I'm glad we're not going to Estero. This is our home. And we've been through enough."

Birdie rested her chin on her knees and closed her eyes. Her father's dying words pulsed in her ears like a heartbeat. *Find. Your. Mother.*

THE CRATE

Kneeling on the hard-packed dirt floor of their cabin the next morning, Birdie pulled out the hand-hewn crate that held her father's personal items. *Find your mother.* Why? How? That wasn't the plan. Why wait until your last breath to say *that*?

A few years before, Birdie's mother, Elena, and Mr. and Mrs. Stone—Cabot's parents—had left their secret tropical hideout to get supplies: Fabric to make clothing. Tools, ropes, and seeds for their garden. Maybe some sweet treats if they had room in their backpacks.

Everyone knew the route would be treacherous. That was one of the reasons the group was safe here on the peninsula.

The three didn't return.

Four more parents, the Palacios and the Cordobas, had followed to search for the missing three—or so they'd claimed. But they hadn't come back, either. That left Louis Golden in the hideout with the five children.

Mourning the loss of the missing ones was rough. But Louis, despite his criminal past, had been a good parent. The kids had been managing—some better than others.

Birdie wiped her eyes and squared her shoulders, then drew her straight black hair back and tied it with a strip of cloth from her pocket. She began to examine the crate's contents.

At first glance there seemed to be nothing she hadn't seen before. On top were her parents' old, dust-covered cell phones. Telephones, as Birdie and the other children understood them, were used by people to communicate from afar, giving you a kind of handheld telepathic ability. There were also some tightly wrapped cords that possibly went with the phones, but Birdie wasn't sure. If so, the whole conglomeration required "electricity" to make them useful. Birdie set the cords aside to give to Cabot—she'd make something *actually* useful out of them.

Dad's wallet sat next to the phones. Birdie had looked through that plenty of times and knew it contained bills with different numbers on them—he'd shown the kids when teaching them about money. But, to be honest, Birdie hadn't paid much attention. They had no need for money here, and the plan was to stay. So why bother?

Also inside the wallet was Louis's driver's license and some plastic cards that he'd said were useless now. Behind the cards was a picture of Birdie's mother as a young woman in Estero.

There was a grassy area with trees around her, and tall buildings off to one side. Birdie touched her mother's face and accidentally left a smudge on the photo, which she quickly wiped clean using the edge of her shirt. Mom's smile was the same as Birdie remembered.

Instantly the lullaby her mother had sung to young Birdie was in her head. It had been a simple tune that Elena Golden had composed—it even had Birdie's name in it. She longed to feel her mother's arms around her and hear her sing it again.

Fresh pain hit like a tidal wave as she imagined telling her mom that Louis had died. She held the photo to her chest and pinched her eyes shut as a sob escaped. How on earth was she supposed to find her? Especially without her dad's help? Louis believed she'd been captured and jailed in Estero. But . . . she could be dead. Sure, she was supernaturally fast and agile, which had made her the obvious choice to make the trek. But she wasn't invincible. None of them were.

Birdie blew out a steadying breath, then opened her eyes and returned to the task. Underneath the phones and wallet rested a small collection of books and journals Dad had brought with him fifteen years ago. Birdie hadn't paid much attention to her father's personal journals, though he'd shown them to her a few times. "Someday you'll want to read these," he'd said not long after he'd gotten sick. "There's some interesting stuff that might be helpful if you ever decide to go to Estero." But Dad's handwriting was hard for Birdie to read. She'd preferred listening to his stories of their sordid past.

She'd read all the books in the crate at least ten times, though. She lifted the familiar worn stack and looked at the books one by one. Sticking out between the pages of her favorite book, the *Encyclopedia Minorica Volume C–D* (which had pictures of all kinds of glorious castles, cathedrals, and cities), were two new notes: one for Birdie and one for Brix. Birdie pulled them out. With trembling fingers, she put the one for Brix in her pocket to deliver later and examined the one for her. It was written on an end page torn from one of the books. Could this be what her father had left her? After his stunning final words, she was nervous to read it. Steeling herself, she opened it.

Dear Birdie,

Now that the end of my life is approaching, I have a confession to make. Fifteen years ago, right before your mother and I and the other adults were forced to leave Estero, I moved our hidden stash . . . without telling anyone. I've created a map that leads to it. When you are of age and feeling especially brave, I want you to go to Estero, find your mother, and give her the map.

Please be careful.
I love you, and I'm sorry . . . about everything.
Dad

The sentences were so shocking that Birdie couldn't totally comprehend them in her grief. The few words that stood out rotated through her mind: *Confession. Stash. Mother. Map.*

Her focus sharpened on a water stain near the words *sorry . . . about everything,* and she choked up. The stain might have been caused by a teardrop. Louis had softened as he lay dying.

Feeling light-headed, Birdie set the note from her father on top of the stack of books to read again later when she could collect her thoughts. Then she moved a pile of loose papers aside and carefully picked through the journals, examining the exterior of each one curiously and noting that they were numbered and dated in the order he'd written them. She opened his most recent one to a page with a sketch of a group of trees and a mound of earth with an iron ring sticking out of it. Words, blurred by Birdie's tears, danced on the page. The entry was dated a few months before—around the time Dad had taken ill.

The ancient lower tunnels of Estero would be a safe place to hide if any of the children decide to go. After years of searching, I found an entrance days before we became fugitives. I told Elena but no one else. I'll never trust Troy Cordoba again . . . and the children shouldn't either.

Another secret? Birdie closed the journal. It was too much. Too soon.

She reached back into the crate. Tucked along the bottom edge was a scroll with charred edges. Birdie picked it up and felt her father's fire-based energy pulsing inside. Her heartbeat quickened, for it seemed as though some small part of him lived on, beyond death.

When she unrolled the scroll, it burst into flames.

MAP OF FLAMES

Yikes!" Birdie exclaimed, dropping it. The map rolled up automatically, extinguishing the flames. After checking her hands for burns and making sure her eyebrows were intact, she picked up the map by the edge and opened it again, this time holding it farther away from her face. The drawing exploded in fire again, then settled. The flames were her father's special touch. He'd probably added them as a deterrent for ordinary people in case the map ever got into the wrong hands. But there weren't any ordinary people here.

Birdie had never seen a map to Estero before. Her eyes were drawn to the southernmost tip of a peninsula—which she realized was the place they called home. She followed the shoreline up, imagining the path her mother and the other adults must have taken to get supplies. Up the cliffs, through the jungle, over the mountain, and around the curve of the bay to the nearest village outside of Estero.

"She could handle the terrain," Dad had insisted. "Something else happened. She's in jail, I'm sure of it." But what about the rest of them? Had they *all* been captured? Or had some decided to go back to Estero without their children? A few of them were pretty rotten people. But not all. Not Mom. Not Cabot's parents.

The mass exodus of parents three years ago intruded into Birdie's thoughts again. She remembered how gray her father's face had gotten when too much time had passed with no one returning. Remembered him wringing his charcoal-stained hands in grief and sorrow as he faced the five young children who wanted him to fix this.

Louis had explained what it would take to search for the seven missing parents. The journey would have been much harder for a single adult with five children. And even if the kids could handle the dangerous terrain, they knew supernatural people weren't safe anywhere in the world. Especially the wanted-criminal kind. Louis's biggest fear was that, if they made it to Estero, he'd be recognized and arrested, which would leave the five young children alone and vulnerable in a strange place, and in danger once their burgeoning abilities developed.

"Maybe when you're a little older," he'd concluded, his voice strained. "Old enough to take care of yourselves if something happens to me." That had been scary to think about, too. They didn't want to lose the only parent they had left.

Over the next few months, Birdie, Seven, and Tenner, all ten, had developed their abilities. As luck would have it, Birdie's wasn't obvious. And Tenner's was so slight, you had to be looking at him up close to see it. But Seven's proved to be highly noticeable and made him especially vulnerable, easily recognizable as a supernatural person.

In light of that, Louis had decided he would make the trip alone when the children were teens. He taught them how to take care of themselves and their camp. And he'd started building a boat.

But then, a few months later, he got sick.

When it became clear Louis was dying, Birdie gathered the other children. "We'll stay here like we planned," she said. "We don't have to go anywhere."

Seven had been relieved. "If our parents are alive, they know how to find us—if they want to." And that was that.

The five would remain indefinitely in the six-cabin village the criminals had built on the tip of a narrow peninsula at the edge of the sea, guarded by cliffs and rocks and a jungle. Sheltered from a civilized world the kids had never known or understood. Safe from a world that hated supernatural people like them. Despite their losses, it was a good life.

Birdie shook her head to clear it, then returned her attention to the map. She narrowed her eyes as she studied it. "That's odd," she muttered. The thickest line of fire was a directional arrow stretching from their camp across the mouth of the upside-down-V-shaped bay, to the small country of Estero on the other side. Estero City, the capital, was near the southern point.

In the bottom right corner of the smoldering page was an inset map, which magnified the city with a grid of streets.

A flaming sketch of a bag of gold was set in the section of the city labeled OLD TOWN, and there were at least ten other points labeled with initials. Intent on studying the map, Birdie didn't hear the footfalls outside the open window.

"You all right, Bird?"

Birdie gasped and turned sharply. It took her a few seconds to locate Seven, since he was standing shirtless outside the window. Seven's constantly changing camouflage skin and hair blended perfectly with the slow-dancing willow branches behind him. When he came in through the doorway, Birdie could see his shorts and shoes, and when he got closer, she could detect the faint outline of his body that she'd learned, over time, to look for. "Didn't see you there," she said weakly, then cringed.

"Story of my life," Seven said for about the millionth time since he'd developed this unfortunate ability. He was brownish gray now, with knots and lines like the split log wall behind him. "Where'd you get that map?"

Birdie froze. Of course he'd seen it through the window. How long had he been standing there? Flustered, she tried to figure out why she felt reluctant to show him—what had Dad's note said? Obviously it was too late now—he'd seen it. Besides, Seven was her best friend. They'd been born a few weeks apart, Birdie the elder of the two, and had spent every day together since.

"It was in my dad's crate," Birdie said, keeping her tone light. "He put a flame charm on it."

"Is that why you yelled?"

"Yeah." She found his eyes. "Is that why you came?" Birdie had told the others to give her some time to go through her father's things privately, as he'd asked her to.

"Yeah," Seven admitted. "I was going to leave you alone, but then I got worried that something happened." He hesitated, and Birdie caught the tiny, swift movement of his blink. "So," Seven asked contritely, "since I'm here, do you need anything?"

Birdie dropped her gaze as sorrow thickened in her throat. "I'm okay. Thanks."

The emptiness inside her made her yearn for little Puerco. She'd found him as a sickly piglet and nursed him to health. It was with him that Birdie had discovered her supernatural ability to talk with certain types of creatures. Since then, she'd interacted with several whales, an octopus, and an old crow, who now blessed her with a variety of shiny pieces of trash plucked from the shoreline. "Have you seen Puerco?"

"Brix has him."

"Is Brix . . . ?" Birdie pressed her lips together.

"He's all right. Sitting under the willows by the grave. I think the pig is making him feel better. Cabot's keeping an eye on him, too. She brought him some lunch and ate out there with him."

"It's past lunchtime already? I got kind of lost there." Birdie sent a quick message of thanks through her mind to Puerco for helping her brother.

"Everyone is struggling today," Seven said.

"I'm sure." Birdie's face flickered. Her mind turned back to the note, and her eyes darted to it on the stack of books. The words *when you are of age* jumped out. She'd stumbled over the phrase when she'd read it earlier.

"What does 'of age' mean exactly?" Birdie asked, glancing up. She detected the two black dots of Seven's pupils—one more thing she'd trained herself to look for. Focusing on those living dots brought her more comfort than almost anything at the moment.

Seven shifted. "I guess it means when you reach a certain age."

"Yes, but *which*?"

Seven laughed. "I have no idea. Maybe . . . old enough to take care of yourself without a parent?"

"That's . . . now."

"Your dad made sure we knew how," he said agreeably. Then he cleared his throat and inched closer. "So, can I see the map?"

Anxiety rippled Birdie's skin as she put the "of age" query out of her mind. "Sure. Stand behind me," she cautioned, then unrolled the scroll again.

After the initial burst of flames settled, Seven rested his chin on Birdie's shoulder and studied the map, then let out a breath and moved to Birdie's side to get a closer view. "This is a map to Estero! Is that bag of gold in the middle of the city supposed to be the hidden stash?"

Birdie stiffened. "Uh . . . it seems like it."

Seven scanned the inset map, and his tone turned fearful.

"Wow. That's, like, a huge city. Look at all those streets. It's probably full of . . . people." He said *people* with a sneer, as if it were a bad word. "We're much better off here." He reached for the edge of the map to study the inset.

Birdie's chest tightened. She tugged the scroll away and let out a shaky laugh. "Definitely," she said. But the last words of her father wouldn't stop ringing in her ears. And the words of the note came rushing back to mind. *I moved the stash . . . without telling anyone.* What would the other kids think? They'd all held up Louis Golden as the model of a good parent. But his underhanded move against *their* parents could tarnish that.

Seven pulled his fingers back. "When did your dad make this?"

"It's probably old," Birdie said. "From . . . before." Her uneasiness grew. She was lying to Seven, and it felt terrible. But she just . . . needed more time to process the note. "Or maybe he did it in case we ever changed our minds and wanted to find Estero. And the money."

Seven snorted. "That stash is long gone by now," he said with a cynical tone that hadn't been there before.

"We don't know that," said Birdie.

"Please. I'm pretty sure at least some of them saw an opportunity to not have to split the money eight ways and went straight for the stash." He didn't say who, but they both knew that Tenner's parents, Troy and Lucy Cordoba, were most likely to do something like that. Louis had held a grudge against Troy

Cordoba that dated back to a heist they did shortly before escaping Estero. They'd broken into a jewelry shop and stolen thirteen flawless diamonds intended for the president's daughter's wedding jewelry. But then the diamonds, in Troy's possession, "went missing." Troy had apologized profusely for losing them and insisted he was telling the truth, but he couldn't hide the smug look on his face. Search as they might, none of the others could find the diamonds. Louis had been wary of Troy ever since.

Seven's parents, Martim and Magdalia Palacio, were easily swayed by Tenner's parents, and they'd taken Troy's side back then and ever since. Louis had shared with the kids his suspicions about the real reason those four had gone after the other three. He'd doubted they searched for Elena Golden and Cabot's parents at all.

"They're probably enjoying a lavish life in Estero right now," Seven said bitterly. "Living it up with the stash and Troy's thirteen diamonds."

"Possible," Birdie said. "I still think my mom got caught. Maybe your parents did, too."

"My dad can go invisible," Seven reminded her. "And my mother—don't get me started. They would *not* get caught. So they're either dead or living it up. And they didn't care enough to come back and get me."

Birdie cringed, knowing what he said could be true. "Well, my mom can run faster than anybody, but my dad still thinks—

thought—she was captured. Our parents' abilities are great, but your theory only works if they know someone's about to grab them. They could've been ambushed."

Seven mulled it over. "Maybe," he said with a sniff. It didn't matter, though. He knew his parents wouldn't be coming back.

Birdie dropped her gaze. "I'm sorry my mom wanted to go for supplies in the first place. We've managed to make it all right without any of the things she wanted to get."

"I'm not blaming your mom. She's cool. She just inadvertently gave the bad parents an excuse to leave." He shook his head. "Look out the window. The trees, the sparkle of the sun on the waves, the cliffs—it's way better than what I can see in the photos that my parents left behind, with all those massive buildings and hardly any trees, and cars buzzing around to run you down. And people everywhere. Who needs civilization and money when we have everything we want right here?"

"Everything except my dad," Birdie said dully. Her mind returned to the note, and more phrases came back to her. *Find your mother. Give her the map.* Dad's last communication. Could she actually complete the task? She'd never considered it possible to do without Dad before, but now . . .

Seven checked himself. "Yeah, of course. Geez. I'm sorry. You know I miss him. A lot."

Birdie nodded. "I know."

Seven moved toward the door, then paused halfway. "Your dad was everything my parents weren't."

Birdie drew her shoulders in and blinked hard at the floor. She loved Seven. And she knew he was hurting, too. But right now, she needed him to go away.

"And I know I'm intruding," Seven added awkwardly. "It was just that I heard you ... yell ..." He gave up.

"It's fine," Birdie said with a quivering smile. Her eyes were brimming again. She couldn't see his expression, and she missed that desperately. But she could hear the compassion in his voice. Complicated emotions pounded her. The grief over the loss of her father felt different from when her mother had disappeared. Back then they hoped that she and Greta and Jack Stone would come back. Then, when they didn't, that the other parents would find her.

There was no hope of bringing Louis Golden back. For the past three years, the five children had leaned heavily on him. Even in his own grief over his missing wife, Louis Golden had done his best to make life normal for them.

He'd taken over Greta Stone's school and taught them about the world beyond their beach, then gone out after class to play with them in the water and toss coconuts back and forth. He'd continued their swimming and fishing lessons, shown them how to hunt for bird eggs in the cliffs, and explained which mushrooms and berries were safe and which were poisonous.

Louis had also taught them how to tend the fire and cook. And, after one harrowing incident, he'd emphasized the importance of cleaning up after dinner. Louis, Brix, and Birdie had been asleep one night after the kids had stayed up late around the fire. They'd heard the hiss of a mountain lion through the open window. Puerco had squealed and run under a chair. A low whine turned into a sharp, growly roar. Cabot had screamed from the next cabin, and Louis had rushed outside, fingers sparking. While Brix and Birdie had watched fearfully from the window, Louis ran at the mountain lion, yelling and sending bolts of fire flying into the dirt around it to scare it. He chased after the giant cat, throwing sparks until it ran deep into the woods where it belonged. When Louis returned, they heard him cleaning up the dirty dishes they'd left out. When he'd come back to the cabin, all five kids were huddled in Birdie and Brix's bed for the night, offering tearful apologies. The children hadn't needed a lesson about cleaning up their dishes ever again.

The reality was that Louis Golden had prepared the children for this terrible moment none of them had expected to come. They were of age. Able to take care of themselves.

Seven continued to the door, seeming unsure if he should offer a final hug or leave, and deciding on the latter. "I'll go check on Brixy. Call me if you need anything. I can . . . be here. For you."

"Thanks," said Birdie with a crooked smile. "I know."

With a pattering roll of his fingers on the log doorway, Seven left the Goldens' cabin and disappeared. Literally.

Once he was gone, Birdie blew her nose, then washed her face in a water basin made from a large shell. She took a few intentional breaths and blew them out between pursed lips. Then she went back to the note from her father and reread his confession. *I moved our hidden stash . . . without telling anyone. I've created a map that leads to it. When you are of age and feeling especially brave, I want you to go to Estero, find your mother, and give her the map.*

Birdie sat down on a log stool that her mother had painstakingly sanded smooth to keep the children from getting slivers. "He moved the stash so Tenner's parents and Seven's parents wouldn't steal it," she murmured. "But why didn't he tell my mom?" Maybe he'd been worried that Mom or the Stones would accidentally leak the information to the bad parents. Or maybe he thought it would only add to the tension between them all, and he wanted to shoulder the blame alone.

This note changed everything. The five loved their little beach village and could live off the land and ocean indefinitely— that had been the plan. Sure, they struggled sometimes, especially when it came to making clothing for the growing children. They'd used up all the parachutes for clothes and blankets, but their parents had left some old clothes behind that were starting to fit. They'd be fine.

But now Dad's dying wish was messing everything up.

Birdie put down the note and opened the map again. This time, with a clearer head, she studied it thoroughly. She focused on the initials written in various places around the city and beyond—what did they mean? Were those the jails where her mother could be?

And the directional line across the bay leading to the hidden stash seemed strange. Why would Birdie's father suggest a route across the huge mouth of the bay when the boat he'd started building was barely a shell and would take skills the kids didn't have to make it seaworthy?

Using a boat seemed fruitless anyway. With all the rocks hidden in the water, it was questionable if they'd even be able to get through the maze without wrecking. But doing that might be safer than traveling by land.

The route skirting around the bay, which their parents had taken, was longer, and there was no arrow suggesting it. Clearly Dad still had grave doubts about the feasibility of going that way.

A whale called from far out in the ocean and filled Birdie's mind, like it was mourning with her. She closed her eyes and sent it a greeting. She'd visit it later.

She looked at Estero again. The children had all heard tales of their parents' former lives in the big city full of old cathedrals and museums and palaces, roads and vehicles, and trains and airplanes that sometimes crashed and hurt people. They'd even seen some planes out here, way up in the sky, the size of birds. Tenner's dad had once told them that the planes were actually huge—one of them could fill their entire beach at low tide and fit hundreds of people inside. It was impossible to believe something that big could defy gravity and fly through the air, so they remained dubious. Especially since the story had come from Troy Cordoba, who thought it was funny to tease the children. Like the time he sent Tenner up into a tree to get coconuts and then took the ladder away and returned to camp. Tenner had been stuck for hours, screaming for help, before Seven and Birdie had found him. Mr. Cordoba had laughed and said it was a character-building exercise.

"Maybe we should do it to you, then," Tenner had retorted.

His dad had slapped him in the mouth.

"Knock it off, Troy!" Louis had shouted, and he went at the bigger man. Jack Stone was right behind him.

"Get away from me," Troy had warned. He'd stuck out his chest and raised his fists, but Martim Palacio had gone invisible and shoved Troy back before he could strike anyone. The other parents pulled them apart and held them. Brix had started crying because he was scared. And Tenner had looked like he wanted to sink into the earth, mortified that everyone had witnessed it.

Troy didn't slap Tenner again after that, but he was still mean to him. Tenner wished his mom had tried to stop his dad. But she never did.

After the Cordobas left, Dad told Birdie that Troy had always been a bully. That his parents had been mean to him, too. And though this group of supernatural people supported one another and hid out together because the rest of the world was a bigger enemy, Louis said they weren't exactly friends.

"What were you like when you were a kid?" Birdie had asked her father countless times. But he'd always answered with some sort of joke, like he didn't want to say. "I've always been an adult." Or, "I was born a bearded man."

By the time he was dying, Birdie and the others had grown desperate to know more about Louis and the rest of the parents. And this time, when they'd asked, he'd answered.

YOUNG LOUIS

want you to understand what it's like being supernatural when you're not on this beach," Louis had said one evening after dinner. He'd sat wrapped in the frayed blanket from his bed, shivering even though it was still warm out. Tenner ran to his cabin and brought out another blanket for him.

Louis smiled his thanks and continued. "I was sent to a home for unwanted supernatural children when I was eleven. It was in the heart of Estero City, right across from a park where I took that photo of your mother when we were about to graduate." He'd glanced at Birdie and Brix. "I nearly burned the park's restrooms down once after I got rejected from *another* job interview. You'd think a welder would have seen the value in a guy like me, but no." He flicked his wrist, sending flames shooting from his fingertips at the fire pit. The burning log split, and ash clouded up and settled. The action started him coughing fitfully, and Birdie had feared that would be the end of the story. But after taking a moment to catch his breath and sip some water, he went on. "The home was filled with young supernaturals in trouble, with parents who couldn't handle their abilities or didn't want to raise them because of the stigma."

"What's that?" Brix had asked. "Stigma?"

"It's like a stain or a black mark," Seven had said. "Since the whole world is against supernatural people, nobody wants to be associated with them. They don't want other people to think they're sympathetic toward them."

"Us," Tenner had said.

"Toward us," Seven agreed.

"But weren't their parents supernatural, too?" Birdie asked. "Like ours?"

"Some of them." Louis dotted the corners of his mouth with a handkerchief, then folded it carefully.

"It's like an epidemic," Birdie mused.

He turned toward her. "What is, sweetheart?"

"Parents of supernaturals leaving their kids."

That had made Louis Golden go quiet. A tear slipped down his cheek, which had horrified Birdie. Brix ran over to him, and Birdie apologized profusely even though it was the truest fact ever uttered. "I'm sorry," she said. "Tell us more about the home."

Mr. Golden had wiped his eyes. "It's where I met your mother and the others." He'd begun speaking slower, gasping for air every few words, as if exhausted after crying. "We were all from different backgrounds, and we didn't always see eye to eye. But we were bonded by our experiences: given up by our parents, sent to this place for kids like us, then shunned by everyone in Estero and the world. We had to stick together. We were family." He closed his eyes.

The five children had looked at one another soberly, all feeling the same sense of relief that they hadn't been forced to grow up in a place like that. Later, Tenner and Seven had helped Louis to bed.

Another evening, Birdie had asked, "Why didn't your parents think they could raise you?"

Her father waved his fingertips, then shot flames into the air, startling Cabot and making Brix shrink back. "I was setting fires left and right—purely by accident, back then. It was too hard to control. I set my mother's sewing room on fire once when we were arguing—the flames shot out whenever I got upset. Thank God we had extinguishers everywhere, or the whole house could have gone up." He took in a ragged breath. "I don't blame my parents. I was a terror."

"Why did you and the others steal things?" Cabot asked.

Mr. Golden closed his eyes. "It started because we needed resources."

"Resources for what?" Cabot leaned forward. "You mean money?"

"Yes—money for food, a place to stay. We'd been registered as supernatural when we got to the home, and after graduation it went on our work permits, our driver's licenses, our identification cards, our passports. No one would rent us a house or give us jobs. Your mother," he said to Cabot, "was the exception. She managed to use her superintelligence to manipulate her way into university and later on get a job as a doctor. She helped us all a little whenever she could."

He coughed, then continued. "For people with obvious abilities, like me and Seven's parents and Tenner's dad, there was no way to make money honestly. Look at Seven with his camouflage, or Brix with his bouncing gait—they wouldn't be able to get work in Estero." The younger boy's eyes widened. It sounded terrible.

"Tell us more," Birdie had begged. But her father had closed his eyes.

That was the last time he told stories around the fire.

TENNER

Tenner Cordoba had just turned thirteen. He was a few months younger than Birdie and Seven, and perpetually a step behind them in everything—that's what it felt like to him, anyway. It seemed like Birdie and Seven had their best talks and private jokes when he was out catching their dinner.

When he was alone with either of them, he got along all right. But when they were together, he felt a little bit like their servant. It was fine. His parents had never fit in with the others, either. Not that Tenner wanted to imitate *them*. But it seemed like he was at the bottom of the hierarchy because his parents were the worst.

No one ever *said* that. But Tenner always felt like he had to do extra to prove that he wasn't like his crappy parents. Or maybe it was all in Tenner's head and he was super insecure. Tenner had learned at a young age that if he kept his emotions in check and didn't cry or get mad, his dad might leave him alone. Now he thought that if he didn't act like a bully, or play awful tricks, or get angry . . . maybe in time the other kids would forget that he was Troy's son.

When Tenner removed his parents from the scenario and tried to look at himself objectively, he could see that the others appreciated him. They thought his extrasensory abilities were cool. And he could hold his breath for a ridiculously long time, which made him by far the best swimmer and fisherperson among them, which was useful. His extra-large, oval pupils allowed him to see long distances *and* in the dark, and their unique shape made him feel special . . . even though the others said the difference was barely noticeable. And his slightly larger-than-normal ear canals allowed him to listen in on their conversations when they didn't know he was close enough to hear. But it wasn't like they were ever talking about him. Maybe he wished they would.

Growing up in a group of families like this, when his parents were the least liked of them all, felt kind of bad. Everyone thought Troy and Lucy Cordoba would use the excuse of finding the missing parents to go back to Estero and steal the stash, and . . . not return. Whenever the others said this out loud, they gave Tenner a pitying look, which made him want to sink into the ground. He wished they understood that he disliked his parents as much as everyone else did. But he didn't know how to say that, or how to explain how guilty he felt about their rottenness. He knew it wasn't his fault. But he wondered if the others thought he might be rotten deep down, too.

Tenner waded into the blue-green water with his spear. His brown skin shone with droplets from a rogue wave that slapped his chest. He wore his wavy brown-black hair shoulder length and tangled by the sea. Louis had called him a surfer boy, and he quite liked the sound of that. Maybe later he'd ask Cabot to help him design and build that surfboard Louis had described, sort of as a tribute to the parent who'd stayed. Then he rolled his eyes. He'd probably crash it on the rocks.

Before diving under, Tenner glanced back and saw Birdie parting the lush green plants, coming up the main path to the beach. He hesitated, waiting to see if she would call to him, but no. She was just walking. Not noticing him. He sighed, noting he should probably trim back the overgrowth sometime. Then he took a deep breath and pressed forward into the ocean. Even in grief, they needed to eat. And Tenner longed for his quiet place where he could be his real self. The ocean wouldn't notice his tears.

"Hi, Tenner," Birdie called, but he was already underwater. She turned to walk along the shoreline where the sand was wet and packed down. The tide was going out, and she could see the tops of many of the rocks that jutted up for hundreds of yards all around in front of their hidden home. The rocks kept ships from coming near enough to see or approach them. That was the reason their parents had chosen this location. This narrow peninsula, with high cliffs and mountains to the north and rocky ocean to the south, west, and east, was virtually inaccessible from any direction except from above.

A crow dropped down from a tree branch to Birdie's shoulder, as if he'd been waiting for her. He deposited a small, shiny piece of metal into her hand. "Ooh, thank you, Seymour," she said, admiring it. The crow preened his feathers, then flew away.

As Birdie pocketed the gift and continued down the beach, the note from her father stayed heavy on her mind. What would it be like to actually go to Estero? To search in a big city for a person in jail? Mom would need the map for when she got out— she'd have no money.

She spotted Brix sitting in the shade of the willows with Puerco. She didn't notice Cabot above her in the treetops, watching everyone.

CABOT

Eleven-year-old Cabot Stone had white skin that was tan from the sun. Her piercing green eyes caught most of what happened in their tiny village, and her pale pink lips were full like her mother's. Cabot found hair to be annoying, so she'd designed and carved a hair-cutting tool out of driftwood. She'd added a spring mechanism she'd taken from a small radio in her mother's crate and some razor-sharp glass from a broken bottle Tenner had found on the ocean floor. Ever since, she'd worn her white-blond hair super short. Louis had called it a buzz cut. Tenner's dad had joked that she was a boy, but Cabot didn't understand why that was funny, and when she didn't laugh, he'd stopped laughing and scowled, then walked away.

Cabot was a late bloomer as far as her supernatural ability was concerned. The other four children had developed theirs at around ten, with Brix recently discovering his. It was possible that Cabot was the rare child of supernatural parents who possessed no extraordinary features.

"Your ability could still come," Louis had assured her a few weeks ago when she'd brought him some tea she'd made from herbs to help his pain. She'd sat next to his bed to help him drink it, and he'd paused halfway and looked her square on. "Sometimes the greatest abilities are slow to develop. And, ability or no, if anyone has greatness in them, Cabot, it's you." His eyes had shone with unshed tears. "You're going to do incredible things."

The idea that her ability could be late in arriving had bolstered Cabot for days. But she knew she might have to settle for being skilled in other ways. And the *incredible things* part—what did it matter here in this hideaway where no one knew they existed?

Cabot had inherited her brains and a photographic memory from her superintelligent mother. Sometimes the kids would play "What page?" with her—they'd open the C–D encyclopedia and ask her what page *castle* or *downtown* or *capybara* was on. She always got it right. She could see the page in her mind.

She'd inherited her handiness from her father, who, in addition to having telepathic abilities, was something of an inventor. Though her father had built the community shower before she was born, Cabot had recently improved it by staining the outside of the water tank with black squid ink. The dark color absorbed sunlight. She'd raised the tank, as well, in order to expose more surface area to the sun. Both improvements heated the water so the children could have warm showers. And the added height made the water pressure seem stronger, too. Now, if she could get everyone to remember to refill the tank first thing in the morning so the sun could beat down on it all day, it would work perfectly.

She'd also started harvesting bamboo. She discovered that by smashing the stalks into pieces and adding water to make a mushy pulp, parts of the grass broke down and she could pull out the soft fibers, which could eventually be wound up to make yarn. It would take a long time to have enough to knit, but bamboo was plentiful and grew fast. That could help solve the problem of the kids' need for clothes.

Everyone came to her with their found treasures and seemingly useless goods to see if she could make something of them, and she always did. Hair ties out of ripped fabric, clotheslines out of frayed rope or useless cords, knitting needles out of rusted aluminum wheel spokes that had washed ashore after a storm.

Cabot often dreamed about what her latent ability might be. She wanted some sort of telepathy that would allow her to send her parents a message to see if they were alive. But she doubted it. If her parents were alive, they would be here with her.

The girl frowned and focused on the activity below. From this particular treetop she could keep an eye on everyone *and* stay away from them at the same time. She'd started coming up here a few weeks after her parents had left so she could cry without anybody trying to hug her. Greta and Jack Stone were the most incredible people Cabot knew. Greta had beat the system.

She'd manipulated documents and people in influential places in order to get a higher education and become a doctor.

She'd taught Cabot everything, from how to clean wounds to placing a tourniquet. And once, when Brix dislocated his shoulder while climbing, Greta had shown Cabot how to help him pop it back in place.

Cabot's mind-reading dad had manipulated the system, too, in his own way, by finding occasional underground work as an inventor back in Estero. He'd said there were a few people there who would look the other way when it came to his supernatural status . . . especially if his work would make them a lot of money. It helped that he could sometimes read people's thoughts, so he knew who to approach. But Jack's successes had been few and far between. Not enough to survive on.

When Cabot was little, she'd caught her parents talking quietly about how much Greta missed being a doctor. How she loved the hideout but there wasn't much to aspire to. "I want to be in a place where we are accepted *and* I can make a difference," she'd said. But that place didn't exist for supernatural people.

Even after Cabot's bouts of sorrow lessened, she kept coming to this tree because she realized she could see almost everything—the outdoor kitchen, the willow trees, the cabins set back from the beach, the creamy brown cliffs to the north, where Seven and Brix gathered eggs, and the ocean to the south, where Birdie spoke to whales. And no one could see her through the thick leaves. It was a quiet sanctuary in which to work on her own nonexistent telepathic skills. She figured she might as well try. But so far she hadn't been able to do anything.

She sat down in the log chair she'd hauled up here from her cabin a few months ago—she'd tied a rope to it, flung the other end of the rope over a branch, and Tenner had helped her pull it up. Then she picked up the binoculars that had once belonged to Troy Cordoba. She'd snagged them after he'd been a jerk to Tenner. He'd grumbled about losing them for weeks while Cabot hid them under her cot. Now she kept them up here and watched approvingly through the branches as Birdie made her way to Louis's grave. It was about time she took care of poor Brixy. He'd been sitting there half the day while Birdie had been in their cabin. By herself first, then talking to Seven, even though she'd asked everyone to give her some space. What had kept her? Just reminiscing? Or needing to be alone? Cabot could understand that. It was a shame she couldn't quite see *into* the cabins.

Sometimes Cabot regretted not starting to spy years ago. If she had, maybe she would have learned more about the grown-ups before they left. Maybe she could have gotten a clue about where they'd be if they didn't come back.

Cabot sighed and settled back on her perch, waiting to cast judgment on whoever happened by next.

BRIX

rix Golden was the youngest person he knew. His fair skin was suntanned like Birdie's and Cabot's from spending time outdoors and had a smattering of freckles across the bridge of his nose. While Birdie had dark brown eyes and straight black hair, Brix's eyes were light brown like his wavy hair, which was streaked with gold highlights.

His supernatural abilities were still developing. He'd always been small and agile and fond of climbing. And he could run pretty fast like his superspeedy mom, so he'd always wondered if his ability would bring his running to a super level. But after a recent fall down a steep cliff face, he'd simply bounced gently on the ground. Then he'd gotten up and walked away, jumping and cheering, because this was clearly a new ability he could use.

Now when he got injured—stung by a jellyfish or scraped by sharp rocks while climbing—his injuries healed quickly. And he walked with a new bounce in his step that he couldn't control, but he didn't mind that, either. It was fun to bound from rock to rock and to jump from heights he never would have attempted before.

Everyone had speculated that either Birdie or Brix would inherit some iteration of their dad's fire-charm ability. But Brix's was definitely more like his mother's. And Birdie's ability to communicate with animals was nothing like either parent's.

Brix's ability to heal quickly didn't seem to work on the pain in his heart, though. Brix had been growing closer with his dad, reading to him from one of his books when he couldn't read for himself anymore. Talking about the future with his cool new ability.

Dad had been excited to hear about what Brix could do— and relieved to know Brix could heal well. But now Brix was floundering. Cabot had brought him lunch and sat with him for a while, which was nice. But there weren't any parents now. It was hard to get used to.

Birdie approached. Puerco saw her coming and scrambled out of Brix's grasp, scraping his leg in the process. "Ouch!" he said, annoyed, but the pain only lasted a second. The scrapes sealed up before they could even start bleeding.

The tiny pig ran to Birdie and circled her, prancing and splashing in the waves. Birdie sent another message of thanks to him and felt the warmth of his answer, which gave her a rush of comfort when she needed it. The pigs and other animals never spoke in words, but they sent feelings to her, which Birdie had learned to read. Puerco was telling her that Brix was sad but he would be okay. That was good to know. She almost asked the pig if she would be okay, too . . . but she didn't think she wanted to know the answer.

"Hey, Brixy," Birdie said. She stood for a minute, shifting cool sand over her feet, then sat down next to him while Puerco nosed around in the dead leaves nearby. "Nice here in the shade."

"It would be nicer if Dad wasn't dead," said Brix. He sniffed and couldn't quite look at his sister. He didn't want to blurt out his worries, or she'd think he was a baby.

"Wow." Birdie gazed over the water, her tears having run dry for the moment. "I found a note for you. From Dad." She fished it out of her pocket and handed it to him. Then she let her eyes rest on the grave while he read it. It was weird that her father's body was right there, under the ground. And Mom and the other criminals had no idea.

Brix looked up from reading. "It's a nice note," he said, his voice shaking. He held it out to her.

Birdie took the note and read it aloud.

Dear Brix,

I love you so much. I'm excited about what a great young man you will become. I wish I could be there to see you grow up.

Birdie put a hand to her mouth and choked back a sob, then continued.

I know that a part of me will always be with you.
Stay safe and listen to Birdie. She's your grown-up now.

Love you forever.
Dad

"Oh," Birdie said. "This is lovely." She handed the note back to Brix, then added, "Especially the part about how you have to listen to me now."

Brix swiped at her, and Birdie laughed through her tears and hugged him, thinking about how different his note had been from hers and feeling a bit hollow from it. After a moment, she ventured, "Hey, Brix?"

"What?"

Birdie picked up a loose strand of a beach plant and smoothed it between her finger and thumb, noticing its milky green and yellow stripes. The note from her father weighed a thousand pounds on her mind. Should she tell him about it? It had been addressed to her, not him. Not both of them. And Birdie still wasn't sure what to do. Dad's confession and how he'd hidden what he'd done from the other criminals made her want to keep it close a little longer. Long enough so she could figure out what to do about it.

"Never mind," she said finally. She loosened her hug and pulled back. "Are you holding up okay?"

"Not really," Brix said miserably.

Birdie leaned up against the bark next to her brother and settled in, then drew him close again. "Neither am I."

Later, Birdie made her way to her favorite rock in the water and called silently to the gray whale. After a moment it rose out of the water in a glorious arc, then hit it with a magnificent splash. It drew closer and did it again, twisting in the air this time to cheer her. Birdie breathed in the salty air with a half smile on her face. Even in the midst of sadness, there were still good things in the world.

THROWING IT OUT THERE

Around the fire that evening, Birdie couldn't keep her father's dying wish to herself any longer. As Seven served dinner, Birdie sighed heavily. Then she blurted out, "I'm thinking about going to Estero."

Everyone turned to stare at her. "What?" cried Seven.

"Why?" asked Tenner.

"How?" mused Cabot.

Brix's face screwed up in confusion. "What are you talking about?"

Birdie gripped the edge of her chair, instantly regretting her decision to speak, but she plowed forward anyway. "It's been on my mind since . . . yeah. So, I didn't mention this before because it was hard to tell you. But the last thing my father said to me before he died was 'Find your mother. Tell her I did my best.' And I . . ." She choked up. "Ugh, my heart. But how . . . ? I need to think about that."

"This . . . is unexpected," said Seven. He went to his chair and set his plate down hard on the table. "We have a plan. We confirmed it last night."

"I'm sorry I didn't say it after it happened," Birdie said. "It was so shocking, and then the funeral..." It felt good to get it out now.

"Birdie," Seven said gently, leaning forward, "Louis was delirious for the past week. Maybe he didn't know what he was saying. He was clear about supporting our decision to stay. He wanted that."

Birdie scraped the toe of her shoe in the dust. "I know. But something must have changed. He left me a note, too. Like, he must have written it weeks ago when he was still strong enough. I just..."

"This is..." Seven's voice tightened, and he yanked his chair forward. "Look. We talked this through. Our parents know how to find us if they want to. We're safe here. We're not safe *there*. I'm not, for sure."

"I know all that," Birdie said faintly. The toll of Dad's death had her faltering and wondering if she was making sense. "Maybe we could find a way for you... Or I guess I could go alone." She didn't want that. It scared her to death.

"How?" Cabot said again, lifting her head. Her green eyes pierced the darkness like a cat's. On the off chance her parents *were* still alive, Cabot might be interested in going along. She was the only one who didn't have a supernatural ability to worry about.

"Like I said, I haven't figured that out yet." Birdie shrank back in her chair. Saying it out loud had made it clear: This had been a bad idea. She glanced at Seven but couldn't see much of him.

He saw her, though. "Have you told the others about the map?" he asked accusingly. His voice grew louder. "Is that why Louis made it? So you could find your mom? Why didn't you—and he—tell me this before?"

"I'm wondering the same thing." Birdie shot an annoyed look in his direction. "I wasn't trying to hide the map." She stood abruptly and accidentally sent her plate and fork clattering to the ground. "Everyone, my dad left me a map to Estero." She cringed. "I didn't know any of this before he died." She should have thought this through a lot more before saying anything. Should have expected the strong pushback from Seven. "Sorry—forget I brought this up. I'm thinking out loud about his final words, you know? Trying to process all of it. Please—I'm tired after . . . everything."

"Well, that was a pretty big announcement," Seven muttered.

"I shouldn't have said it like that."

"Like *that*?" said Cabot, one eyebrow raised.

"At all," Birdie said. She covered her face, frustrated.

"It's okay, Birdie," said Tenner, trying to calm the situation. He picked up her plate and fork and set them on the table.

Cabot remained silent and studied Birdie. There was no easy way for her to make it to Estero, so at the moment it wasn't worth arguing about, but she was curious about what led to Birdie blurting it out like this.

"Seven," Birdie pleaded, "will you say something, please?" She understood why Seven was rattled. "I—I don't want to go anywhere but to bed. It's been a hard day. My mind has been all over the place."

"Sure," said Seven coolly. Then, more kindly, "I mean it. It's forgotten."

Cabot shifted but didn't take her eyes off Birdie.

"Cabot," Birdie said quietly. "Are we good?"

"We're good," said Cabot, measured. "I mean, but how did you anticipate getting there when you brought it up five minutes ago?"

"Cabot," Birdie said with a frustrated sigh.

"Okay, sorry."

"So we're solidly back on plan?" Seven asked.

"Yes," said Birdie miserably. "Solidly."

"Good," said Seven, sounding relieved.

"Okay, well," Birdie said, "thanks for being understanding on a hard day. Tomorrow will be better. Sorry if I upset anyone. I didn't mean to." Birdie took Brix's hand and pulled him out of his seat. "Come on, buddy. Let's go to bed." Birdie put her arm around her brother, then whistled for Puerco. They walked away as the others called out their good-nights.

After Birdie and Brix were out of sight, Tenner let out a breath. "That was intense."

Cabot turned to Seven and leaned in. "Did you see this map?" she asked.

"Yeah," said Tenner, turning to him. "What's it like?"

Seven was quiet long enough to make Cabot wonder whether he was scrambling for an answer or if he'd slipped away unnoticed to argue more with Birdie. But Tenner, with his night vision, could easily see his clothing. Seven's chair creaked as he picked up his plate and fork. "It's some map Birdie found when she was going through her dad's things. It had a bunch of markings on it. A big one that pointed to where the stash was hidden." He took a few bites and chewed. "Which," he pointed out, "we all know is long gone by now. So."

Tenner nodded, ready to be done with the conversation. "Okay. Well, I guess I'll clean up."

"Thanks." Seven quickly finished the rest of his dinner. Then he scraped his chair away from the table and got up. "I believe Birdie. She was tired. And what her dad said about telling her mom he did his best—I don't blame her for wanting to do what he asked. But after a good night's sleep, she'll see it's a bad idea."

"Sure," Cabot assured him.

"I'm going to bed, too," said Seven. "Good night." They heard him moving down the path in the direction of his cabin.

"Night," they echoed.

Tenner looked at Cabot. "What do you *really* think?" he asked.

After a split second, Cabot shrugged. "Birdie's feeling the

weight of the past few days. I would be, too, if my parent said something like that to me before . . . dying." She cringed.

"Me too, I guess." Tenner flinched because it wasn't true. He moved to clean the dishes as Cabot went for water to douse the fire. Then they split up and headed for their cabins. Tenner fell right to sleep. But Cabot lay awake, staring at the log ceiling, thinking things through. She couldn't imagine that Birdie would give up this easily when it came to fulfilling her father's dying request.

NOT NOTHING

Birdie woke up with her heart thudding and an overwhelming sense of loss. Dad was gone. She wondered if the shock would hit this hard every time she woke up. Why couldn't she remember it during her dreams so waking up wouldn't be as sad? She lifted her head and glanced at Brix, still asleep on his cot, and her heart broke for him—he'd go through the same thing.

She rolled to her side and let her thoughts wander to the note and map. Last night she'd blurted out her half-baked idea of going to Estero and then immediately canned it, mostly because it had upset Seven. But having the detailed map made imagining this journey much easier than earlier, when she'd only had a vague understanding of Estero being out there somewhere to the west.

Dad's belief that Mom had been captured and was being held in Estero clearly hadn't wavered. Otherwise he wouldn't have told Birdie to find her. The thought of seeing her mom again after three years was mind-blowing. Could it be possible for Birdie to do this?

Birdie sat up with a sense of clarity. If Mom and the other criminals had actually gotten captured and were in jail, they'd definitely need the stash when they got out in order to survive . . . and to be able get back here. And if Mom was the one with the directions to the stash, she'd be sure to get her portion of it, and she could decide who to share the rest with.

After Brix got up and went to breakfast, Birdie looked at the map. She thought about what life might be like in a city with people everywhere. With huge buildings and old palaces and cathedrals, and cars and buses and trains, and cell phones . . . and money. Would she blend in? Or would the people of Estero sense that she was supernatural and do something to her?

When the kids were little, Cabot's mom had spoken wistfully about her former life working at the hospital in the big, busy city. Birdie thought it sounded intriguing, though it seemed scary, too. She couldn't figure out how a car could roll along on a road with nobody pushing it—even uphill. Her dad had told her plenty about what vehicles looked like, and there had been a whole section on cars in her encyclopedia, but she wanted to see them—see for herself how they worked. See the places her parents had spent time in, now that Dad was gone.

Yes. She was going to do it. Find her mother. Tell her the sad news and that Dad had done an amazing job raising the kids. Give her the map to the new stash so she could distribute it.

None of the other kids needed to know that was what this was about. It would only make Tenner feel bad that Louis had thought it necessary to move the stash because he didn't trust the Cordobas to share it. Besides, the kids had the best memories with Louis—they didn't need to think he'd double-crossed their parents. It would leave a stain on his memory.

Birdie would call a meeting as soon as she figured everything out, like how to follow the route across the sea. Could she continue work on the boat Dad had started building? Was that what he'd had in mind when he drew the map?

And would any of the others support her? Go with her? Brix would want to see Mom, but he'd also be scared, especially since his bouncy gait might be suspicious to anyone on the lookout for supernatural people—Birdie would be scared for him, too. But, then again, he might prefer to stick with Birdie. Cabot was probably a yes. She seemed convinced her parents were dead, but she'd still want to look for them—just in case they weren't. And she'd be curious about Estero. Birdie could probably talk Tenner into going, like she'd talked him into being the chief fisherperson so she didn't have to do it. He wouldn't want to search for his parents, though, because they were the worst. But Seven?

Birdie's shoulders slumped. He was obviously supernatural, and there was no way to hide it unless they wrapped him up like a mummy, and that would be obvious, too. Birdie would never want to put him in that kind of danger. But he was her closest friend. Maybe she could convince him to confront his parents. It would be nice to have him around for support.

Birdie and Puerco went out to the sharp point of the beach at low tide, near where a few large rocks poked up above the surface. She climbed onto her favorite flat-topped one and sat like a monkey—feet flat, knees bent all the way, bum tucked, and arms wrapped around her shins. She felt the warmth from the stone through the thin, slightly-too-big dress that her mother had left behind when she disappeared. It was starting to fit her.

Strange. Mom had been the first to go, and Dad, the last. Like bookends that contained all sorts of mysteries. Were they at the end of the first volume, embarking on the next?

Birdie glanced at the distant willow tree that marked the location of her father's grave, and a horrible thought crossed her mind. What if Mom had actually abandoned them on purpose? Birdie gripped her shins tighter as doubts crept in. It might be easier to stick to the plan and stay here.

But Mom would never do that. She, like the Stones, would come back if she were able. As the waves lapped the rocks, making the long strings of moss attached to them flow like a mermaid's hair, Birdie moved her hand to Puerco's pinkish-gray back and felt his breathing and occasional grunts and tiny, adorable snorts. She thought about the map.

Birdie tried to imagine finding her mother behind bars and was alarmed that she couldn't quite remember the contours of her face. Thankfully, after a moment, the image came back to her. But the thought of going to an actual jail in an actual big city was terrifying. Especially without friends she could count on. She *had* to convince Seven that this was a good idea.

She turned to the ocean and wondered again what the city looked like in person compared to the pictures in her books and the photographs Seven's parents had left behind. Did it have water all around or jungles nearby filled with animals Birdie could speak to? The pictures didn't show that.

As if on cue, a dark red octopus tentacle reached up around the point of a rock near Birdie's foot, its suckers tasting everything. Soon the bulbous portion of the octopus's body broke the surface. Birdie reached her hand near the tentacle, and the octopus took her fingers. "Hello," said Birdie. She didn't recognize this one, but she spoke kindly to it through her mind. *There's room for you here on this rock.* She could tell the octopus wasn't afraid, and it climbed up and regarded Birdie and Puerco. It sent a warm greeting, stayed a moment longer, then slid back into the water.

Puerco had fallen asleep on his side, his back curved and his short legs extending into a crescent moon shape. Birdie sensed movement on the beach and glanced over her shoulder to see Tenner coming toward her. She sighed. Tenner was great, but he was a lot to deal with sometimes. She turned back to the low waves, looking for other signs of life. A small hump rose up in the distance, then disappeared.

I see you, Birdie said to it. *Hello. Come closer.*

It rose again, gray and enormous this time, like before. It flipped in the water, letting its tail slap down and causing a huge spray. "Wow," said Birdie, in awe. *You're beautiful.* She waited to see if the gray whale would approach on its own, but it didn't, and Birdie was too weary today to try harder.

"That was cool," said Tenner uncertainly from behind her. "Did you ask it to do that?"

"We've been communicating a lot lately. I said hello. Maybe it was waving."

Tenner shifted on the sand, then eyed the slippery seaweed growing on the rocks and hopped carefully to the one next to Birdie. "So, how are you doing? Do you need anything?"

"What would I need?" Birdie asked without looking at him. She was starting to grow tired of people asking how she was doing. How did they think? Her father, the caretaker of all of them, had just died. She was doing poorly, thank you very much. Everyone was. It was a terrible situation.

"I don't know," said Tenner. "Maybe a hug? Or lunch? You didn't eat lunch yesterday." Louis had fondly referred to Tenner as the grandmother of the group because he was constantly feeding them, and ever since then, Tenner had done it even more.

Birdie closed her eyes. Tenner was being nice, but his niceness chipped away at her more than usual today. "I had a huge breakfast," she said, holding back tears for the hundredth time in days. "Did you go fishing yet?"

Tenner tapped something on the rock until Birdie finally turned. He had his spear in hand. "That's where I'm going now. Do you want to come?"

"Uh, no thanks." Birdie wrinkled up her nose. "Watch out for the dark red octopus. He's new."

"They change color," Tenner told her. "Besides, I wouldn't hurt an octopus. You know that."

"I know." She squinted up at him. "You're a good guy." It was true. When Birdie's ability had become apparent, Tenner had made a pact with her not to kill any creatures that Birdie could communicate with.

"Thanks."

"Do you know where Brix is?" Birdie asked.

"He's back by the grave."

"Oh." Birdie squinted in that direction, and now she could make out a spot of black under the tree that was probably Brix's shorts.

The gray whale breached again, farther out. Going away. Unlike Tenner.

Birdie stood up and balanced on the rock. Then, with a mischievous grin, she jabbed her hand out, hitting Tenner in the shoulder. He lost his balance and fell in. The splash startled Puerco, and the pig jumped to his feet.

"Hey!" Tenner cried when he surfaced. "I could have landed

on rocks." He whipped his head around, spraying Birdie with water from his hair.

"I knew you'd miss them," said Birdie, though she was relieved he actually had. She probably should have thought about that before knocking him in.

"I do know where they are," Tenner said agreeably.

"You've actually cheered me up," Birdie said. "So thanks. And sorry about that."

Tenner flashed a forgiving grin. "Byeee." He turned and slipped under the surface, still smiling as he weaved through the underwater obstacle course with his spear.

Birdie hopped across the rocks, back to the point of sand, and headed in, knowing Tenner would stay underwater for up to a half hour until he had enough fish to feed everyone. His abilities came in handy here by the sea. But if they ever left . . . if they ever went to the city, where supernatural people were not welcome or treated nicely . . . what use would his abilities be? Could he protect them by holding his breath and seeing in the dark? She almost laughed, picturing it. At least his sensitive hearing might come in handy.

"Seven!" she called as she reached the beach near their cluster of cabins. She may as well give this idea another try. And Seven would be its biggest critic—if she could convince him, the rest would be easy. She turned toward the sound of running water coming from the shower hut. "Seven!"

"I'm in the shower! Sheesh. Give me a minute."

"Come here!"

"Hang on while I get clean clothes." The water shut off.

"It's not like I can see anything," Birdie called out. She couldn't even find him, much less see anything he didn't want seen.

"I don't care," Seven muttered. "It feels weird. Why don't you get that?"

Birdie waited a moment, then glanced down the shoreline. "I can come back in a bit. I'm going to go see about the baby." She realized how silly it was to call Brix that now that he was ten. But his nickname had stuck.

"I'm coming." Seven's voice was closer now. "Is he okay?"

"He's hanging out by the grave again."

"So that's a no." Seven emerged from the shower area wearing shorts, and he had a towel around his neck. He came up to Birdie, close enough for her to see his eyes—she always liked to be able to see his eyes, she'd told him once. And he liked being with her. Most of the time, anyway. When they weren't at odds, like last night. Because even though he could be easily overlooked, Birdie never forgot to seek him out first whenever they had a decision to make. With her, he felt like he still existed. Even so, Seven wanted desperately, more than anything, to be visible like he used to be. Not just his clothes. Him. It had been a hard three years. Louis had been there for him, though.

"You're like me," Louis had told him a few weeks before he

died. Seven had brought him some cold water from the creek, and he'd waited at his bedside to help him drink it.

"I am?" said Seven, surprised.

"We've got an extra burden with our abilities. You especially. At least I could put fireproof gloves on to stop my fingers from randomly sparking. Only one body part. But I couldn't do much with them on. I couldn't write; I couldn't operate my phone. I had to take off the gloves to fill out any sort of paperwork, and then suddenly I was a menace. Shunned immediately."

Seven had nodded. "I'll be shunned wherever I go. Immediately."

"Yes," said Louis. "Unless something changes. But people have to *want* change in order to bring it about." He'd coughed violently, then sipped the water. "You're safe here in the meantime."

It had been a thought-provoking conversation. But somehow it had made Seven feel less alone.

He turned to study Birdie. "So, last night was . . . different." He toweled off his hair, which changed and blended like the rest of him. Then, as they turned to walk, he slung his arm loosely over Birdie's shoulders, which they'd done with each other since they could walk.

Birdie's shoulders stiffened. "That's kind of what I wanted to talk to you about."

"Okay . . . what about it?" Seven dropped his arm.

Birdie winced. "The map. And—" She could sense Seven's body tensing.

"And what?" he asked, guarded.

She stopped walking and faced him. "And my father's dying request. I think he needed my mom to know he'd kept his promise to take care of us when she left."

Seven's pupils didn't waver, but his heart sank. After a minute, he blinked. "Birdie," he said, like he had so much to say and didn't know where to start.

"What?"

"You know what."

"I think I'm going to do it. And I want you to come." The moment she said it, pain and longing seared through her. She wanted it very badly. She'd never been away from Seven before. And this was scary. She needed him.

Seven let out a deep sigh. "Last night you said you weren't thinking straight. You said—" He gripped his hair. "Ugh. I cannot do this. It's too dangerous. We already decided to stay. Can't you understand what this means for *me*?"

"We can figure out how to keep you safe."

"I don't want to live like that! Besides, you'll be in danger, too, if anyone finds out you're supernatural. And Brix won't be safe bouncing all over the place. Heck, even Tenner could be noticed if somebody looks too carefully at his eyes."

Birdie blew out a frustrated breath. "I don't want to fight."

Rogue tears pricked her eyes. "I still need to figure out how to do it. You have time to think about it."

"I don't need to think about it."

"Think about it anyway, please," Birdie said through gritted teeth. "Don't you want to find out if your parents are alive?" Her emotions were still high after her father's death, and she could feel anger and sadness and fear welling up and complicating things. She took a deep breath and let it out. "Let's talk more later," she said, her voice strained.

Seven didn't answer. His feelings about his parents were complicated. Sure, he wanted to know if they were alive. He also wanted to yell at them for not caring about him.

Birdie watched for him to roll his eyes, but he didn't—not that she could tell, anyway. She reached out to find his arm again. "I need to go see Brixy."

"All right, all right," he said quietly. "I'll think about it." But there was no way he was going to change his mind. He wasn't leaving here. Ever. Not even for Birdie.

CAMOUFLAGE

Seven's ability had come on slowly. His body had become translucent, and his skin began to take on the traits of its background. Unlike his invisibility-gifted father, Seven couldn't turn his ability on and off. And he also wasn't *completely* undetectable, though it grew harder and harder to notice the narrow blur of his edges and the black dots of his pupils unless you knew what to look for. He hadn't been able to talk to his parents about his ability—they'd disappeared right before the big change had begun. They might never learn what had happened to him. Did they wonder? Did they even care? Were they alive? How could they have gone away and not come back, knowing Seven's ability-reveal was imminent? But Tenner's parents had talked them into going on the search for the missing ones. So they went. And Seven believed they'd kept going all the way to Estero City to get the stash.

He wouldn't put it past Tenner's parents. And his own? They slid into a similar category. They weren't outright mean to Seven, like Tenner's dad was, but they didn't seem to enjoy having a kid, either.

Sometimes when Seven had wanted them to play with him, his dad would go invisible and sneak away. And his shimmering, hologram-projecting mom would cast an image of herself onto the sand near him, like a fake babysitter, while she was actually hanging out somewhere else with the other adults.

Louis had pulled Seven aside when the camouflage was developing. "I know this is scary. How do you feel?"

"I . . . don't know." It was hard for Seven to express what was going through his mind. "It's not what I was hoping for. I mean, I'm glad I'm not constantly shimmering like my mom. But this is just as bad. At least my dad could look like a regular person most of the time and go invisible when he wanted to. I thought I might get invisibility, too. Not . . . *this*."

Louis nodded. "Your dad had problems controlling his ability for years—he could choose to go invisible and hold it. But he also sometimes went invisible accidentally, when he didn't mean to. Because of that, he only went out at night when we were doing heists. I think the isolation took a toll on him. He finally managed to control it here in the hideout." He paused. "What ability were you hoping for?"

Seven dipped his head. "I didn't care what it was as long as I looked normal. Now, if we lived anywhere else, I'd have to isolate, too. Forever."

"You could always go freestyle like your dad did on our heists," Louis said. "In case you ever decide to go elsewhere, I mean. Nobody would see you."

"Freestyle?" Seven gave a quizzical look. Then his eyes widened. "Oh. You mean naked?" He felt his face burn. "No way. I'm not doing that. Ever."

Louis nodded. "I understand. I wouldn't want to, either."

To be honest, Seven was crushed. His ability was so . . . loud. And it didn't seem useful at all. Maybe if his dad had been here to support him, or tell him it was going to be okay, or offer suggestions on ways to control it based on what *he'd* learned, Seven would have handled it better. Louis was a great comfort, but he wasn't his dad. So Seven had buried his confused and dismayed feelings about it inside. Right next to all the other feelings about his parents' disinterest in him, and their disappearance.

In Seven's mind, there was little chance of a hologram-projecting woman or man with an invisibility trait being eaten by animals or captured by police—they could outwit anyone. Unless the two had fallen off a cliff, they'd probably made it to civilization. But then what? Had Tenner's parents talked them into going after the stash? Had they chosen money over him? It had taken a while to accept it, but now Seven was sort of glad they were gone. That way they didn't have to see him . . . like this. He'd been fading away from his parents his whole life. They'd probably be glad they didn't have to see his face ever again.

Good riddance to them all. The kids didn't need anybody's stolen artifacts to have a good life here. And they didn't need a big city full of horrible people who hated supernaturals like them. Like him. This beach was a place where a camo boy could be safe.

Maybe someday Seven would feel braver about it. Brave enough to face his fears and go after his parents to say how disappointing they were. This place was a paradise. But forever was a long time. Seven left room in the future to change his mind.

For now, it was better to stay.

Convincing Birdie would be another matter. He understood her wanting to go. And maybe . . . maybe she'd have to do that without him.

He closed his eyes and tamped down the fear that threatened at his throat. Seven was safe in the hideaway. It was the only place in the world he could live freely. Without ridicule. Without having to defend who he was to a frightening, angry sea of nonspecial people day after day after day. Without being a camo-skinned freak in pants.

SNEAKING AROUND

Cabot hadn't forgotten about the map, and she wanted to see it badly. She'd waited to give Birdie a chance to show it to them—after all, the five normally shared everything with one another, didn't they? Or at least they had before Mr. Golden died. It was hard for Cabot to bring it up because she got a lump in her throat every time she spoke about the dad who'd stayed, but her curiosity brought out the question anyway. She spotted Birdie by the creek washing her father's bedding and grabbed the near-empty water container from the shower. She went upstream from where Birdie worked and knelt to fill it.

"Hey," Birdie said in greeting.

"Morning," said Cabot cheerfully. "Sounds like that map your dad made was pretty special—he put flames on it or something?"

Birdie shrugged. She lifted a soaked blanket and twisted it to get the water out. "It was probably something he did because he was bored. Did Seven tell you that?"

"Yeah. I still don't totally get it, though. Is it a map to where Louis thought your mom is?"

Birdie twisted the blanket so hard, her face turned red with effort. "Ah," she said, panting as she put the blanket down. "No, I guess not . . . Not *that*, specifically."

"Then what is it a map *to*?"

"It's just—I don't know, Cabot. It's a map, okay? A map *of*."

"Of what?"

"Estero! And, like, the whole bay, and our hideout area and stuff."

"And the stash?"

"There are markings," Birdie said vaguely. She got up hastily and grabbed the wet blanket. "You're making too big a deal of it. And I need to put this in the sun to dry before bedtime." She left abruptly.

"Can I see it?" Cabot called after her.

Birdie kept going and didn't answer.

"Hm." The way Birdie was acting made Cabot suspicious. Was there something more to this map that Birdie wasn't talking about? Why wouldn't she want to show off a map made of flames? That was so cool!

Something was fishy. And while Cabot wanted to respect Birdie and Brix's space while they were grieving, she was absolutely determined to have a look.

Cabot watched and waited in her favorite tree perch until

the right moment came. Brix and Seven had gone hunting for bird eggs and berries on the cliffs and wouldn't be back for hours. Tenner had waded out to catch fish and would no doubt be cleaning them immediately after, so that took him out of the area for at least thirty minutes. Birdie was on the farthest-out rocks, talking to whales or dolphins like she'd been doing for hours each day since her father had died. Today she'd managed to coax a gray whale closer and closer toward the maze of rocks until it was only a short swim away. She would be occupied there for a while.

Cabot climbed down the tree and ran stealthily to Birdie and Brix's cabin. She pushed the door open and slipped inside, then hesitated for a moment to get her bearings in the dim light.

She spotted the family's crates—her father had built storage crates for all the criminals when they first came here. Cabot went over to them and knelt next to the fullest one, which looked like it might have belonged to Louis. Carefully but swiftly, she pulled the crate out and removed the items, noting the order so that she would be able to replace them exactly. At the bottom she found what she was looking for: The scroll with singed edges must be the mysterious map in question.

Cabot took it out, then checked the windows to make sure no one was coming. Seeing Birdie still occupied with the whale, she unrolled it.

The map erupted in flames. "Holy coconuts!" Cabot exclaimed, throwing the thing to the floor. It rolled up, extinguishing itself. "That's some charm." Cabot blew out a few heavy breaths and collected her wits, then picked up the map and tried again, unrolling slowly this time and holding it at arm's length. When the flames died down, Cabot quickly realized it was exactly what Birdie said it was—a map of Estero. And there, in the center, was a symbol of a bag of gold. Probably the location of the hidden stash. But there was no obvious mark that showed where Elena Golden might be.

Cabot frowned at the other markings. She couldn't decipher them . . . but she could memorize them and think about them. Her skin tingled and her instincts kicked in. She scanned every line and detail, even the letters that didn't make sense. Then she calculated various distances based on the key and the terrain. Within a few minutes, she had the entire thing committed to memory. Cabot would never have to look at it again to recall what it contained.

She was startled by Tenner whistling as he sloshed ashore and up the path into the cabin area carrying a string of fish. Cabot's chest pounded even though she knew his routine—he wouldn't be coming past this cabin any time soon. Sure enough, he stopped at the fish cleaning station with today's catch.

Cabot took one final glance at the map, closed her eyes and saw it in her mind, then rolled it up and put it back inside the crate. She replaced everything else exactly as she'd found it, ending with a few papers and a folded note on top. The name *Birdie* was written on the outside.

Cabot hesitated, bit her lip, then picked up the note. She yearned to open it and see what it was, but something made her hold back. Instead she slid it open slightly until the words *Dear Birdie* appeared at the top. She cringed, then slid it further to read the first line.

Now that the end of my life is approaching, I have a confession to make.

Her eyes widened.

"Cabot!" Tenner called. "A little help?"

Cabot gasped. She dropped the note, feeling like she'd crossed a line. The note from Louis to his daughter . . . it was sacred. She wished she'd had a special note like that from her father. And she'd never want anyone else touching it. "Coming!" Hastily she shoved everything into place.

Shaken by the whole experience, she left the cabin and helped Tenner dispose of the fish bones in the compost bin. Then she went back to her observation treetop. She sank into her chair and gazed over the ocean, pondering what she'd done.

It wasn't too bad, she concluded, now that the mission was over. Yes, she'd gone into Birdie and Brix's cabin uninvited and looked at the map. But their door had been standing open. And the map was just a map. And yeah, maybe she'd read a *tiny* part of a private note, but she'd stopped reading when she realized it was personal . . . thanks to Tenner.

"It's fine," she said, sitting up. "I'm keeping Birdie honest."

But now the words she'd read in the note were burned into her mind. Louis had a confession. What was it? And . . . could that be what was making Birdie act strange?

Cabot blew out a frustrated breath and told herself to forget about it. Maybe Birdie would tell them in time.

Out in the ocean, Birdie slid into the water and swam out past the rocky barrier, presumably toward the whale, which wasn't visible at the moment. The move was uncharacteristic and unsafe, and it caught Cabot's attention. She tipped her head to one side and watched closely, forgetting the map and note for the moment. "That's curious," she murmured. None of them went swimming beyond the rocks alone—it was very deep, and the currents were strong. But then the whale surfaced and pushed up underneath Birdie, lifting the girl onto its huge, broad back. Cabot gasped.

"Birdie!" she shouted. "What the—"

But Birdie was too far out to hear. She looked tiny compared to the great gray creature. And while she seemed to be mostly in control of the situation, it was a shocking sight. Cabot watched slack-jawed as Birdie stayed low on the whale's back. Waves splashed over her, but she held on. Cabot grabbed the binoculars and focused, then set them down and started down the tree.

"Birdie!" Tenner called from the ground, and headed toward the sandy point. "You all right?" He'd been watching, too. Cabot scrambled the rest of the way down and emerged onto the beach.

She and Tenner ran up the point as far as they could. Puerco stood alone on the tip of land, his pink snout pointed into the breeze and his little tail in a loop, waiting for Birdie to return.

"Would you look at that," Cabot murmured. Her hand grazed her short crop and stopped above her eyes to block the sun that bounced off the waves. "Amazing." The older girl had used her ability to ride a whale, and it was magnificent.

"How the heck did she do that?" Tenner marveled. "I can't believe it."

"Was she trying to ride it all this time? She's been talking to it for days."

"I guess." Tenner hesitated and adjusted his parachute swim trunks, which were almost dry. "I hope it doesn't hate me."

Cabot frowned. "What? The whale?"

"Yeah." He gathered his damp hair into a knot at the back of his neck and absently tied it in place with a rope made of braided strands of seaweed. His brown shoulders and upper back were speckled with sand that had dried in place.

"Why would you think that?"

"Because I'm always hunting for fish. Stealing from the sea. Or . . . maybe I'm kidnapping its friends?"

Cabot gave him a quizzical glance. "A whale would probably understand the concept of survival of the fittest."

Tenner looked at her sidelong, eyebrow raised. Half the time he had no idea what Cabot was talking about.

"But oh!" Cabot exclaimed. "Look!" Tenner turned back to

Birdie. The whale raised itself out of the water, making a perfect, achingly beautiful arc. Birdie stayed on, but barely. Was she asking it to do that? Out of nowhere, a pang of jealousy hit Cabot. What if *her* supernatural ability never developed? She might never have an amazing moment like this in her life. She tried to shrug it off, but it smoldered beneath her skin.

"The whole thing seems a little dangerous, doesn't it?" Tenner asked, now that the shock had worn off. His hands made fists and loosened again, over and over. "I'm not sure I like it."

"She'll holler if she needs help." Cabot nimbly hopped onto the rocks to get closer. She teetered on the tip of one—her favorite, the one with the sharpest point—and deftly found her balance on one foot. She loved the way the point dug into the sole of her sandal as if it wanted to pierce right through her. She held the position to try to improve her balance while watching the whale-and-Birdie show.

Tenner followed her to Birdie's favorite, the flatter rock next to it, and stood like a worried lifeguard, ready to go in after her if needed. Though he wasn't sure how he'd fare against a whale. What Birdie was doing seemed terribly reckless. She was sliding all over the place. This kind of whale wouldn't eat a human, but what if it batted her with its tail? She could die!

Cabot noted Tenner's tense face. "She's using her ability the way it's meant to be used," she said quietly.

"With *whales*?" Tenner muttered. "I'm going after her."

"No." Cabot grabbed Tenner's arm before he could enter the

water. "Don't. She's fine—just *look* at her. She'll have this memory forever, and she won't want you barging into it."

Tenner grimaced. But he kept watching the whale and reluctantly agreed. "Okay. Yeah." He blew out a breath. "You're right."

Cabot switched feet, making a mental note that her right side felt slightly weaker than her left today. Though she was naturally left-handed, she was working toward complete ambidexterity in all things. Louis had once told her that the world was made for right-handed people, which seemed rude (of the world, not him). Cabot thought that maybe by being ambidextrous, she might be able to see things from the others' perspectives.

The whale swam steadily now, and Birdie pushed up on the creature's back to a sitting position. She wiped the spray from her eyes, then turned toward shore to get her bearings and noticed the two standing on the rocks. Her joy was visible, and she waved, her arm sweeping the backdrop of the deep blue sky. She held her finger to her lips so Cabot and Tenner wouldn't shout or disturb whatever strange sorcery was at play here, for it was magical. Majestic. Birdie was riding a whale.

After a while, the creature sank with Birdie still on its back. Tenner tensed, ready to jump in, but seconds later, Birdie resurfaced alone. She struck out toward home.

When she reached the rocks, Cabot and Tenner bent down and helped her out of the water. Birdie's chest heaved from exertion, and water streamed down her body. Her legs trembled. But her grin went on and on. "Did you see me?"

"Yes!" Cabot told her, pride and curiosity swelling and dousing the jealousy and suspicion she'd felt earlier. "How did it feel? Tell me everything."

Birdie adjusted her swimsuit, which was made of shorts and a tank top she'd cut and sewn from a long floral, bohemian-style dress her mother had loved to lounge in when the kids were small. The swimsuit hung a bit limp around the arm and leg holes, for Birdie had used all of the dress's elastic for the waist to keep the shorts from falling down. "Absolutely indescribable. Like I've made the most amazing friend."

"You were great," Tenner said, jumping to the next rock. "Were you scared?"

"Not much," Birdie said, though her limbs still quaked. The three started back to the sandy point. "I couldn't think about being scared. It was the best thing I've done in my entire life." She was quiet for a moment as she stopped to pick up Puerco and looked over her shoulder across the expanse of ocean where the whale had taken her for a ride. "I can't wait to do it again."

Hope stirred in Birdie's heart. Had she found the answer to her problem of how to get to Estero? Could this be what her father had meant when he'd drawn that arrow across the sea?

LONGING FOR SOMETHING

After Birdie dried off and got dressed for dinner, she started to go outside to help with the food prep, but something in the cabin seemed ... off. She stopped at the door and turned back, sweeping her gaze around the small space. Then she went over to the bookshelf and studied her father's crate that sat beneath it. The hard-packed dirt in front of the crate had fresh lines scraped in it. Birdie thought they had to be fresh because she'd swept the floor since the last time she'd pulled it out. Had she accidentally skipped this spot? Or had Brix been looking through Dad's things? He'd been missing their father—maybe he'd gone in search of something to comfort him.

Birdie's heart leaped to her throat. What if he'd read the note and seen Dad's confession? She pulled out the crate and reached for the folded paper. It didn't look like it had been disturbed. And if Brix had read the shocking stuff Dad had written, he would have definitely come to her.

Maybe she was being paranoid.

She hid the note inside the encyclopedia, then dug through

the crate to the bottom. The map was in its usual place. None of the kids knew where the original stash had been located, so it was probably safe to show them the map to the new one. Maybe it would satisfy Cabot's curiosity.

She called to Puerco and gathered the pig in her arms. She wiped the sand off his snout and pressed her cheek against his warm side, closing her eyes and trying to draw strength from the feelings the pig was sending her. She wouldn't be able to bring him with her.

Together, she and Puerco went to help Seven prepare a meal out of the eggs he and Brix had collected and the fish and seaweed from Tenner's dive. She found Seven on a stool in the open-air kitchen and dining area, cracking eggs into one of the skillets their parents had brought when they'd built this hideout.

"Hi," she said brightly.

Seven looked up. "Hi. Did you have a good day?" His top half was blue-green and moving like the ocean behind him, and his legs were sand and waving beach grass.

Every time Birdie saw Seven, she thought he was beautiful in a new and different way. She wished he loved his camouflage as much as she did. Birdie hesitated, not wanting to tell him about the whale ride quite yet . . . and about what it could mean. "Yeah. Good. How is Brix doing on the cliffs?"

"He's smashing it. I'm actually jealous. He'll be quicker than me soon."

"He's got a gift," Birdie said in agreement. "Our mom was a great climber, too. Me, not so much."

"The thing is, he has no fear. Today the kid jumped down from a fifteen-foot ledge, hopped a few times, and was fine. His built-in suspension system is developing quickly." Seven cracked open the last egg into the skillet, then held the handle out to Birdie. "Can you season this? My legs are so tired from chasing him that I can barely stand up."

"Did he talk about . . . our dad?" She took the skillet.

"Yeah," said Seven, pausing to look at her. "He's processing. Doing okay."

"I appreciate you working so hard at everything. You know." Birdie turned sharply as tears stung her eyes. She walked the eggs over to the counter where they kept herbs. "And I definitely wouldn't want to watch him jump from those heights. I don't think my stomach could take it."

"I trust him to know what he can do."

"That makes one of us," Birdie said, forcing a laugh.

They each focused on their work for a moment while Birdie steeled herself for the conversation they'd both been avoiding. She glanced sidelong at Seven. "Did you have time to think about what I asked you to think about?"

"Come on, Birdie."

"Just answer me."

"You still want to do this?" asked Seven. His fruit cuts got louder.

"Yes." Birdie took a large pinch of dried herbs, crushed them, and sprinkled them over the eggs, then reached for the salt they'd mined from evaporated ocean water.

Seven put down the knife and pressed his fingers on the edge of the table. "I can't go with you. You know? I'm not—I can't."

Birdie's heart thudded in her ears. She knew he'd say that, but it was still sad to hear. She wasn't sure how to answer.

Seven looked at her. "I wish you wouldn't go, either."

They could hear Cabot not far away by the stream, muttering as she filled the water container for the shower again because nobody else remembered to do it. Then she snapped it back into place and turned the handle so it would be ready for the next person.

"I need to," Birdie said. "My heart won't let it go."

Seven threw her a hard glance. "I took an extra-long hike on the cliffs in that direction. The route is tough for someone who's not a climber. You won't make it."

"There are other ways." Birdie was glad Seven had made some effort, but her insides started to ache. She wanted him—all of them—to go with her. But that couldn't happen. "You're sure you can't go? Not even with different clothes? Cabot could design something special."

"I'd look like a . . . like that beekeeper in one of your books. You'd have to cover every inch of me. It would be more noticeable than anything. I'd rather . . ." He didn't say what he'd rather do.

Birdie fell silent as she put the skillet on the fire. "I wanted us to do this together," she whispered. Pleaded. "We're a team, Seven. You and me. We'll lead the others."

They caught each other's gaze and held it until they heard footsteps coming up the path toward them. "I can't," Seven said, his voice breaking.

Brix bounded into the clearing after a quick swim. His wet hair was standing up all over, and his arms were laden with coconuts and figs. He put them in the produce bin. "When's dinner ready?" He looked expectantly at the two.

Seven pressed his lips together. He'd made up his mind. Birdie couldn't make out his expression, but she could feel the finality in the air. She dropped her gaze. She'd made up her mind, too.

Dinner was tense. Cabot was unusually quiet and threw measured glances at Birdie, worried she'd detected the break-in and wondering about Louis's confession. She was starting to regret not reading more of the note.

Brix talked about the climbs and jumps he'd made, and Birdie tried to sound excited about them, but her heart and head weren't in it.

Tenner seemed to want to tell Seven and Brix about what had happened with Birdie and the whale but knew enough to let her bring it up, which she didn't do. And Seven stared moodily at the fire, then went to his cabin early.

After sunset, when the sky was still orange and pink, Birdie went alone to the sandy point. It was high tide, so the rocks she'd stood on earlier were barely submerged, and the sandy point was more like a small bump-out. There were no whales or dolphins in sight, but she could sense them in the waters, and she sent out a good-night message to them. Thinking about the map and the note, she turned and looked in the direction of the arrow and imagined following the flaming line across the ocean. The bay was vast enough that she couldn't possibly see the land. But she knew where it was. She knew how to get there.

Now she needed someone to go with her.

SIMMERING

W hy didn't you tell me you rode a whale?" Seven demanded
when Birdie appeared for breakfast. His voice had been
changing for a while, and the word *whale* came out in a
two-tone squeak.

"How did you hear about that?" Birdie asked while shooting
daggers with her eyes at her brother, who was sitting at the table
already.

Brix's eyes widened. "I thought you'd tell him before you told
me!" He slurped the rest of his coconut water so fast that a drib-
ble ran down his chin. He wiped it up with his sleeve. Birdie had
told him about her major accomplishment last night before they
went to sleep.

"I guess I forgot to tell you," Birdie said apologetically, "since
we had a lot of other things to talk about. But I'm heading out
now to work with my whale friend again, if you'd like to come."

"I'll come," Tenner called from afar. Anyone else would have
been out of hearing range. Soon he walked into the clearing.
"Where are we going?"

"Nowhere," Birdie muttered. She grabbed some fruit and a scoop of the root vegetable hash Seven had cooked, then sat next to Brix to eat.

Tenner's face fell, and he turned away.

"It's a little unsettling when you do that," Birdie explained.

"Okay. Fine. I'll stop." Tenner hovered over the skillet, taking his time selecting his breakfast as he tried not to feel defensive. He'd only done it to be funny.

Birdie frowned. She studied Tenner's blank expression. Was he hurt? She couldn't tell with him. "Sorry. I'm feeling cranky at the moment."

Tenner stirred the hash.

Birdie sighed. "You can come with me. I'm going to try to ride the whale again."

"Oh." Tenner sat down at the table and started eating. He struggled to put his feelings in check. And he didn't want Birdie to think he'd drop everything to do what she wanted . . . even though that was *always* what he did. This time would be different. "I'll think about it."

"Why is everybody so tense?" Brix asked. He bounced his feet on the ground, shaking the table, and looked down the path, waiting for Cabot to come and lighten things up. But she hadn't shown her face yet today.

"I know what you're doing," Seven said evenly.

Everyone looked up. "Who, me?" asked Birdie.

"Yes, you."

"I'm utilizing my ability," said Birdie. "Trying to get stronger."

"What are you two talking about?" Brix demanded.

Seven and Birdie didn't answer. Brix rolled his eyes and sank into his elbows on the table. "Annoying," he muttered.

"What do you think she's doing?" Tenner asked Seven. "I don't get what's happening."

Birdie glared holes through Seven to warn him to keep quiet, but he wouldn't look at her. Their talks about going to Estero were private. Now that he was for sure not going, Birdie had to figure out who was. And she didn't want to talk about it with the others until she'd thought it through this time.

"Never mind, everyone," Birdie said with finality. "This conversation is over." She stood up, then looked down at Tenner with his plate of food. "Are you coming or not?"

Tenner gulped down a bite of his breakfast, trying and failing to feign indifference. "I mean, yeah. Can I just go to the—"

"No." Birdie tossed her last bite of hash to Puerco, then set her dirty plate down hard in the wash bin next to Seven. She turned and started toward the sandy point with the pig at her heels.

Seven pretended like nothing was wrong. Tenner and Brix exchanged a look of mock panic, then Tenner got up and sheepishly trotted after Birdie, carrying his plate of food. "Sorry, boys," he said over his shoulder. "Gotta go."

Maybe he'd get a chance to find out what they were fighting about. Maybe Birdie would see that he was the less combative friend, the one she could count on. And confide in. And eventually she'd see he was more like a partner and less like a servant. Maybe she'd start to rely on him a little more than Seven and start having secrets with him while Seven was away, rather than the other way around. Maybe.

Probably not, Tenner thought with a sigh. The camouflaged person was the only one Birdie seemed to see. He slowed his pace to a trudge and shoveled another spoonful of food into his mouth. But he kept following, holding on to the hope that one day his luck would change.

FLAMES ACROSS THE SEA

Birdie stood on her rock, trying to calm the upheaval in her thoughts so she could call to the whale she'd ridden the day before. Tenner dropped his bowl and spoon on the sandy point and hopped onto the rock next to her. Birdie's eyes were closed and her lips slightly pursed, almost as if she were about to whistle. She rotated slowly, then stopped with her back to him.

A whale breached in the direction Birdie was facing. Tenner knew better than to say anything to disturb her, but a nervous thrill went through him. Was she actually going to let him ride it with her? Or . . . was this merely an invitation to stand here and watch her do something great?

Sometimes Tenner was annoyed with himself for not being able to break into the tight bond between Birdie and Seven. But he wasn't all that close with the younger two, either. He and Cabot often helped each other out with kitchen duties, but they hadn't exactly bonded. Her intelligence was intimidating, and that sent Tenner's insecurities into overdrive.

Did that mean *he* was the problem? What would it be like to go someplace else and make new friends?

The whale appeared again, much closer. After a few minutes, Birdie opened her eyes, then slid off her rock into the water and started out.

Tenner watched her, confused. Felt the air being let out of him again. He thrust his tongue into his cheek to stop himself from calling out to her, *What about me?* He wasn't going to cave and be the first to say something. He'd rather stand there until she came back and noticed that she'd left him.

Yeah, that was what he'd do. He'd wait and confront her. Tell her that he was a human being with feelings and say that she didn't treat any of the others like this—like they were . . . expendable. And he shouldn't have to put up with it.

He'd never dared tell his father those things. But he would tell Birdie. Soon.

Birdie started swimming, and Tenner stood there, awkward and embarrassed. He looked over his shoulder toward land to make sure nobody was watching, then pretended like he was shaking his head because that felt embarrassing, too.

His plan to stay until she noticed him started sounding bad. It could take hours. He'd look even more ridiculous if he did that. After a minute he turned and checked the shore again. Of course Cabot was there now, standing by one of the trees she liked to climb, waiting for him to make a move. She pretended not to be watching him, which was generous, but they both knew the truth. Cabot was always watching everyone.

"This is super annoying," Tenner muttered. He gave up and started back across the rocks.

Birdie stopped swimming and turned in the water, looking back. The sun lit her path across the water—a big white glaring path, with the ripple of waves making sharp teeth along both sides. "Did you forget how to swim?"

Tenner turned. "Huh?"

Birdie blew a stream of water from her lips. "Aren't you coming? Our ride is here! Geez, I don't understand you sometimes."

Tenner blinked. Had he missed something? She was the one who'd gone off without a word.

"Tenner!" she exclaimed. "What is going on with you? Don't you want to swim with the whale?"

"I'm coming!" he said. Heat flooded his cheeks. Annoyed. But . . . Yeah. Whatever. Before she could see how flustered he was, he jumped to the farthest rock and dove expertly into the space he knew was clear of hidden obstacles. Underwater, anger boiled and fled through his eyes with their extra-large pupils, through the bubbles of his exhale, as he swam to her. Not *to* her, but past her. And on toward the whale.

Soon *she* was trying to catch up to *him*.

Birdie was right—she didn't understand him sometimes. And he didn't always understand her. He wished he could accept that. But could it ever be okay that they didn't get each other when their whole world consisted of five people?

After his burst of frustration, he slowed down in the water and let her pass him. After all, he didn't know how to approach whales. But hopefully he'd shown her how rude it was to leave people behind. He didn't have to point it out face-to-face. He could only imagine her reaction—confusion? Anger? He didn't want that. He wished he could say something to her and then pause the world so she couldn't respond.

Tenner didn't surface, and instead watched from underwater as he swam behind Birdie. The water was clear today, and he could see the bottom way out here—the beauty of it made him ache inside. There was something about the ocean that allowed him to feel things in a way he couldn't on land. The ocean was supportive. It didn't scrutinize him or judge him.

The gray whale moved closer. What a beast! It threw a huge, ominous shadow over the sea plants and fish below them. Some fish swam alongside it, and others scattered. Tenner caught a glimpse of the new octopus, who seemed to have made a den in a cove of rocks and plants. The octopus didn't appear bothered by the whale or the humans. Tenner's heart pounded, and for once he fought to catch his breath, but he took his cue from the octopus and stayed steady.

He could see barnacles populating the whale's underside— they would be sharp, so they'd need to take care not to cut themselves. Tenner put aside his list of grievances with Birdie. This whole experience, compared to his normal fishing expeditions, was a once-in-a-lifetime thing.

Birdie swam up, touched the whale's fin in greeting, and went to float above its slick back. Tenner followed, situating himself behind Birdie. When the whale moved up, it caught the two floating humans and brought them above the surface.

Was Birdie directing all of this? Or did the whale already know its riders needed to be above the water? Whales were mammals that breathed air like humans did. How long would it ride this close to the surface?

Soon they were moving forward. The top of the whale's back was out of the water, leaving Birdie and Tenner sitting together, one in front of the other, both sliding a bit but glad for the parachute material of their shorts, which clung to the whale's skin.

Birdie looked over her shoulder with a blissful expression. Water droplets shone on her eyelashes. "Can you believe this?" It was clear to her who would be the best companion across the sea. Tenner wasn't her first choice, but he was an expert in the water. That was exactly what she needed to stay as safe as possible.

Tenner shook his head and brushed the wet hair off his forehead. Sometimes he felt like he belonged in the ocean. He wished he'd gotten Birdie's ability to talk to animals, because there were a lot of them out here. He'd never been this close to a whale before, much less riding on its back. "This is incredible."

"Well, you might want to get used to it," Birdie told him.

Tenner frowned. "What do you mean?"

Birdie smiled. She gazed out to the west, thinking about that blazing arrow across the water. "Oh," she said, "you never know."

"If you think you're going to do this a lot," said Tenner, "you might want to wear full parachute pants that will give you more surface area to connect with the whale's skin."

"That's a good idea," said Birdie. She eyed him appraisingly, then faced forward again. Maybe he wouldn't be so bad.

Tenner lifted his chin. Perhaps she'd gotten the message.

They rode around for several minutes before the whale submerged near their rocks. They swam to the surface and floated, unsure if they were done. But then it came back and lifted them up again. "Can you tell the difference between the whales you've been talking to?" Tenner asked.

"I can in my mind—they sound different. And they grow . . . warmer, I guess, the longer we communicate. But physically? All I've noticed is that this one has eight little knuckles on its dorsal ridge back there," Birdie said. "There's another that has six, but I haven't touched that one yet."

"Interesting." Tenner glanced back, noting the bumpy ridge near the tail. He leaned forward as the whale picked up speed. "What are you and Seven disagreeing about?"

Birdie sighed. "You'll find out soon enough. I think I'm going to call a meeting when we get back."

Tenner grimaced. "Is this about finding your mother?"

"Yeah," said Birdie. "I know I said everyone should forget about it, but I can't. And I feel like I have to go. I talked to Seven . . ." She flashed Tenner a guilty look, as if apologizing for doing what she always did. "He won't go. So . . ." She bit her lip. "I'll either go alone, or maybe . . . you or someone else would want to come along." She hesitated. "You'd be the best choice."

"Oh." Tenner coughed into his hand, then cleared his throat. "Wow. Okay. Something to think about, for sure." It was hard to mask his surprise. Go to Estero? The best choice? It was something he'd given up thinking about. Now it sounded scary . . . but exciting. His mind whirled, but he knew better than to fire questions at her—that would be annoying. And then she'd pick someone else.

Once they reached dry ground, Tenner looked to see if Cabot had noticed how much fun he was having with Birdie. Instead he saw Brix storming down the path toward them, holding something that appeared to be on fire.

THE CONFRONTATION

Birdie muttered under her breath as Seven and Cabot followed Brix, all three coming toward them.

"What's he got?" Tenner asked.

"It's the map," Birdie said. Her stomach churned, worried he'd found the note, too, but she'd tucked it out of sight.

"Why didn't you show me this before?" Brix asked, holding it up and shaking it, making the flames sway. "This is neat!"

"Careful!" Birdie said. "Don't wreck it!" She grabbed his wrist and pried the map away, then held it above her head so he couldn't grab it back, but he started bouncing to reach for it.

Seven stepped in and gently held Brix back.

"I was going to show you all today," Birdie said. "But I've been preoccupied with the whales."

"Seven told us you're definitely going to Estero," Brix reported.

"Seven!" Birdie exclaimed. "Why did you tell him that?"

"He asked what we were talking about at breakfast." Seven said. "I got tired of keeping it a secret when it didn't need to be."

"I wanted to figure out a few things first," Birdie grumbled. "How did you find the map?"

"It wasn't me," Seven said, holding up his hands.

"Cabot told me what it looked like," Brix said.

"Cabot! How would she know?" Birdie turned sharply to look at her. "You snooped around in our cabin? How would you like it if I did that to you?"

Cabot shrugged. "You couldn't get past my security system."

"Your *what*?"

"I'm . . . joking." Cabot wasn't joking. She had a trip wire at her cabin door she could employ, and nets full of rocks at both windows that would hit anyone in the face if they tried to open them from the outside. And why not? There were wild animals out there. And maybe even police searching for supernatural criminals. She threw Brix a snide look for getting her in trouble. She'd been hoping Brix would find the note, too, but he said there wasn't one. Now what was she supposed to do?

Birdie made a frustrated noise. "Stay out of my private stuff!"

Cabot took a step back and put her hands up in defeat. "You're right. I'm sorry."

"Sheesh, Cabot," Birdie said, still rattled. If Cabot had found the map, did that mean she'd seen the note? It had been right on top until Birdie had buried it in the encyclopedia. Hopefully she hadn't snooped until after that.

Cabot eyed her back, eyebrow raised as if issuing a challenge. Birdie was the first to look away. "Okay," she said. "Let's have a group meeting at the fire pit in ten minutes. We need to talk about this . . . and about what we're doing next."

She and Tenner walked toward the cabins so they could change. Birdie pressed her lips together as she watched Seven peel off from the group, heading for the fire pit. His eyes flickered back. This was going to be interesting.

SEVEN WAS TENDING to the fire when the rest of the kids gathered. Birdie held the rolled map tightly in her fist. Seven remained standing, unnecessarily prodding the logs with a stick, while the others sat. "Does this mean we're going to Estero to look for Mom?" Brix asked.

"I will be," said Birdie. "Seven will stay here."

Cabot's expression flickered. She closed her eyes and sank back in her chair, trying to decide how she felt. Believing her parents to be dead had given Cabot a reason to forgive them for not returning. And knowing they were going to stay here indefinitely had doused all thoughts of going to Estero to look for them. But now that Louis had opened that door and told Birdie to find her mother, maybe it would be smart to go along with her.

"We can't stay here forever," Birdie was saying.

"Why not?" said Seven. "We have everything we need."

"But there's much more out there," Birdie said, sweeping her arm to the west, in the direction of the mainland.

"A lot more," Tenner chimed in. After what she'd said earlier about him joining her, he was all for it. But she hadn't mentioned him to the group yet. Was she going to? Or was he supposed to declare he was going? He never knew what to say.

"I want to find Mom," Brix said.

"It would be hard, though," Cabot said, seeing where she was needed to balance the discussion. "We have no money. From what I understand, you need money for everything. Like, even for food."

"My dad's wallet has money in it," Birdie said. "Remember? He taught us about it."

"That's weird," said Brix, shaking his head. "Do you pay when you slosh up to the shore with your fish or what? Who would trade a piece of paper for a whole fish? It doesn't make sense. Unless maybe if you don't have any paper."

"My parents also left money behind," Tenner announced, and they all turned to look at him in surprise.

"They did?" Birdie asked. "Are you sure?"

There was Birdie, right on cue. "Yes, Birdie," he said, sounding more impatient that he meant to. "I'm sure it's money."

"You never mentioned it before," Birdie explained.

"That's because I just found it in one of my dad's pants pockets when I went to make shorts out of them. Folded in a clip. It's, like, a hundred and twenty, or whatever," Tenner said, sounding less sure now about how to speak about the bills. "Which seems like a lot."

"Are you going to look for the stash, too?" asked Brix, sounding confused. "It's marked on the map."

Tenner shook his head. "I keep telling you. My parents would have gotten it already."

Birdie threw him a pitying glance that Tenner intentionally ignored. "This trip is about fulfilling my father's dying wish," she said. It wasn't a lie.

"That's it?" Cabot asked. "You're going to find your mom and then come home?"

Birdie softened. "We can look for the other parents, too, if that's what you're asking."

"Hm." Cabot narrowed her eyes. "Maybe I'll go with you. When are you leaving? And *how* . . ." Then she blinked and looked out to the ocean. "Oooh. I get it now, you clever Bird."

"We can ride a whale there," Birdie said, filling in the answer for those who hadn't figured it out.

"I knew it!" Seven tossed his stick into the sand. "Ridiculous."

"Yeah," said Cabot. "It's cool in theory but super unpredictable in reality."

Birdie flinched. "I'm serious."

"I know you are," Seven said. "But it's such a long way. You'll never make it."

Birdie's cheeks turned red. "I've been working with the whale, and I think it can be done."

Cabot slumped as reality set in. While she was all for searching for her parents, Seven was right about the transportation.

It was a ridiculous idea. Cabot wasn't a strong swimmer, so the prospect was extremely frightening.

"How far is it?" Brix asked anxiously. He wasn't a great swimmer, either. And Seven seemed to be making more sense than Birdie right now.

"I don't exactly know," Birdie admitted. "I can probably figure it out, though."

Sixty-three miles over water, thought Cabot. *Ninety-eight by land, unless you swim part of the way where the bay is narrowest, which shaves at least twenty miles off the trip.* Her brow furrowed. *Doing that could save a couple days of walking, depending on the terrain.*

"You can all go without me," Seven announced. "I'll be here when you come back. I don't care." It wasn't true. He cared a lot. But he wasn't going to force anyone to stay with him.

Birdie went over to him. "I care," she said, and tears sprang to her eyes. "I wish it were safe for you."

Seven pulled away. "That whale isn't safe for anybody."

"I agree with Seven," Cabot said. Her chest felt heavy. "I'm staying."

"Tenner?" Birdie said, trying to be patient. "You'll come with me on the whale, won't you?"

Finally. Tenner looked up, trying to be nonchalant. "Yeah. Sounds fine to me."

"Brix?" Birdie asked. "We have to be prepared to do a lot of swimming out in the deep water, where it can be very choppy or have high swells. What do you think?"

Brix looked at Seven with a fearful expression. The whale freaked him out, and the whole trip over the ocean was frightening. "Will you bring Mom back with you?"

Birdie flashed a small smile. "I'll do everything I can," she promised.

Brix nodded. "I guess . . . I'll stay here with Seven."

Birdie nodded. "That's probably for the best with your bouncing. Seven will keep an eye on you."

"I'm not a baby," Brix muttered.

"I know. If you want to write Mom a letter, I'll give it to her if I find her."

That cheered Brix slightly.

Birdie glanced at Tenner. "I guess it's just us," she said with a wan smile.

Tenner shrugged. "Looks that way."

Cabot closed her eyes, wishing she dared go with them. She longed to know something more of her parents. "If you see my parents . . ." she started to say, but then she choked up.

"I'll find out what's keeping them," Birdie said quietly.

Cabot nodded. "Thanks." The memory of Louis's note flickered before her, and again she wondered what his confession was. Maybe it had nothing to do with his dying wish.

Seven slumped into his chair. "What if you drown?" he blurted out. "I'm scared for you."

"It's going to be okay," Birdie said, pushing down the fear that jumped into her throat. "The whales are my friends. They won't let that happen." She glanced at Tenner. "We'll leave in the morning."

That night, Birdie dozed uneasily with the map clutched in her hand. Brix cried in his sleep. Tenner slept soundly with the hint of a smile on his face. Seven stared at the ceiling of his cabin for hours, then got up and packed a bag. He stared at it for a long time, and then, with a sigh, he unpacked it and put everything away. And Cabot tossed and turned, wondering what Louis could have possibly confessed to his thirteen-year-old daughter . . . and if it had anything to do with Birdie and Tenner leaving.

ONE LAST MOMENT

B rix got up first and woke his sister. "You're not really leaving, are you?"

"I really am," Birdie said, and the feeling of calm that washed through her gave her the confidence she needed. She got up and dressed in full parachute pants and a long-sleeve shirt. Then she took some of her mom's old sneakers and put them into her backpack. Mom's shoes fit her now, even if some of her other clothes didn't quite yet.

Brix frowned.

"Aw, buddy." Birdie gave him a hug. "We'll be gone less than two weeks," she promised. She whipped open the flaming map to show him. "We'll travel across the bay and figure out the layout of the city and how to buy food and stuff like that. Then we'll check out all the marked spots on the map. I think they're places where Dad thought Mom might be."

"But where are you going to sleep?"

Birdie shrugged. "There's probably a beach there, since the ocean touches it. I'm not worried."

"I'm worried. What if . . ."

Birdie tipped her head to one side and regarded him with concern. "What if what?"

"What if the bad parents are there, too? Like Tenner and Seven think they might be?"

Birdie had thought about that. If they'd figured out that Louis had been the one to move the stash, they'd be mad. Hopefully they thought it was stolen by someone else. "If we see them, we'll talk to them. They might know where Mom is. But Estero is a big place with thousands of people," Birdie said. "Maybe *millions*." The thought was overwhelming, and she couldn't picture it. "There's not much chance we'll run into them."

"But what if you do?" Brix asked. "What if they're mad that you left the hideout?"

Birdie felt a pang strike her chest. "They won't find us. They don't know we're coming. Besides, I doubt they'd even recognize us. We've grown up since they left."

"What if you talk to them and they . . . do something to you?"

"Brix," Birdie chided. "They're thieves, not murderers. We're coming back. I *promise*."

Brix's face remained clouded as the siblings went to the dining table.

Tenner was already there with a waterproof backpack. Their camp had two of the high-tech packs left from when the criminals had parachuted here—the one belonging to Louis, and an extra one that had held supplies. Tenner had filled his halfway with necessary items and didn't squeeze out the air before he'd sealed it—it would act as a life preserver and keep him afloat if necessary. "I've got the money," he announced to Birdie, patting the pack. "The big One-Two-Oh Money. Dollars."

"Great," said Birdie. "And I've got the bills from my dad. We should have enough for ... things."

Tenner bounced on the balls of his feet. "I packed food, too, in case it costs, like, a hundred or whatever and we run out. I got up before sunrise and smoked some fish so it'll stay fresh for a few days. I made extra for breakfast."

"Wow," said Birdie, blinking. "You've been busy."

"I packed a few oranges, too, and some wild carrots I found at the edge of the jungle last night. Oh! And I brought a pair of sunglasses from my dad's crate. I don't want anyone to notice my extra-large pupils."

"All right, Tenner," Birdie said, moving to the counter. She rummaged in the silverware bin for a fork and grabbed a plate, then loaded it up with sauteed mushrooms and the smoked fish. She didn't think anyone would notice the minuscule difference in his eyes, but he was convinced of it. It would be easier for her to appreciate Tenner when he was the only one she had. She glanced around. "Is Seven up yet?"

Cabot spoke from the turned-around chair, startling them. "He's on the beach." She turned around on her knees to face them, then decided to go for it. "Is there anything else going on with this trip, Birdie?"

"Like what?" Birdie's eyes widened. She took a bite of food as she moved toward the table, then chewed slowly as her stomach twisted.

Cabot's face wrinkled in consternation. She didn't want to admit to reading the first part of the note and had exactly zero reasons to question Birdie's intentions other than an overactive brain. She chickened out. "Nothing. Like I said, Seven's on the beach."

"Ooh-kay." Birdie shook her head, then stubbed her toe on the chair leg and caught herself on Tenner's arm. "Thanks," she said, and she and Tenner exchanged quizzical glances. As Birdie went down the path, she looked back at Cabot, who was watching her go. It was time to get out of there.

"I gotta go write my note to Mom," Brix called to Birdie, and went bounding back to the cabin.

The morning tide was coming in. Seven was standing where the frothy waves could lick his feet. His body was the sea, except for his shorts and part of his feet, which blended with the wet sand. Birdie cleared her throat as she approached so she wouldn't startle him.

"Hey," she said.

Seven turned. "Hey."

"You okay?"

"Not really."

A pang struck Birdie's heart. "I told Brix we'll be back in two weeks, tops."

"Two weeks," Seven said thoughtfully. "I've never actually been away from you for more than a few hours in my entire life. So . . . it's hard." He hesitated, almost wanting to tell her he'd packed a bag in the night. Almost. He'd come to his senses once the morning sunlight had streamed through the window and landed on his arm.

Birdie felt the distance between them. Seven meant everything to her. It seemed wrong to be leaving without him. "It's strange for me, too. You can still come if you want."

Seven was quiet for a moment. "I actually thought about it, you know?" he said. "I thought maybe I was being selfish or something."

Birdie frowned. "Well . . ."

Seven continued. "I hope things have changed for supernaturals there. If they have . . . maybe I'll go next time."

"Deal," Birdie said with a grin.

"If you happen to see my parents . . . just . . . I don't even know."

"I'll kick 'em in the teeth for you," Birdie said. "Though I'll probably miss on both counts if your dad goes invisible and your mom's only a projection." She gave him a sympathetic smile. "Are you going to be okay while I'm gone?"

"We'll be all right." Seven didn't sound fine now, though.

Unsure what else to do, Birdie reached her arms around her best friend and gave him a hug. "I need to go get my things. We have a long day ahead of us."

Seven slid his cheek alongside Birdie's. "Please don't drown."

"We have the special backpacks. And I won't be alone—Tenner will be there," she said. "That's the main reason I'm bringing him along. I'm being careful."

"I know."

"And I'll be careful while we're in Estero, too."

Seven smoothed her hair, then turned and took her hand, and they started back toward the cabins.

BON VOYAGE

Brix handed the note for his mother to Birdie. She put it in her backpack, then gave Brix a solemn look. "Take care of Puerco for me."

"I will," said Brix. His face was etched with worry.

Birdie gave him a hug. "I'll miss you."

Brix nodded against her shoulder, and then they released each other. It was time to go.

Birdie grabbed her backpack and took a last look around. Four family cabins set among the trees. The school cabin, the kitchen, two toilet rooms, and the shower. All built by people who were no longer there. The thick bushes and beach grass around the cabins were startlingly more overgrown than Birdie remembered. Even the trees seemed taller—when had that happened?

It was her first time leaving this place. First time for any of the kids. She glanced at Tenner, who was intently scraping something sticky off the bottom of his shoe as he waited for her. "See you soon," she whispered to the hideout. And then she slung the backpack over her shoulders and headed to the beach.

Birdie's pack contained essentials like clothes and food, and she'd also packed the earliest of her father's hideaway journals. She hadn't gotten very far because Louis's long entries were filled with tight, cramped lettering. But it might help to read it if she was having trouble getting to sleep in Estero.

Birdie began mentally calling to the whales while Tenner hugged the others goodbye.

Cabot shifted from one foot to the other in the cool sand, squinting at Birdie while she wasn't looking. Sweat glistened on her forehead, even though the heat of the day was not yet upon them, and her skin looked pasty.

"Are you feeling sick?" Brix asked her.

"I . . ." said Cabot. She stopped shifting. "No, I'm fine."

The gray whale surfaced nearby, surprising them all with its quickness to respond. Birdie didn't want to make it wait, so their final farewell was hurried.

"What if something happens?" Brix asked for the umpteenth time.

"Oh, I'm sure something will happen," Birdie said, moving to the sandy point and pulling Tenner with her. "And we'll tell you all about it when we get back. You'll hardly miss us."

"We might miss the fish for dinner," Seven pointed out, trying to lighten things up for Brix's sake, but his voice was shaky.

"That's all part of my plan to make you appreciate me more," Tenner called over his shoulder.

"Love you all!" Birdie said with a wave, and Tenner echoed her. "Love you! See you soon!" They hopped across the rocks, then jumped into the water.

"Bye!" cried Brix. He followed them across the rocks and stopped, peering anxiously after them. Seven came after him, while Cabot trailed behind.

Birdie and Tenner swam out to the open sea. Soon the gray whale rose up, and they found their seating. In seconds they were heading west.

When they were out of sight, Brix sighed and turned back. "I have to clean my cabin," he said. "I threw things everywhere trying to find a blank piece of paper."

Cabot looked up sharply. Maybe the note was still in the crate. "I'll help you."

Seven followed, feeling out of sorts. "I may as well help, too." The three went to the Goldens' cabin and started picking up all the journals and books that had been in Louis's crate.

Cabot riffled through the first journal, then casually shook the other ones, hoping the note would fall out. She put them in order the way Louis had numbered them. The most recent journal was open to the last entry. The page opposite had been roughly ripped out—probably the piece of paper that had become Brix's letter to his mom. Cabot shook that one in case the note was there.

It wasn't. But she glanced at the final journal entry title, which was written in shaky, bold letters dated a few days before Louis had died. *BIRDIE & BRIX: In case you go to Estero.* Cabot set it aside to read later—it was more important to find Birdie's note without appearing to be sneaky.

She reached for the worn-out C–D encyclopedia. She picked it up and flipped through the pages carefully, in case the note was tucked deep inside there somewhere. "Remember when we used to play 'What page?'?" she asked.

"Do you think you could still do it?" Seven reached for the book.

Cabot's smile faded. She handed it to him, trying to shake all the pages loose, but it was too heavy. Nothing fell out. "Uh, sure," she said. "Give me a word."

Seven let the encyclopedia fall open to the *Ch* section. There was a folded slip of paper inside that he thought at first was being used as a bookmark. He pulled it out and opened it. "What's this?"

Cabot's eyes widened as Seven examined it. She casually leaned in to read it, too.

Dear Birdie,

Now that the end of my life is approaching, I have a confession to make. Fifteen years ago, right before your mother and I and the other adults were forced to leave Estero, I moved our hidden stash . . . without telling anyone. I've created a map that leads to it. When you are of age and feeling especially brave, I want you to go to Estero, find your mother, and give her the map.

Please be careful.
I love you, and I'm sorry . . . about everything.
Dad

Seven stared at the words. Cabot's throat tightened. They looked at each other.

"I don't think we were supposed to read this," Seven said quietly.

"What is it?" said Brix. He took the note out of Seven's hand and bounced around the room, reading it out loud. "Whoa," he said when he finished. "That's a lot different from the note he left me." He stopped bouncing and looked uneasily at the other two.

The confession slammed into Cabot. "Louis . . . rehid the stash? So no one else could find it?" She was flabbergasted. "Not even my parents? How could he do that to them?"

Seven turned away as betrayal and fear seized him. "Birdie didn't tell me anything about this."

"Was it because she's doing something underhanded, too?" Cabot said sharply. "Like her dad?"

Tears sprang to Brix's eyes. "My dad didn't do bad things."

"Of course he did," Seven said. "He's as much a criminal as

the rest of them." He blew out a breath and put his hand on Brix's shoulder. "Look. He was good to us, but this is a *confession*—even he says so. I'm sure there's an explanation for why he did it. But Cabot's right. It's kind of suspicious."

"Kind of?" Cabot said with a snort. "Birdie lied to us!"

"She didn't lie," Brix retorted. "She just didn't tell us everything."

Seven sat up on his knees, thinking. "If Troy and Lucy and my parents went searching for the stash three years ago and it wasn't there . . ."

"They must have been mad," Brix said anxiously. "Would they know my dad was the one who moved it?"

"Louis would be the obvious guess," Seven said slowly. "He was pretty open about not trusting Troy." He imagined the implications, then shook his head. "Birdie is being reckless. If Troy found out she and Tenner were in Estero with a map to the new stash location, he'd go after them."

"And Troy has X-ray vision." Brix's eyes widened, and he shivered. "There's nowhere for them to hide."

"Do you think Tenner knows what Birdie is up to?" Cabot asked.

"If not, he's even more vulnerable than Birdie," said Seven. "I hope she told him for his safety."

Cabot agonized. "What if my parents *are* alive, and they needed their share of the stash to get back?" Her hand rose to her throat. "What if that's what's keeping them away?"

Brix's face went gray. He'd always been afraid of Troy Cordoba's booming voice. "I'm scared for Birdie and Tenner."

"Me too," said Seven. He started pacing, then took the note from Brix and read it again. "Maybe they won't run into anybody. It's a big place. What does a thousand people look like, especially if they're all moving around? Or . . . a million?" Try as he might, he couldn't fathom it.

"I'm more worried about my parents," Cabot said. "The note doesn't say Elena will distribute the money. Did Louis do it this way so she could keep it all? Is that why Birdie didn't tell us?"

"I don't think Louis would want that," Seven said firmly. "And I don't think Birdie would want that, either."

"Then she should have told us," said Cabot.

"At least now our parents can find it if they need it," Brix said, trying desperately to smooth things over with Cabot.

"It's not *our* parents who can find it," Cabot said. "It's yours."

"But I know my mom will share," Brix insisted.

Cabot shoved the crate, disgusted. The crate sent the journal spinning in front of Seven. "I *knew* I should have gone with them," said Cabot. "I had a gut feeling . . ." A gut feeling that had started when she read that first line a few days ago. She didn't think the boys needed to know about that. She regretted not reading a little bit farther. Maybe she could have stopped Birdie.

"I feel sick," Seven said. He couldn't get the picture out of his head of Troy coming at Tenner and Birdie in some unfamiliar place. Not understanding what Estero was like made it all worse.

"I'm mad," Cabot said, though she managed to flash a comforting look at Brix. "But not at you, Brix. Okay?"

Brix nodded. "Okay."

"I don't know what to do," Seven said as conflicting thoughts pounded him. And then his eyes landed on the journal.

NEW MOTIVATION

Seven picked up the journal and read the last entry aloud. Parts of it were hard to read because Louis's hand had been very shaky in his final days. It was more like a note to his kids than a journal entry.

BIRDIE AND BRIX: In case you ever go to Estero

The ancient lower tunnels of Estero would be a safe place to hide if you are in danger. After years of searching for an entrance, I finally found one days before we came to the hideout. I told your mom but kept it a secret from the other parents. I don't trust Troy . . . and you shouldn't either.

The entrance is a near-invisible, moss-covered door in the ground. It lies in the shadows and overgrowth of trees on the edge of the park across from Sunrise Foster Home.

"A safe place to hide," Seven murmured. "One that Troy doesn't know about." That was exactly what Birdie and Tenner needed. He looked up at Brix. "Do you think Birdie has read this journal?" He held it up so Brix could see the cover.

"Not that one," said Brix. "My dad kept telling her to read them, but she only just started the first one after he died—that's the one that's missing."

Seven's heart wouldn't stop racing as he imagined how angry the bully would have been to discover the stash missing. "I know Estero City is a big place. But if one of the bad parents runs into them as they're scouring the streets . . . Birdie and Tenner are definitely not safe with that map."

"And if they get ahold of it," said Brix, turning to Cabot, "your parents for sure won't get their share."

Cabot gripped her head in angst. "Should we—" She lowered her hands and looked at Seven. "Should I—" She got to her feet and put her hands on her hips. "I'm going after them."

Seven dropped his head into his hands. "Cabot . . ."

"Somebody needs to make sure the money gets distributed fairly. And I'll tell them about the secret hiding place in the lower tunnels, too. I'll take the land route, obviously." She reached for the journal.

Seven gave it to her. But he couldn't let Cabot go alone—she was a good climber but the weakest of the three of them. And she was eleven. Brix could help her, but what kind of guardian would Seven be if he let her go with a ten-year-old? Birdie would never forgive him. And even though he was hurt and angry that

she didn't tell them what the note said, he wouldn't put Brix's life in danger because of it. He'd have to go.

His throat closed in fear. Even if they made it through the treacherous journey, he'd be in even worse danger than Tenner and Birdie because of how he looked. Brix wasn't much better off. He broke into a cold sweat. "We don't have a map," he said weakly.

"I memorized it," Cabot said. Sensing his turmoil, she added firmly, "We have to make sure Elena—or the other criminal parents—don't find the stash and keep it for themselves. It belongs to *all* of our parents."

Brix nodded and let a sob escape. "Birdie and Tenner are in danger. We need to tell them about this hiding place. I'm going with Cabot."

"Augh." Seven closed his eyes and filled his chest with air. Then he let it out slowly between pursed lips. He didn't care if his parents got cheated out of their part of the stash. It was Brix's argument that got to him. And Brix and Cabot's insistence on going that forced his hand.

"Okay," he said. It sounded like another person's voice. "We'll all pack up and go. Now . . . before I change my mind." He got to his feet, then picked up the rest of the journals to take with them in case there was more important information inside. "Are you both up for the hardest journey of your life?"

PART TWO

NO LOOKING BACK

The whale went at a steady clip as Birdie directed it. She and Tenner had talked excitedly at first about what they faced, but the farther they went from the land, the more Birdie started to think Seven had been right about worrying over this trip. They were out on the open sea, far from everything. She felt tiny.

Tenner pointed to a distant spot. "Dolphins," he said. Then added nervously, "Or sharks."

When they got close enough for Birdie to see the fins, she shivered. *Hello, dolphins.*

There was no response. Did that mean they were sharks? "Real life hitting us in the face right now," Birdie muttered. She kept up a mental conversation with the gray whale they rode, but after about thirty minutes, it submerged without warning, leaving Tenner and Birdie skidding through the waves. They bobbed in the water, their backpacks puffed up behind them and keeping them afloat. The bright morning sunshine made the water seem turquoise on the horizon, but it was murky green here in the depths. There was no land in sight. They felt like two tiny dots in the giant ocean.

Come back! Birdie called. But the whale was gone—needing to eat, or perhaps attending to the call of another whale. *Thank you!* Birdie added, trying not to project her distress in case sharks were able to pay attention. She looked at Tenner as they treaded water and tried not to think about her legs getting bitten off. "I was afraid this might happen. I'm going to try to find another whale."

"I'll have a quick look around for sharks," Tenner said. He flipped out of his backpack and gave it to Birdie to hold on to while he dove under. His vision focused in the dark water, but he still couldn't see the bottom. Brightly colored fish, speckled and striped, shimmered past, and plankton floated all around. A large swordfish, longer than Tenner was tall, appeared, making Tenner bolt toward the surface and wish for his spear. He didn't think it would attack them . . . but if it did, that needlelike sword would hurt.

It kept moving. A moment later, a pod of dolphins interrupted his sight line. He could hear their trills. He surfaced next to Birdie. "Dolphins?"

"They're coming?"

"Yes! Thank goodness." He didn't tell her about the swordfish. He took his backpack from her and wriggled into it. "How do we ride them? They have a dorsal fin about halfway back."

"I'm not sure. We'll figure it out. Maybe they'll show us."

Soon nine dolphins surrounded them, gray and silvery and shiny with intelligent eyes and boopy snouts. "Wow," Birdie said. "Grab a dorsal fin or two. And prepare for some spray to the face." As she reached both hands around a dolphin's dorsal fin, she spoke to the pod, directing them due west toward the mainland, which was still far away. In a moment they were speeding along much faster than they had with the whale, but also with great discomfort as water pounded them in the face. The dolphins occasionally submerged without warning, dragging them with them. Their backpacks fought to keep them afloat, making their ride even more of a struggle, but the fear of letting go of the dolphins and being left behind kept them hanging on for dear life. Birdie pleaded with them to stay closer to the surface, which they began to do.

Once they stopped submerging, Tenner swung himself around so that the water hit him in the back of the head instead. He lodged the dorsal fin into one of his armpits and held on with the other hand. "Turn backward!" Tenner called out to Birdie, who was still floundering.

Birdie's face was being pummeled with water so hard, she couldn't get a breath to yell for help. Her grip began to slip, and she feared she'd drown if she didn't let go. Tenner lunged for her to try and boost her up above the spray, but he couldn't reach. Finally she let go.

"Birdie!" Tenner cried. "Tell them to stop!" He didn't know what to do.

Before he let go to help Birdie, two lagging members of the dolphin pod scooped her up between them. They rode together until she could stop coughing. She lifted her hand to Tenner to let him know she was okay and thanked the dolphins who'd saved her. As they sped up, Birdie turned to face backward so she didn't get drowned by spray again, and soon everyone was together and moving swiftly.

"That was a learning curve," Birdie joked once her nose and throat stopped stinging from the saltwater rinse. She was still shaky from the experience, but she had to concentrate on directing the dolphins to keep them on task. She hoped they would travel more miles than the whale had. "Dolphins will protect us from sharks," Birdie told Tenner. "I read about it in the C–D encyclopedia."

"I remember that, too," said Tenner. He kept a wary eye out.

The dolphins continued, constantly switching places to allow each to fully submerge in turn, for the better part of an hour. But Birdie still couldn't see land. This was a lot farther than Birdie had imagined. She had no frame of reference, no real understanding of distance, since they'd spent their entire lives on the narrow peninsula.

As they traveled, Birdie began pinging other communicative sea creatures, saying hello and making sure there were more around in case this pod of dolphins decided they'd gone far enough.

Tenner, sensing Birdie at work, remained quiet, but he longed to talk about this process with her. They'd hardly had a conversation since the giddy few moments after they'd left. This wasn't how Tenner had pictured this trip. He'd imagined a leisurely ride where they would plan out what they were going to do once they reached the mainland, because those details were pretty sketchy to Tenner. But now all sorts of fears mingled in his mind. There were dangerous creatures out here. Were they even going the right way? What if they accidentally veered too far south and missed the land completely? Was Birdie paying attention to that? How do you tell a sea creature to go due west? He had a lot of questions.

As they rode, Tenner started imagining what Estero would look like and how the two would be received. Fear niggled at him. Would the people of Estero have some sort of sensor that would detect supernatural people? And what if he saw his parents? There was no easy way to hide from Troy Cordoba and his X-ray vision.

"Tenner," Birdie said in low voice, jolting him back to the present. "Look ahead. Do you see a shark fin, or am I imagining it?"

Tenner sat up, immediately feeling bad for not being a better lookout. His father had given him one good thing—amazing eyesight. "You're right," Tenner said, spotting multiple fins. Then his eyes widened as he scanned the ocean all around them. He gasped. "They're great whites."

"What do you mean, 'they'?"

"It's a whole shiver of them."

"A . . . wow," said Birdie, drawing her legs up. "A shiver? Did you make that up?" She couldn't imagine he'd know something like that.

Tenner eyed the fins, trying to count them, but they appeared and disappeared too often to tell. "I did not," he said, too busy to be annoyed by Birdie assuming he wasn't smart. "Greta taught us that when we were seven." Then his voice cracked. "Where are our dolphins going? Tell them to come back!"

Birdie swiftly glanced around as two dolphins left the pod. She pleaded with them. *Please don't leave us. We're in danger!* But how could she convince the dolphins not to save themselves? More dolphins peeled away from the group.

"This is bad," Tenner said. He reached over to Birdie as their dolphins slowed down. "Grab my hand. If our rides go under, we need to stay together." For the second time he wished he'd brought his fishing spear, but there'd been no way to carry it safely.

Birdie lunged for Tenner's hand as their dolphins submerged, leaving Birdie and Tenner bobbing in the water like bait with sharks circling. *Help! Help!* Birdie screamed through her mind. Was there a whale nearby that could rescue them? Birdie's breath came in short bursts, like she couldn't get enough air. She was panicking. Tenner put his face under.

"What's happening?" Birdie cried.

Tenner lifted his head and swung his hair around. "They're swarming around us! Kick their noses! Punch them in the gills! Go underwater so you can see!"

"I can't catch my breath!" Birdie tried to take in a deep breath, then did what Tenner told her to do.

Then the water in front of them exploded. Dolphins slammed into the sharks from beneath, striking them in their tender bellies, then swam down and did it again. Tenner realized the dolphins hadn't abandoned them—a few had stayed nearby to protect them, and the others were fighting.

A shark made it through the maze of dolphins and came straight for Tenner and Birdie. Tenner swam at it, then flipped around and kicked it in the snout. Birdie twisted and connected, though she wasn't sure where. Her lungs burned. Then Tenner was shoving her legs away and slamming his fist into the shark's gills. Its sandpaper-like scales sliced a layer of skin off his knuckles.

Finally two dolphins came at the shark and plowed into its belly like they'd done with the others. The sharks retreated. A moment later, the dolphins came together once more around the two. Tenner surfaced and took in a long breath. His hand was bleeding, and his face was contorted in pain. "You okay?" Tenner asked, breathing hard. Four dolphins came up alongside them to continue their journey.

"We could have died," Birdie said, her voice breaking. "Is your hand all right?" She thanked the dolphins for protecting them.

Tenner inspected his bleeding hand, then nodded. He ripped off a strip of his shirt and tied it around his knuckles. They didn't need to attract more sharks.

Then they slipped into place between dolphins and kept going.

ON FOOT

Seven, Cabot, and Brix, with Puerco peering out of Brix's backpack, moved swiftly on adrenaline and worry. They wore boots belonging to their parents—anything with a tread was going to help them. Seven's fit nicely, and he'd also packed clothes from his father's crate. Brix's and Cabot's boots were too big, but they wore extra layers of old socks, despite the holes in them, to help with the size issue.

Those two were too small to wear their parents' clothes, so they stuck to layers of the parachute variety. They trekked north at a jog, using the path they'd created over the years through the heavy woods, heading toward the cliffs where Seven and Brix often hunted for eggs. They had their parents' climbing tools, like ropes and grappling hooks, and they also carried food and water, medical supplies, and the aforementioned pig, who might be good for digging up truffles but not much else. However, Brix had refused to leave him home alone, so here they were.

"It almost seems like we're making a rash decision," Seven joked, trying to keep the mood light. He'd committed to doing this. Now he had to step up and lead the younger ones. The dirt path began to ascend and grow narrow, leading them right to the edge of the land as the trees grew thicker, crowding beside them. If they tripped on the path, they'd fall straight down onto giant rocks at the edge of the sparkling bay. Thirty minutes later they were at a dizzying height above the water. They stopped to catch their breath. Brix tossed a branch over the edge and watched it fall.

"It's a long way down," Cabot said.

"We can always go back if it gets too hard," Seven said hopefully.

"I'm not going back," said Brix. "No matter what happens."

"Easy for you to say," Cabot remarked. "If you fall, you can bounce to your feet and try again. But me? Splat."

"You're not going to fall," Brix said.

"You don't have a clue what you're in for," Seven warned. "You haven't gone as far as I have."

"What if we get lost?" Brix asked.

"That's the one thing I'm not worried about," Cabot said, visualizing the map. "All we need to do is keep the bay in sight the whole way." They picked up the pace in order to get to the top of the cliffs before it was too dark to see. There'd be no place to camp for the night until they got there.

The unknown terrain worried all three. But what Birdie and Tenner might face worried Seven even more. He began to wonder aloud as they inched along the narrowest part of the path, going around a huge jutting rock. "I hope Birdie and Tenner are okay." In the distance he spotted the sheer cliff they needed to climb and could see a few trees at the top of it. They would come in handy later.

"If they're not, it's Birdie's fault," said Cabot. "Tenner is an unwitting accomplice. Along for the ride because Birdie needs him."

"I object to your assumptions," Seven said loftily—he'd read that phrase in one of Cabot's mom's books and liked it. He continued up the path, moving along a narrow ledge, and peered down. One false step, and he'd be falling to his death. "Careful here, okay?"

The other two inched along with their hands against the sheer rock, and soon they were on a wider path once more. The forest opened up again, but it was thinner here, and cooler.

"Assumptions about Tenner?" asked Cabot, picking up where they'd left off. "Why do you object?" She was truly curious. In her mind, she possessed the most well-rounded impressions of everyone else because she could see them when they didn't know they were being watched. But she was also begrudgingly glad to be challenged, because it kept her from boredom. "What don't I understand?"

Seven trudged on, reaching to move the occasional branch that crossed their path. He frowned and stopped for a moment. "It sounds like you think Tenner is, well, not very smart. And that's not true."

"Hmm," said Cabot, unconvinced. Of course another not-very-smart person would say that. But at least Seven and Birdie were good for a lively debate now and then. They reached a wide fissure, and Seven pointed out the way they would climb down into it, then up the other side. Once they were on their way, Cabot continued her thought. "I don't see how Tenner *is* smart, so you need to explain."

Brix listened curiously. Tenner *seemed* pretty smart. He loved it when the older four had deep discussions around him. Sometimes he tried to participate, but more often he preferred to listen.

"Just because Tenner doesn't have your vocabulary doesn't mean he's not smart," Seven told Cabot. "He probably has the most common sense of all of us. And common sense is severely underrated. It's more important than intelligence."

Cabot sniffed, mildly offended. The scent of pine trees filled her nose. "Don't you think I have a *lot* of common sense?"

Puerco snorted inside Brix's backpack and rammed around, then calmed down and poked his snout out again.

"I think we all have enough to get by," said Seven agreeably. "You? I think your intelligence can get in the way of it sometimes."

Cabot frowned. She weighed the likelihood of that theory and was silent. Seven had a point.

The route became steeper, though it moved slightly away

from the edge, between the trees. But the biggest challenge was still ahead. They could hear a low rumble and climbed their way up to the base of a waterfall. "This is the water source that feeds our creek," Seven told them. "If you ever get lost out here, find the creek and go downhill. It'll take you home."

"My dad taught us that," Brix said.

Seven nodded. "Glad you remember." They stopped to refill their canteens.

"I spy wild carrots," Cabot said. "We can have them with dinner." She picked them and rinsed them in the waterfall, then sniffed the air. Spearmint mingled with the pine trees. She located the plant along the bank and grabbed a few leaves to chew on later.

"Let's stay here for a few minutes and eat," Seven said, squinting through the trees to judge the time of day. He let Puerco out of Brix's backpack to forage. While they ate and rested, Seven peered over the edge at the bay below. It was a long way down, and they'd made good progress. But not far ahead of them was the spot he was dreading. The place where they'd have to make a tricky move: jump a deep, three-foot-wide fissure and grab on to a tiny handhold all in one fluid movement, then scale a sheer rock wall. One slip would dump them into the fissure, and he didn't know how deep it went.

That was where Seven had stopped the other day, when he was alone. It was the farthest he'd ever been. He knew that if he wasn't able to jump high enough to grab the handhold, he would fall into the fissure. And no one would have found his body down there.

With all three of them helping one another, their chances of making it were decent, especially with Brix along. As they packed up the pig, Cabot spied more wild carrot tops off the path. She ran to pull them and kicked something in the overgrowth. She bent down to see if it was anything useful, then picked it up and shook off the decaying leaves and dirt. When she realized what it was, she dropped it with a shriek.

"What's wrong?" Seven asked, alarmed. "What is it?"

"Ugh," said Cabot with a shudder, "it's a human bone."

A CLOSE CALL

There were more bones in the overgrowth. They found six altogether. Cabot, Brix, and Seven looked down at the short row of them. "Boys," Cabot said, "the whole thing—it's . . . a leg. That big one is the femur. Tibia and fibula—I can't remember which is which. There's a kneecap . . . and those little bones are from the foot, I think."

"How could there be only one leg?" asked Brix, wrinkling his nose. "Where's the rest of the body?"

"And more importantly, whose leg is it?" Seven said.

"It's not . . . one of the parents," Brix said, his face growing pale. "Is it?"

"I don't know," Seven said quietly. He watched Cabot, knowing the conclusion she'd jump to. It was the story she'd been telling herself for three years.

Cabot's stomach clenched. She was already calculating. "Three years. Exposed to the sun and rain. And with wild animals tearing things up . . . Which, by the way, is probably why it's just a leg, Brix—some big animal tore off a manageable piece and ran off with it." Cabot pressed her lips together as her heart sank. "This could totally be one of my parents. I told you they'd have to be dead to not come back." Hot tears sprang to her eyes, and she willed them away. She didn't want pity or comfort—it only made her feel awkward on top of sad. When Cabot cried, she cried alone.

Seven didn't know what to say.

Cabot continued even though her throat started to ache. She picked up the largest bone and held it alongside her thigh. It was a little longer than hers. "The femur is pretty short. I think it could be a woman's." She'd had her mother's medical books to thank for that knowledge.

She was hit by a sudden wave of longing. She missed her mother and father *so* much. And the bones, even if they didn't belong to her parents, made death real.

"It could be *my* mom," Brix said, his voice quavering.

"It could also be a complete stranger," Seven said gently. "A police officer or someone else who was searching for the criminals. Or these bones could have been here for decades. We don't know."

Cabot turned away until she could compose herself. "Maybe." It was possible. But it seemed more likely that it was one of their parents who'd fallen or been attacked.

They combed the area for identifying features, and Brix thought he spotted a bit of cloth . . . which turned out to be coconut husk.

"We should keep going," Seven said gently. The ground was too hard to dig into without tools, so they left the bones in the hollow of a tree near the river's edge.

Cabot's mind wouldn't settle. Her father was pretty tall. It probably wasn't him. The feeling that the bones belonged to her mother was so strong that she couldn't stop the looping, intrusive thought that her theory about her parents must be partially true.

At least she could be distracted by the fissure and the rock wall.

Seven scanned upward. None of the children had ever ventured beyond this point. "There are trees up there," Seven said. "I saw them when we were a bit farther back." They were too close to the wall now to see over it.

He tried launching a rope with a grappling hook. At first he couldn't get it high enough. Then it wouldn't catch on anything. After multiple tries, he gave up. "Brix, you should go first. Once you get up there, you can leverage the rope around a tree like I showed you the other day. Remember?"

Brix nodded. "I can do it."

"I'll take Puerco," said Seven. If Brix fell, he'd be able to heal. But the pig wouldn't be that lucky. He fished the animal out of Brix's backpack and set him on the ground.

"Be careful, Brixy," Cabot said quietly.

"I will." Brix hopped in place a few times as he eyed the gap he needed to launch over and the handhold that he'd need to grip securely to help him stick to the wall and allow him to climb up the rest of the way. His ability to bounce when landing also worked in his favor when jumping—he'd be able to easily clear the fissure. But his hands were small, and his grip strength wasn't the strongest. He was most worried about that.

Seven clipped a rope to Brix and held it loosely so he could pull him to safety in case he fell and kept going down into the fissure. Cabot leaned over to see. Were the rest of the bones down there? It was too dark to tell.

Brix took a few deep breaths, shook out his hands, and flexed his fingers. Then he bounded for the wall. He sprang on his bouncy feet, easily clearing the gap. Instead of grabbing on to the lowest rocky handhold, he landed with one foot on it and kept going, running up the wall a few steps. He reached the next handhold and clung to it with one hand, his legs dangling as he twisted in the air. Then his feet found the wall, and he reached for the next handhold, and the next, all the way up until he grabbed the edge. He hung there for a moment, then pulled himself over the top. Seven and Cabot craned their necks to watch.

Brix peered over. "I'm just getting started," he called down. He unclipped the rope from his waist.

Seven laughed. "Good. Is there anything up there to attach the rope to?"

Brix disappeared. "There's a little tree," he called.

"How little?" asked Seven, looking up. All he could see was the overhang and the sky beyond that.

"Thicker than my leg. It's the only thing close enough. I'll clip the rope around it. Then I'll help pull you up."

"Perfect." Seven turned to Cabot. "You ready?" He gave her some pointers on how best to do it. Then he clipped her to Brix's rope.

Cabot wiped her hands on her pants and tried not to look down into the deep, dark gorge.

"Here I come!" she called. Brix watched from above. She backed up as far as the rope would allow, then ran forward and jumped, legs extended, over the gorge. She missed the handhold, hitting the wall with her feet flat and bouncing off. Holding the rope, she swung there, stunned she'd made it, then lunged for the handhold the next time she swung near it. This time she got it.

"Great job," Seven encouraged. "The hard part is over."

Cabot started climbing. She tried to stop imagining her mother doing this same thing and falling to her death.

"Almost there!" Seven paced along the fissure, sounding worried.

Cabot moved slowly but steadily and finally flung herself over the edge to safety. Brix helped her up. "Climbing trees is more my thing," she called down. This experience had unsettled her, but she'd made it.

Below, Puerco seemed agitated and ran around in circles like he sometimes did when he thought Birdie was in danger. Seven chased him, then scooped him into his backpack, and the pig settled down. Cabot unclipped and tossed her end of the rope to Seven. He clipped it to his belt and did much like what Cabot had done—he took a short running leap with the rope and planted his feet against the vertical rock. The force against the tree made it crack.

Brix and Cabot turned sharply at the sound and saw the tree bending, threatening to break off. With a yell, they lunged for the rope.

Seven didn't hear the crack, but he knew a yell never meant anything good. He glanced down, weighing his options—climb fast, or try to jump back down across the gorge to safety without falling in or smushing Puerco. He started climbing as quickly as he could. As he neared the top, he heard the other two grunting and exclaiming, "Hurry, Seven!" Spooked, he continued up and lunged for the ledge.

The force of his lunge yanked Brix and Cabot to the edge. With another yell, they let go of the rope to stop themselves from plunging over. Seven hung from the edge. One hand slipped. "Help!" he screamed. "Pull me up!"

A BLEAK DISCOVERY

Puerco squealed from inside Seven's backpack.

Brix and Cabot desperately felt around, trying to locate Seven's camouflaged arms. Seven reached for Cabot's hand and connected. Cabot latched on and pulled. Brix grabbed Seven's backpack strap and pulled that, too. Finally, with no help from the little pig ramming around, Seven clawed his way up and over the edge to safety.

The three lay heaving, staring at the sky as the sun began to set. "That was scary," Seven said, flexing his fingers and wrists as the immediate pain started to fade. "Thank you. What happened?"

Brix told him how the tree had bent and cracked, and he and Cabot had hung on to the rope and slid across the loose dirt as Seven climbed up.

"You saved my life," Seven said.

Cabot tried to imagine life without Seven and broke into a cold sweat. "That was a close one," she whispered as tears sprang to her eyes for the second time that day. Something about this, about Birdie's lie of omission, about finding the bones and the looping thoughts of her mother, about Seven's near tragedy, made her emotions stick near the surface. "Glad you're okay."

After a rest, they got up and looked around. The trees were sparse in this rocky area. There was a cave nearby, and the rocks surrounding it were light orange and red, like clay. To the left, the rocky ground gave way to the ocean bay, even farther below them now. The journey ahead looked fairly flat for a quarter mile, then the trees thickened and grew into a great tangle of jungle. Beyond it, Cabot knew from the map, a mountain rose up. And after the experience they'd had so far, she was starting to wonder how they would make it.

Brix checked the sky. "It'll be dark soon."

"We'll camp here," Seven said. "And tackle the jungle tomorrow." He opened his backpack, and Puerco clambered out. He shook his body, then dropped to the dirt and rolled around to scratch his back. He snorted and sneezed. Orange-brown dust scattered.

"Good," said Cabot. "I'll draw the map for you in the rock dust. I know exactly where we are." She calculated the distance in her head. "We've gone about twelve miles today, but that's okay—we did a lot of climbing. Tomorrow's route will be flatter. We should shoot for twenty." Her feet hurt imagining it. She went to the edge and looked down at the bay, thinking aloud. "There are rocks lining the edge of the bay as far as I can see. Once we're through the jungle and approaching the mountain, it might be smarter to go down instead of up, and walk across the rocks. Then maybe we can swim across the narrowest part of the bay. We'll save a lot of time if we do that."

The boys listened half-heartedly. Not knowing the map like Cabot did meant her musings didn't make a lot of sense. Brix wrinkled his nose at the thought of swimming across the bay. But his mind was on the nearby cave. "Do we want to check out that cave and maybe use it for shelter?" Brix asked slowly, as if he thought it might be a bad idea but wasn't quite sure.

"Ah, no," said Seven. He shivered as evening fell and reached into his backpack for a thin sweater his dad had left behind—tan, soft, lightweight but warm. The neck was stretched out, and the elbows had holes in them from age and overuse, but it wasn't way too big on him anymore. "Let's stay away from the cave. We're near the jungle, so we don't want to disturb anything that might live there." He scouted around, steering well clear of it, and eventually called to the others. "This is a good spot—we've got some rocks around us for protection. We'll keep watch in shifts tonight. That way we can each get a decent amount of sleep. Cabot, you do the first watch, then wake me up when the moon is overhead. Brix, you can do the third watch. Let's skip the fire and eat something. That'll lighten our loads a bit. Then we can go at sunup. We've got a big day tomorrow."

As Cabot searched for a stick to sketch the map in the dust of the red rocks, she came to an abrupt stop. Lying in the dirt was a cracked human skull.

Cabot cringed. It probably went along with the other bones they'd found. She looked all around—was there anything else? Clothing? An earring or anything else to identify who this person was? Other bones? But there was nothing.

Cabot went to nudge it into some overgrowth with her foot but stopped and picked it up instead. She looked into its eye sockets. The skull had been cleaned by animals, birds, maggots, the elements . . . whatever. It had been here a while. Was three years long enough for it to be in this condition? Maybe in Estero Cabot could find a book about human body decay. She placed the skull by a tree and pushed dead leaves over it.

While the others fell asleep, the thought kept coming back. What if that was her mom?

A DIFFERENT KIND OF EVENING

The dolphin pod carried Birdie and Tenner into late afternoon, then signaled to Birdie that it was time for them to go. Soon Birdie and Tenner were alone again in the sea, looking to hitchhike with the next creature who would give them a lift.

As Birdie concentrated on finding another ride, Tenner alternately scoped out the water for sharks and scanned the horizon. There were clouds ahead. A single gray wisp of smoke rose up to meet them, and Tenner wondered if that meant land was near. "I think we're getting close," he said.

Birdie didn't respond at first. But then she turned sharply. "Heads up, Tenner!" A moment later Birdie gasped in surprise as a huge black-and-white orca rose up beneath them.

"Oh my God, what have you done?" Tenner shrieked. He'd never seen a creature like this before. Its broad back was slick and rubbery, and the black-and-white design startlingly distinct. But its mouth wasn't too big, so that was a relief. "Does it eat humans?"

"I hope not," Birdie said, trying to get a look at the thing's teeth. "I didn't realize what I was talking to." The two water-logged kids clung to the frightening creature's large dorsal fin, wondering if it would be better to let it go and have Birdie try for dolphins again.

But the orca didn't try to eat them, and it seemed to like when Birdie rubbed its skin. Eventually Tenner calmed down enough to realize land was in sight. This turned out to be the most pleasant ride of all of them, for they could both face forward, side by side, holding the dorsal fin between them.

As the sun dropped low in the sky and a beach and city appeared before them, the orca drew close enough for the two to swim the rest of the way. Birdie said goodbye, and they struck out toward shore. They were *here*. In Estero—or at least that was where Birdie thought they were. Countless buildings rose up beyond the beach. The buildings were in layers, each taller than the last. Lights shone brightly from them even as darkness descended.

Their skin was wrinkled, and both shivered as they swam. Swimming had helped them warm up a little, but by the time their feet could touch the bottom, they were exhausted, sore, hungry, and afraid. They were in the world, and the world was against them. Would anyone approach them? Would people be able to tell they had supernatural abilities? What would happen if they could? Birdie grabbed Tenner's wrist before he went barreling onto land, and she shrank in the water, pulling him with her. "Look!" she whispered. "People everywhere. Can you believe those buildings?"

"And the lights," said Tenner. "I wonder how they do that."

There were groups of people on the beach, and some of them had dogs—they'd never seen a real dog before, except in the C–D encyclopedia. The groups tossed or kicked bright-colored balls to each other, or sat on blankets watching the sunset, eating dinner, joking, and laughing. The tallest structures in the distance were so shiny that they reflected orange from the setting sun. Birdie stayed low, chin riding the gentle waves. "What if they see us?"

"We run," said Tenner, nodding emphatically.

"No. We're not going to run."

Tenner felt his face heat up, and he scrambled to change the subject. "Do all of these people know one another?" How did that work? Both of them had a hard time understanding how big everything was compared to what they were used to. "We can't stay in the water, though," he added. "I'm freezing."

Birdie blew out a nervous breath. "I didn't imagine that people would be right here staring at us. Don't they have cabins? Dinnertime?" Back home the five would have finished with the dishes before it got too dark for most of them to see. Here, more and more lights were turning *on*.

"Let's walk ashore," said Tenner, shivering in the water. "If anybody talks to us, we'll pretend we live here."

"Yeah—we'll say we live at the beach. That won't even be a lie."

"Well . . . I'm not sure people would believe it," said Tenner. "Remember our parents talked about their houses? See all those short buildings? I think those are houses. We'll say we live 'up the street' or 'in the city.' Something like that. Those are the kinds of things your dad said when he told us about life here."

Birdie nodded, then tried out the phrases casually. "Oh, we live up the street," she said with confidence. "You know, in the city." She took a deep breath and started forward. "Okay. Let's go." They went together, rising out of the water in their gray parachute clothing and backpacks. When they were waist deep, Tenner stopped to pull the sunglasses out of his backpack and put them on. Then they casually walked ashore.

"Smile," Birdie hissed. Tenner and Birdie smiled brightly as they reached the sand, ready to greet strangers who might talk to them and defuse any confrontations they might face. But no one paid them any attention. Did they look like they belonged here?

"What's happening?" Birdie said through gritted teeth.

"I don't know," said Tenner. "Keep walking."

They did. A few people looked curiously at their dripping backpacks, and one woman in a bright green swimsuit eyed their clothes, but the rest gave them no more than a passing glance. They were watching the sunset. A group of kids about Tenner and Birdie's age were eating triangular, crunchy items out of very crinkly bags, using their fingers, which were covered in an orange substance that they occasionally licked off with a smacking noise. "A lot of noisy food," Tenner murmured, aghast, as it was all amplified inside his ears. He wasn't sure he would want to be friends with people who ate such crunchy things. It would be too stressful. The smell made him hungry at first, then nauseous after the scent grew overwhelming.

He turned to watch a man throwing a ball to a dog, and the dog brought the ball right back to him. Tenner poked Birdie with his elbow. "You need to teach Puerco to do that." They continued walking, and Tenner took in more food smells from the groups as they passed by, but nothing smelled as good as the fish and root vegetable hash they made at home.

"I thought . . ." Birdie began, but then realized how silly her thoughts were. She'd imagined that people would come running over to them. Ask them who they were. Did they look different, like they were from another land, like these people looked to them? Almost everyone here wore colorful things. Stripes and patterns, some like ones on their parents' old clothes, but very unlike their dark-colored parachute pants and tank tops, and Tenner's tan cutoff dad shorts. Though Birdie saw a few black swimsuits. Maybe, because everyone looked different, they fit in already.

But they wouldn't fit in when people found out about their abilities. Still, if they didn't use them or talk about them, maybe this wouldn't be hard after all. They could be like Cabot's mom, who managed to beat the system and trick people into treating her better than other supernaturals.

Birdie stopped when she saw a man on a blanket. His black hair was shoulder length, wavy, and graying at the temples, like Louis's had been. He looked around the same age. As she stared, two teenagers plopped down on the blanket next to him with an oval-shaped ball, talking at top speed. And then a woman joined them, too, in a long, flowing dress. The adults laughed at what the kids were saying. Were they a family?

Birdie swallowed hard and looked away. They crossed over the beach and made it to a hard, surprisingly level surface.

"Do you see any toilet cabins?" Birdie asked.

"I peed on the orca," Tenner confessed.

"Tenner, gross!" Birdie hissed. "That's not respectful of our ocean friends. Or me."

"Actually, more in the water above it," Tenner went on, remembering.

Birdie rolled her eyes, but the truth was, she'd peed, too. All the sea animals did. It was fine—they didn't have a choice. But she didn't want to announce it to the world, especially since they didn't understand this place yet. She imagined a conversation:

What were your first words in civilization?

I peed on the orca.

Terrific.

Soon her annoyance was replaced by awe as her eyes

strayed to what was beyond the beach. The shorter buildings, or houses, were much bigger than their cabins in the hideout. And there was a long stretch of hard, black road separating rows of them. There were cars parked on both sides. The cars didn't look like the ones in the encyclopedia, but they were still recognizable.

This beach and the edge of the city, with all these people and blankets and dogs, felt vastly bigger than home. But the kids had a few things to take care of. "I want to change into dry clothes," Birdie said. "And I need to open the map in a private place so we can figure out where we are. But I don't think I should do it out in front of people, or they'll know we're supernatural."

"Right." Tenner adjusted his sunglasses and watched people standing in line to enter a small, flat-roofed building. Light flooded out the open door. There was a small sign on the outside wall depicting a stick person. "I wonder what's going on in there?" He shrugged, and they started walking up the street, looking curiously at the structures around them but keeping their exclamations to a whisper so as not to draw attention to themselves.

"Why so tall?" Birdie mused as the buildings grew in size.

"Maybe people are bigger here," Tenner guessed. They stopped in front of a small building with a huge window. Light flooded out. Inside, two women wearing nets on their heads were working, with steam or smoke rising around them. A curly word blinked on and off in the window. *"Tacos?"* Tenner said.

The word sounded familiar, like maybe one of the parents had said it before, a long time ago.

"It smells good," Birdie said, but she was too afraid to venture in. "Maybe it's someone's house. Like the Tacos family."

They went farther, finding no toilet rooms, until they came upon an empty bench. "Can we stop to eat something before I die?"

Overwhelmed, Birdie nodded. They hadn't wanted to risk opening their backpacks on the bay for fear of water getting inside, so their last meal had been breakfast that morning, which felt like a lifetime ago. "Sure. Maybe I'll have a chance to steal a quick look at the map." Her expression flickered. She'd hardly thought about the map all day. But now they were here, and she had to find her mom. She glanced at Tenner, feeling a twinge of guilt from omitting the whole truth. "Hey, Tenner?"

"What?"

She sat down on the bench. "Never mind. Let's eat first." She pulled her backpack to her lap, then unsealed the water-tight flap and rummaged around the interior, careful not to let her wet hair drip onto anything inside. The cell phones were there. Dad's first journal. Tenner's smoked fish and coconut wrapped in a palm leaf. She doled out a portion to Tenner and started inhaling the rest. A couple walked by from the direction of the beach, giving the two sodden children in strange cloth-ing a lengthy glance but saying nothing and continuing on their way. By the time Birdie was finished eating, more people were coming.

The sunset display was finished, and foot traffic picked up. A few people stopped at the Tacos' house and went in. The rest swarmed the street and started opening doors of cars, getting inside, and slamming them shut in a startling manner. The vehicles roared to life—even more startling—and bright headlights blinded Birdie and Tenner as an acrid burning smell filled their nostrils. Birdie could feel the vehicles' energy vibrating in her chest, and she had the urge to run for her life as they passed by. The two were half-mesmerized, half-fearful as they watched the large containers carry people who were rigid and facing forward inside them. When people got into the car nearest them, Birdie stood abruptly and moved behind the bench for safety.

If people here thought that kind of energy and power was perfectly normal, it seemed even more horrible that they would have a problem with a girl who could talk to animals or a boy who had heightened senses and could hold his breath. Or even a boy you mostly couldn't see.

A CONFESSION

N obody said a word to us," Birdie marveled as they started walking back to the beach. She was amazed by how invisible they were. After what Dad had implied, she'd worried she and Tenner would be stopped and questioned or checked over upon arrival. But they'd seemed to blend in with the crowd.

"Can I take these glasses off now that it's dark?" Tenner asked.

"Yeah, I think you're fine."

"I'll keep them in my shirt pocket."

Birdie closed her eyes. "Okay, Tenner. I honestly don't believe anyone will notice your pupils even in the light, but *especially* not in the dark, when everyone's pupils are big."

Tenner frowned and put the glasses in his pocket in case of emergency.

Most of the cars were gone now, and the crowd had thinned. Back at the entrance to the beach, a woman in a dark blue uniform hung long chains on poles across the road in what seemed a half-hearted attempt to block access to the beach. When people walked around the poles to avoid the chains, there were no consequences.

"Why . . . ?" Tenner started to say as they both watched.

"No idea," said Birdie. "Does it keep the cars out?"

"What, that little chain? I think a car could probably push right through."

When the woman was gone, Birdie and Tenner slipped back to the empty beach and cased the area for a private spot to sleep. They found a place behind some tall grass not far from the building where Tenner had seen the line of people earlier—they were gone now. Birdie unrolled a parachute blanket and spread it out on the ground.

There was a light fixture stuck to the wall of the building. They knew that somehow, through electricity, the fixture could stay lit without fire being involved, but they still didn't understand it. Tenner was curious enough to go up to it. But it was bright and hurt his eyes, and there were at least ten moths fluttering around by it, which was unnerving. After that, he hesitantly poked his head inside the building and discovered what he determined to be very fancy toilets and washbasins.

"A whole room full of them?" Tenner questioned aloud. The toilets back home were made of wood: flat and uncomfortable. The basins in here were white, like the toilets, and there were curious knobs at the tops of them. But there was no water in them. "How the heck . . . ?" Tenner wondered. What good was a basin without water? He called Birdie over to let her know about the facilities, and she joined him.

Using the booths for privacy, the kids changed into dry clothing. After Tenner relieved himself and moved away from the toilet, it emitted a deep-throated gurgle. A rushing sound accompanied a wild swirl of water in the bowl. Tenner shrieked and backed up against the door as it drained and refilled.

"What's happening?" Birdie called anxiously from the stall next door just as hers roared to life, too. "Yikes!"

A tiny red light blinked near pipes that led into the wall. "It's stopping now," Tenner called over the noise. "It's like it *knows*." Tenner, who'd put on the shorts he'd made from his dad's old trousers, cinched his belt tight to keep them from falling off and exited the stall. He stopped in front of the mirror and studied his reflection. "These shorts look like a skirt on me," he said after a moment, adjusting them. "I wish I'd sewn the waist up a little."

"Too late now," Birdie said, joining him. There was only a small mirror back home—she'd never seen one this big before. She gazed at herself and adjusted the oversized sweatshirt that her mom had left behind. Then she found her brush and worked it through her tangled hair.

Satisfied, she started messing with the knobs on the basin, and soon a gush of water was hitting the bottom and splashing over her dry clothing. She shrieked and jumped back. "It's like a waterfall," she said once she realized what was happening. She turned the knob the other way, and the water ceased. Then she turned it on again, and off again. "Okay," she said. "This is how water works here." Tenner tried it, too, and they put their mouths to the stream of water to get a drink. The water tasted strange, but it was refreshing. They filled their canteens and went back to their blanket on the beach. At least the beach part of this experience felt like home.

Thinking about home sent a pang of longing through Birdie. She missed the others already. She lay on the parachute fabric, thinking of Seven and Brix and Cabot. And Puerco. She'd sensed the pig checking in when they were fighting the sharks, but she'd been too busy to respond, and then she'd forgotten about him. Could she communicate with him from this far away? She faced the direction they'd come from and sent a message of love to the pig, letting him know they were safely on land. After a few minutes, Birdie thought she felt him respond, but the feeling was coming from a slightly different place than she had anticipated. Or maybe her bearings were off. "What do you think the others are doing?" she asked Tenner.

Tenner put his hands behind his head and glanced at the sky. "By now? Sound asleep. Counting the days until we get back."

Birdie thought about how they'd get back, and groaned. "I'm not ready to jump back into the ocean quite yet." She lay quietly for a moment and thought about their task. "Tenner?"

"Yeah?" He turned his head toward her and realized this was the calmest he'd felt in a long time.

"There's something I didn't tell you and the others about my dad's final request." She cringed.

Tenner's calm feeling dissipated. He sat up on one elbow. "What is it?"

Birdie told him everything the note had said.

Tenner's face twisted as he listened. He was quiet for a moment, thinking it through. "Why didn't you say something?"

Birdie searched his face. "Because the way it's written seems like my dad wants me to give the map to my mother so she could get the stash and keep it for herself. But you know my dad. He wouldn't do that. I mean, maybe he would have a long time ago, but he changed. I'm sure he meant for my mom to find it and distribute it to the other parents."

Tenner nodded slowly, taking it in. He thought about how his dad had probably stolen the thirteen diamonds from the others a long time ago. He didn't think Troy would have changed at all. But Louis surely had.

Birdie continued studying him, but his expression wasn't giving anything away, as usual. "Are you mad? I promise I won't give my mom the map if she seems like she won't share the stash." She gave him the standard sorry-your-dad-is-a-horrible-person pitying glance.

Tenner scratched his head. "To be honest, I don't care whether my parents get any of it—in fact, I hope they don't. And

I don't blame Louis for moving the stash in the first place. He knew my parents weren't trustworthy. You could have explained this to the others."

"I know," Birdie said miserably. "I should have. I just—it made my dad look bad, and I didn't want anyone to be suspicious of me wanting to come here." She hesitated. "I'll explain it all to everyone when we get back."

"I'm sure it'll be fine," said Tenner. "Really." He smiled to let her know he was okay with it. Then he rolled onto his back and shifted around on the blanket, making a comfy spot in the sand. He closed his eyes. "Good night, Birdie."

"Night." Birdie settled in, too, feeling much better now that she'd confessed.

Soon Tenner's breathing evened out. Birdie closed her eyes and drifted to sleep to the sound of waves. Just like home.

STRANGE COINCIDENCES

n the morning, Birdie awoke to mournful bird calls. A raven landed on the top of the toilet building, and Birdie greeted it sleepily. For a moment she didn't know where she was, but then she remembered. She sat up on the parachute blanket in the beach grass and saw the orange-and-pink sky over the bay. She knew there were mountains somewhere curving around the bay and disappearing into the mist, but she couldn't see them with all the buildings in the way.

Birdie turned toward the city. The buildings were stark and gray now, lit from behind by the sunlight. Not as glitzy or enticing as last night. Everything in that direction felt cold and uninviting. Perhaps, when more people were bustling about, it would be better.

Tenner stirred and rolled over, bumping Birdie's thigh with his elbow. He opened his eyes and groaned. "More sleep," he mumbled.

"Go for it." Yesterday had been exhausting, and it was still early. Birdie got up to go to the toilet building and put on her now-dry parachute pants and top from yesterday, along with her mom's old sneakers whose laces had worn out and been thrown away long ago. They were a little bit big on her, but not much anymore. Her heels slipped out, but most of the time they stayed on, even without laces.

As she dried her hands on her pants, a man pushing a large yellow bucket on wheels came in and started at the sight of her. "This is the men's bathroom," he said, pointing to something on the wall outside that she couldn't see. "You can't be here."

Birdie's eyes widened. "The . . . what?" A bathroom for men? What was the point of that? Everyone had to use the bathroom.

"The women's is on the other side." The man jerked his thumb out the door. "Beach isn't even open yet." He grumbled something about what she was doing here at this hour.

Birdie tried not to panic or say anything odd. She'd never spoken to a stranger before—unless animals counted. "Sorry," she murmured, and fled past him. She went around the building and saw there was another room that was a mirror image of the first. On the wall outside, the blue sign was different—this stick figure had a triangle bottom half.

"I'm a triangle?" Frowning, she went inside and washed her hands. It was a mystery. Back home they had two toilet rooms, and anyone could go into either one. There were no stick figure signs, with or without triangle bottoms.

She went back to the sleeping spot and found Tenner sitting up and eating an orange from his backpack. His hair was fuzzy, and he had a spot of sand stuck to his cheek. "Hey," he said. "Can we make a fire and cook some real food?"

By "real food," he meant fish. They'd eaten all of the smoked fish last night. Birdie looked around worriedly. "I don't know. It doesn't seem like there are any other fires around, and I don't see any remnants, either. Maybe we have to buy a fish."

"How do we cook it, though? Why buy a fish when I can catch one? I'm starving." Tenner was always starving, and after a light meal day yesterday on top of the stress of all the new things they were experiencing, they were both getting a little bit cranky.

"I'm not sure how the rules work here," Birdie said. Hunger pangs stabbed as the scent of the orange wafted her way. She pulled out the wild carrots and split them between herself and Tenner. It wasn't much.

Tenner carefully picked up the orange peel and the carrot greens and found a tall can with the word TRASH on the outside to put it in, even though back home they'd feed those items to Puerco or use them in their wild garden as compost. He didn't see any gardens or compost bins around here.

The smell of something cooking wafted their way and spurred them on as they packed up their things. Tenner put on his sunglasses, and they headed toward the city to find out what it was, trudging up the sidewalk alongside the road, past the Tacos' house, which was dark now. They went farther than they'd gone last night, until they came to another street, this one running crosswise. Cars were moving along both streets, stopping and starting randomly but managing to not hit each other. "There's got to be some code," Tenner said, trying to make sense of the traffic.

"Yeah, code," said Birdie. "Like with the toilet rooms." She told him what had happened with the yellow-bucket man and described the blue signs with stick figures. Tenner stopped walking and looked at Birdie. "You don't look like a triangle," he said.

"Thanks?" said Birdie. Unsure what the street symbols meant, they simply waited until there were no cars anywhere before cautiously crossing the street. There were round, colored lights everywhere—red, yellow, green; and flashing red and solid white stick figures by the street corners. No triangle-bottomed people here. "Estero loves stick figures," Birdie noted. There were lights on cars even though it was daylight. More words in windows lit up, blinking OPEN or CLOSED. Streetlamps faded off by themselves, as if they knew it was daytime now.

They stopped in front of a huge screen above a shop, on which tiny people were running over a green field, chasing a black-and-white ball. Other tiny people crammed into a space off the field watched and screamed in excitement. Then a big man's face came on the screen and words scrolled across the bottom at a dizzying speed. Tenner's jaw slacked. "What is happening here?"

Birdie couldn't take her eyes off it. Where did the green field and running people go? Who was the big-faced man? She was repulsed by the size of him and puzzled by how all the others were so tiny. "Is this a computer?" She'd seen computers in the encyclopedia. "Can they *see* us?"

"I don't think so," said Tenner. "Hey, maybe the big-faced people live in the tall buildings."

Finally they pulled themselves away and continued on. As they crossed a second street, they saw a large sign with arrows pointing in different directions. RESTAURANT ROW straight ahead. CORDOBA MUSEUM a mile to the right. And PALACIO DE MAGDALIA two miles to the left.

"Hey, look," said Tenner. "There's a museum named after me."

Birdie giggled. "That's funny!" Then she stopped laughing. "And Palacio, like Seven's surname." She frowned. "With his mother's first name—Magdalia." The two went silent. Three extremely familiar names, all on one sign?

"This seems like too much of a coincidence," Tenner said. He glanced around uneasily. "Are these places on the map?"

Birdie tried to remember the initials she'd seen, but they all swam around in her mind. "I'm not sure. Maybe? I think *CM* was one of the markings—that might be Cordoba Museum." She started toward the museum excitedly. "Let's check it out."

"What about food?" Tenner asked, pointing straight ahead like the Restaurant Row arrow to where the tantalizing smells were coming from. He hoped *RR* was on the map.

But Birdie was already crossing the street.

ANOTHER SHOCK

Seven, Cabot, and Brix got up bright and early, too, and they picked their way through the jungle as fast as they could manage. Soon they were surrounded by a prison of tree trunks and thick vines. The canopy overhead was often too dense for them to see even a tiny patch of sky unless they looked toward the bay. It was gloomy and dark, and they stayed on the jungle's edge, keeping the bay in sight so they wouldn't get lost.

Periodically Seven peered at the treetops for mountain lions or other animals that could tear their faces off. "We need to pick up the pace a little," he said.

They sped up, hopping over vines and dodging clusters of trees, prickly bushes, sticky vines, and other overgrowth. Brix bounced his way through. There was no path to follow in this remote place. The jungle vines spilled over the cliff, leaving tangles of ivy crawling down the sheer rock wall as if inching toward the water or trying to escape. Birds squawked, and squirrels leaped over their heads.

Everyone froze when they heard a high-pitched, raspy shriek.

"What was that?" Brix whispered.

"Could be a mountain lion," Seven replied. "Keep moving." Puerco squealed and ducked inside Seven's backpack.

"Quiet, Puerco," Cabot whispered, touching his side through the fabric to comfort him. The pig would only draw a mountain lion toward them.

"What do we do if it comes after us?" Brix asked.

They heard a thud, like the sound a mountain lion might make when jumping from a tree to the ground. Then a flurry of crunching noises, which grew louder. They couldn't see anything in the gloom.

"I think it's doing that now," Seven replied, starting to tremble. "Where is it? I wish Tenner were here." He tried to shush the pig, too, but Puerco sensed the predator and squealed again.

"Or Birdie, to quiet Puerco down." Brix headed for a tree and started to climb.

"No, Brix," Cabot said, picking up a stick. "They're climbers, too. And we can't outrun it. Just . . . act big! And scary! Roar at it!"

"Roar at it?" Brix scoffed. "That won't work."

The three finally located the giant cat coming at them. Its eyes glowed yellow, and its mouth was open, with short, sharp fangs coming down. Its tail swished.

"ROAR!" Cabot screamed at it, waving her arms and the stick. "Come on, you guys! Be big! Hands up!"

"It's not like it can see my hands," Seven muttered, but he did it anyway. Brix abandoned his skepticism and roared as loudly as he could, and then all of them did it together. Cabot took a step toward it, still screaming and waving her stick. Brix, worried, stepped in front of her—if the mountain lion came at them, at least he could heal fast. But Cabot and Seven would bleed to death. And end up being more bones scattered across this land.

The creature seemed confused. It stopped ten feet away. Puerco squealed again. The mountain lion shrieked and charged.

"No!" shouted Seven. The camo boy found a stick, too, and ran at the mountain lion as Brix lowered his head and tried to ram into the creature's chest. Cabot stormed toward the clashing bodies, shouting and waving her arms, trying to be big. She kicked the creature in the ribs, causing it to swipe at her and knocking the stick out of her hand. She fought her way out of her backpack and swung it around, walloping the mountain lion with it.

Puerco snorted and squealed.

All three kids, yelling, screaming, bleeding, held their ground until finally the creature had had enough.

"Roar again," Cabot whispered.

They all roared and waved their arms in the air, then charged at the mountain lion.

After a long moment of staring them down, the creature turned and loped away, licking blood off its chops.

"Holy coconuts," Cabot whispered. "Who got bitten?"

"Me," Seven said. "It's not deep." He grabbed her and Brix by the hands, and the three ran together in the opposite direction. Eventually they stopped to take a breath. "Are you okay?" Seven asked, checking them over.

They'd both been swiped by the creature, too. Brix's cuts were already closing up, while Cabot's were bleeding bright red. Seven was bleeding, too—they could tell by the drops falling to the jungle floor beneath his elbow. Cabot got the first aid kit from her backpack—the one her mother had left behind, filled with their homemade bandages and herbal remedies. She cleaned and bandaged her wound, then held out the antiseptic to Seven.

He took it and apparently found the right spot, based on the sharp intake of breath.

"How big a bandage do you need?" Cabot asked him.

"About a two-by-two-inch patch will cover it," Seven said, feeling the edges of the injury. Cabot pulled the appropriate bandage and readied it for him to put on. He did so, and they could see the bandage affixed to his arm, but not the arm itself.

They made sure Puerco was okay, too, and let him out. Then they took in some water and food, collected their things, and continued. Eventually the trees thinned and they could see occasional patches of sky. Brix charged ahead, happy to get out of the jungle. The other two followed.

Finally they emerged from the jungle and entered a triangular meadow. There were a few large trees and lots of long yellow grass. The kids could see a big mountain range that ended abruptly at the water, as if some huge god—or a glacier—had sliced the rock away. The floor dropped away to the calm bay. The open ocean was too far away to be visible behind them.

Cabot observed the mountain with trepidation. It was much bigger than she'd expected—the terrain was *not* to scale on Mr. Golden's map. Then she knelt at the edge of the land to gaze down at the bay below them.

Seven pivoted to take in their surroundings, then took a long drink from one of the canteens and sat on a rock to rest and check his wound. Constant dull pain pounded around it. The heat of the day and the brisk pace had him sweating. He took his sweater off, rolled it tightly, and put it in his backpack.

Cabot and Brix traded vantage points, had a quiet chat about options, then came back together with Seven.

"What's the consensus?" Seven asked. His bandage had a few dark red stains on it now, but it looked like the bleeding had stopped. He looked up expectantly.

"The what?" asked Brix.

"Did you decide on the best way to go?" He whistled to Puerco, who'd strayed a little too far for comfort. The pig bounded back to them.

"Oh. Yes," said Brix.

"We did," Cabot agreed. She took her long-sleeve parachute

shirt off, leaving her in a tank top and baggy parachute pants. She could feel a blister on her little toe from the too-big boots and sat down to adjust her layers of socks. "The rocks that line the water's edge stretch as far as we can see. If we can scale down to them here, we can avoid climbing the mountain . . . which I might not be able to handle. It looks hard."

Brix nodded in agreement, though he seemed slightly disappointed.

"And what happens," Seven said, "if the rocks run out?"

"Then we either climb back up if there's a ledge to get to, or swim across the bay to the other side." Cabot put her boot back on and beckoned the boys to come with her to the edge of the cliff. The view from here was stunning—sparkling bay, sheer cliffs, light blue sky with a few wispy clouds. She pointed toward a misty spot far across the bay, where the land curved around. "We'll cross at the narrowest part and head toward Estero," she said. "Once civilization begins, it'll be easier."

"How long before we get to Estero?" Brix asked.

"Two or three more days should do it," said Cabot.

Seven grimaced, though the others couldn't see it. *Once civilization begins.* Cabot's "easier" was Seven's nightmare.

They set up the rope, then determined the order of descent to the bay. Brix went first again. "Down is always easier," he called out, taking fearless bounds down the side. He let out the slack of rope generously until he reached the rocky area at the water's edge. He stepped out of the way so the next person could go, then turned to look around the pile of boulders on which he stood. Waves slapped them and sent sea spray to cool him off.

As Cabot called down to let him know she was coming, Brix spied something in the shade of a small cove. His eyes widened. More bones.

And a high-tech backpack.

THE CORDOBA MUSEUM

Birdie and Tenner circled the museum, not daring to approach as other pedestrians streamed up a walkway toward its open doors. Next to the doors was a daunting army of guards in uniform, apparently protecting whatever was inside. Other people seemed unbothered by them. But Tenner shivered. The guards had weapons.

There was a sign at the entrance to the grounds that told about the history of the building and what it held. Birdie began reading:

THE CORDOBA BEGAN AS A MUSEUM OF FINE ART BUT WAS FORCED TO CLOSE AFTER THE THEFT OF A NUMBER OF VALUABLE PAINTINGS AND SCULPTURES. PRESIDENT FUERTE MOVED THE REMAINING ART TO HIS RESIDENCE, THE MAGDALIA PALACE, ALONG WITH THE PRICELESS STONE CROWN, A SYMBOL OF PEACE. THE CORDOBA MUSEUM RECENTLY REOPENED

TO HOUSE LOCAL AND FOREIGN RELICS, AS WELL AS
CURRENCY NO LONGER USED IN ESTERO.

"Relics and currency?" interrupted Tenner, wrinkling his nose.

"That part where it says valuable paintings and sculptures
were stolen . . ." She turned to Tenner and raised an eyebrow.

He gave her a knowing nod.

"Listen to this," said Birdie, continuing to read the plaque.

THE CORDOBA MUSEUM GAINED INTERNATIONAL
NOTORIETY FOR HOUSING AN EXTENSIVE COLLECTION
OF GOLD, JEWELS, AND GEMS DATING BACK CENTURIES
TO THE EARLY RULERS OF ESTERO AND OTHER PARTS
OF THE WORLD. BUT SUPERNATURAL CRIMINALS ARE
BELIEVED TO HAVE MADE OFF WITH THE MAJORITY OF
THE COLLECTION.

"Supernatural criminals!" Birdie exclaimed too loudly. A
couple of people nearby turned to look at her with a hint of
disdain—for being loud or for talking about supernatural
criminals, she wasn't sure. She clamped her mouth shut.

Tenner scrambled to say something that would make the
people stop paying attention to them. "Can you even imagine a
stone crown?" Tenner said. "Sounds like a headache waiting to
happen."

"Good one," Birdie said with a groan. The people turned back to their companions. Birdie flashed Tenner a grateful look. They'd been getting along well. He was easier to deal with when it was only the two of them. When he wasn't trying so hard to grab her attention all the time. Was there a nice way to tell him that? She'd have to figure out how to phrase it.

Tenner blushed and kept going. "I mean, think about it. Try to hold your head up after wearing that thing all day." He laughed alone this time. Thankfully he stopped. "Do you want to go inside?"

"I don't know . . . relics and currency?" She made a face.

"It must be at least a *little* interesting if these people are going in," said Tenner. "And with all of those guards there—they have to be protecting something important."

Birdie glanced at the guards and the open door, watching what the people did. They either held a small piece of paper that didn't look like money or a device that they showed to a person standing inside. Birdie shifted uneasily as she imagined her parents staking out a place like this, preparing to steal things and sell them elsewhere. She felt guilty by association just standing outside the building.

Birdie focused on the guards. They weren't interacting with anyone, and their weapons were in place in their belts, so the situation wasn't quite as alarming as it could be. But one of the guards seemed to be looking straight at the two, noticing their hesitation. Birdie felt caution welling up inside. Her father hadn't spoken highly of people like them. They'd gotten in the way of the heists. From Birdie's perspective, they were sort of the bad guys, even though she knew her parents were the actual criminals. It made everything confusing.

"The people are showing something to that woman inside," Birdie said in a low voice. "It seems like you need to either give them a paper or hold up a device before you can go in."

Tenner lifted his glasses and squinted to focus on the transaction. "They're holding up cell phones, kind of like the ones your parents had. You brought them, right?" He dropped his glasses into place.

"Yeah." If holding up a cell phone was all it took, it would be easy to go inside. But her stomach did a little flip. "Let's keep exploring Estero and learning about how to do things. We can go inside the museum another time. I think we should find food."

Tenner lifted his eyebrows and straightened his shoulders. "And I think you are right."

He hitched up his too-big skirt-shorts, and the two headed back the way they came. When they got to the corner with all the lit-up circles and blinking symbols, Tenner studied the one directly in front of them, across the street.

"I've noticed that the white symbol is a walking stick person," he said. "It changes at the exact same time the circle lights above the road change. The cars stop when there's a red circle in front of them."

"Oh, interesting!" Birdie smoothed her hair back and tied it with a frayed rope as the wind whipped around near the speeding vehicles.

"Watch," Tenner said. "The cars slow down when the yellow circle appears, then stop when the red one comes. After that, the white walking figure turns on, which I think means we can cross the street."

"Even though the cars are so close?" Birdie eyed them anxiously. Dead bugs spattered their bumpers. The cars were big and fast and not to be trusted. Drivers peered through their windshields at them, not smiling. As she and Tenner ran across the street in mild fright, looking in every direction, a giant flat-faced vehicle groaned to a stop a few feet away.

"Yikes!" Birdie sped up, and they leaped safely to the curb. A line of people got into the giant vehicle.

"Now watch," Tenner said, stopping and pointing up. "The walking person will disappear and the red hand will appear, which means stop. And then the circle lights will change to green, and the cars and that big monstrous thing will move again. That's how they don't hit each other. It's all a bunch of symbols. Like, everywhere. It's exhausting." But he lifted his chin and smiled with satisfaction at figuring it out.

"I'm glad you're paying attention," Birdie told him. "I didn't expect this to be so hard. Why make roads that cross other roads? Very dangerous."

"At least the people are leaving us alone," said Tenner. He

lowered his voice. "It doesn't seem like there's anyone checking to see if people are supernatural. Or detectors that beep if a person like us walks by. I was worried about that."

"Me too," Birdie said. "But nobody notices us, except to look at our clothes. Or, you know, when I shouted 'supernatural criminals' back there." She started to giggle. And then she couldn't stop. Soon Tenner was laughing into his hands. Then he snorted really hard, and they had to lean against a building and pull themselves together. Hunger plus exhaustion plus Birdie practically announcing their special interest in supernatural criminals had done them in.

They kept walking, Tenner's keen sense of smell leading them to food. A low hum of anxiety returned as they headed for more new experiences. The buildings there were the super-tall kind, which in Birdie's mind made them useless and seemingly inaccessible. It didn't make sense—what was the purpose of something this tall? Maybe Brix and Seven could climb well enough to look out some of those windows, but why bother? At least on the ground floor, there were little shops. Each one had a delightful name. "Magda's Produce," Birdie said, and marveled at the perfect displays of fruit and vegetables they'd never seen before. Who was Magda? What was she all about?

They went up to a shop called Bootsie's Boutique. The second word had Tenner stumped. "What's a bout-i-cue?"

Birdie shrugged, then gasped. Inside the window was a head-less plastic person. It was wearing neon-colored clothes and jewelry, and standing with arms and legs bent in unnatural positions. "Whoa," Birdie exclaimed. The headless person—was that supposed to make you *want* to go inside? She made binoculars with her hands and pressed them against the window so she could see inside. Did they dare enter? She saw racks and racks of clothing, purses, and more headless people, sparkling jewelry, shoes . . . "I'm going in," she declared. "Come on, T. Just for a minute, and then I promise we'll eat."

She pulled on the door, but it didn't open. Then she tried pushing, and it swung open fast, flinging her forward and making her trip over the threshold and lose one of her sneakers. A bell sounded, and the two froze. Was that supposed to happen? After Birdie got her sneaker back on, she continued into the shop. Tenner walked stiffly behind her, senses heightened. He could hear a person moving around somewhere inside the shop, but he couldn't see anyone. He eyed the fake headless person in the window with suspicion. The bright-colored clothing made him glad for his sunglasses.

A woman with light brown skin and long straight black hair like Birdie's came out from a back room. She was wearing a bright pink skirt and blouse, with several necklaces and sparkling rings. Everything she wore looked like she'd gotten it in this store. "Welcome," she said with a bright smile. She was wearing a lot of makeup on her face, and her eyelashes were like the hairy spiders they sometimes found inside a cracked coconut that had lost its water. Seven's mom had put on makeup from time to time to tone down her shimmering when she wanted a change from everyday, but the other parents had either run out of product years before or preferred not to wear it.

"Let me know if I can get anything down for you," the woman said, sounding extra cheerful.

Birdie smiled hesitantly. "Thank you," she said. Talking to the stranger gave her goose bumps. She rubbed her arms and walked past a full-length mirror, then returned to it and looked at herself—her parachute clothing looked out of place in this shop. In the reflection she also caught the woman looking at her with a strange expression on her face. Birdie felt her stomach twist. Did the woman suspect anything? Or did she just think her clothes were weird? Birdie tiptoed backward to position herself behind a rack of dresses and bumped into one of the headless people, making it wobble on its stand. Spooked, Birdie whirled around and grabbed at it, thinking it was going to topple over. She clutched it to her chest. "Ack!" she said, realizing how odd she must look. She let go of the fake person and zigzagged for the door, banging into a rack of earrings with her shoulder and sending it spinning, flinging earrings around the store. She didn't stop.

As the woman—no longer smiling—came swiftly over, Tenner scurried to help pick things up. "Sorry," he said. He shoved the earrings into the salesperson's hands and fled. Back on the street, Birdie and Tenner snickered into their hands and then ran down the block to get farther away.

Delicious smells made them stop in front of Cosimo's Bistro. They peered through the window. There were several tables inside. A few were occupied by people who were talking and eating. Birdie's stomach growled wildly. "Should we go in?"

"Yeah," said Tenner, but he seemed unsure. "I'm nervous after the bout-i-cue incident."

"I'll do better," Birdie said. "What's the worst thing that could happen?"

"That's the problem," Tenner said. "We have no idea what the worst thing is."

"Let's get it over with." Birdie put her hand on the shiny brass handle and took a second to examine it. It was cool and solid and seemed unnecessarily large compared to the clothes shop. She pushed it, then pushed harder, but nothing happened. She stood back and tried pulling it, and the great door swung open. It was ten times heavier than their swinging cabin doors at home. "Doors," she muttered. "They should all swing both ways, like at home."

Inside was dimly lit. A man stood a short distance away behind a raised desk and nodded at Birdie and Tenner. "Hello," he said. "Welcome to Cosimo's. Are you waiting for your parents?"

"What?" Tenner said, alarmed. He looked around.

"No?" The man smiled. "Perhaps you are alone? Table for two?"

Birdie was also thrown by the "parents" line. Could the man possibly know something about their parents? "It's just us," she said, her gaze darting around the place. Big lights with green shades hung from heavy gold chains hooked to the ceiling. There was a long wood counter with little circular red seats on the right, and tables with chairs on the left. And in the center of the room was a wide, hulking . . . something, with platforms that went all the way up toward the ceiling. Birdie searched her mind, trying to remember what that thing was called. And then she realized that was how people climbed higher in these tall buildings. You could step up on the platforms like they were rock formations.

She turned her attention back to the man as he pulled two large, shiny cards from a slot and started walking. "Follow me, please," he said. "Is this your first time at Cosimo's?"

"I—yes," said Birdie. She went after him. "How much do things cost, please? We have, um, about twenty." Her voice shook, and she wasn't sure why she said that, other than knowing that at least one of their money papers had a number twenty on it.

"The prices are on the menu, miss," said the man, eyeing her with a bit of concern now. He frowned at her rope hair tie and her worn-out sneakers, which were missing shoelaces. Then his eyes widened as he took in Tenner's oversized dad shorts that hung on his narrow frame. "You might want to split a main course or order from the à la carte menu."

Birdie gulped and nodded. "Yes. Right. Okay." *The what menu?*

The host came to a stop. "Along the staircase?" he said, as if that were a real question.

But at least it gave Birdie the word she was looking for. She smiled, and he took that as a yes. He set the shiny cards on the table in front of the padded bench seats and left them to sit down.

Birdie and Tenner each let out a breath of relief and slid into the seats. The staircase wound around next to them, and they could look up into the space above. It seemed like there was even more restaurant up there. "Everything is enormous," Tenner remarked, bouncing on the seat. He'd never had a springy, cushiony seat before.

Birdie nodded and bounced, too, but less obviously. She looked at the shiny card, which had the word *Menu* written on the top. "Oh, cute," she said. "It's like when we were little and played chef, making up dishes to serve our parents and putting pebbles on plates instead of food. Remember?"

"I guess our parents taught us about restaurants without us realizing it," Tenner said. He deciphered the curly script carefully. "I have no idea what half of this stuff is. Toast?"

"I'm looking at the cheapest things in each section," Birdie said. "I assume the numbers mean how much it costs." She was silent for a minute. "Oh! Eggs only cost three. Way down at the bottom, see? And fruit. And near the top there's some kind of hash. Brisket?"

"What's brisket?"

"No idea, but the picture shows a lot of food. If we get one brisket hash and two eggs, it's less than twenty."

"Where are you even getting twenty from? I thought you made that up."

"I saw it on the corner of the money, and I only wanted to use up one of them."

"Oh." Tenner settled back in his chair. "That sounds good. But you should remember I can eat, like, twelve bird eggs."

"We're just trying to figure this out, okay?" Birdie said. "I have a few more snacks in my backpack if this isn't enough. We don't want to spend all the money in one meal."

The man walked up. "Are you ready to order?" He gave Tenner a mildly puzzled glance, since he was still wearing sunglasses, but he didn't say anything.

"Y-yes," said Birdie.

"To drink?"

Birdie froze.

The man narrowed his eyes. "Perhaps water?"

"Yes," Birdie said. "Yes, we love water. Fresh, right? Like . . . from a . . ." She trailed off, sensing "from a stream" didn't sound like the right thing to say here, but she didn't want to drink ocean water, so she wanted to be sure.

The man blinked. "Yes, very fresh from the tap, okay? It's free. And to eat?"

Birdie consulted her menu again. "Two eggs, please, and brisket hash."

"To split?" the waiter prompted.

"Yes."

"And how would you like the eggs prepared?"

"Uh . . ." Birdie looked at Tenner.

"Cooked, please," said Tenner.

The man took in a breath and let it out slowly. "Perfect." He smiled condescendingly, indicating Tenner's answer was somehow not perfect at all. Then he took their menus and left them to sit.

"Are we supposed to go get it somewhere?" Tenner asked. He looked around for the kitchen but didn't see anything.

"I think they bring it out," Birdie said, eyeing someone bringing plates to a different table. She recalled a conversation with her father from long ago when he told her about meeting someone famous at a restaurant. He'd said the servers had kept bringing out more and more food.

"I feel bad," said Tenner. "I could go get the food if I knew where it was. When do we pay?"

Birdie shrugged. "Wait until he asks for it, I guess." The two sat in silence for a moment and looked around. "Staircase," Birdie said aloud, tapping the exterior of it. "That's how you climb to the top of the building. This ceiling is like the floor for up there."

"Why not stay on the ground? There are plenty of places there, all crammed next to each other."

Birdie nodded. She picked up a fork and examined it. They had some of these at home, and a few spoons, and a hatchet and a sharp, dangerous knife, and a couple of other knives. Some had broken or gotten lost over the years, but Seven had whittled more spoons from sticks. This fork was metal.

A woman came out of a doorway nearby, and Birdie caught a glimpse of what was inside—a toilet room. On the door it said LADIES and had a triangle person, like the sign at the beach. A little farther down was another door that said GENTLEMEN with a stick person. Between the two doors was a shiny metal box sticking out of the wall. The woman stopped in front of it, pushed a button on the box, and water came out in an arc. She bent down and drank from it.

"Whoa," said Birdie. "It's like they rerouted a stream to come out of that little mechanism. And you can turn it on and off."

"It's a little like our shower valve," Tenner said. "And the basin knobs in the toilet room at the beach. The lever is like a dam that you can move. It controls the way the water comes out."

"Oh yeah," said Birdie. "That makes sense." It was nice to be able to equate something to the world they knew.

Birdie looked around at the people in the restaurant. They all had different skin colors, like the criminals and kids had. But no one bounced when they walked or had bodies that shimmered or fingertips that sparked fire. And there were definitely no people here that looked like Seven.

She was glad, now, that he hadn't come with. He'd have been absolutely miserable. She remembered the way the people had looked at her when she'd said "supernatural criminals." And she thought about the server who'd taken their order. Would he look at Seven with a sneer and say he was perfect, too? Or maybe he wouldn't have let him come in at all.

A BIT OF A PROBLEM

Soon the food came. "Enjoy," the server at Cosimo's said. He set down a large plate of brisket hash between them, then two separate smaller plates with one sunny-side-up egg on each.

"Thank you," Birdie said primly as the server filled their glasses with a pitcher, then left.

Tenner lifted his sunglasses and stared at the eggs. "Those are the biggest eggs I have ever seen," he said. "And that hash looks weird, but it smells good."

They each slid their egg on top of the hash, then portioned out their food onto their empty egg plates and began eating.

"I love brisket," Tenner declared after a while. "It's my new favorite thing."

"This is delicious," Birdie said. "Seven and Cabot would like it, too. Brix might be a little picky about the huge eggs." She paused and took a drink.

Tenner wiped his mouth and sat back. "I don't see Seven ever wanting to come here."

"Here, to this restaurant?" asked Birdie.

"Here, to this city," Tenner said. "He'd stick out. Badly."

Birdie nodded. "I was thinking that, too. Do you like it here?"

Tenner glanced around. "It's not bad. But I'd rather be home, where I don't have to worry about doing something wrong." He frowned and realized that wasn't exactly true—he did have to worry about that at home. Birdie was often rolling her eyes because he'd talked too much or about the wrong things according to her. He was constantly trying to perform a certain way there. It had made him self-conscious, which usually led to him getting flustered and her looking down on him even more. Today was going pretty well, though, he realized with a note of satisfaction. Maybe it was because this was all new and scary to Birdie, too.

Birdie sighed and placed her fork carefully on her cleaned plate, then wiped her mouth. It seemed normal. A meal at a table. It was almost a letdown. "The mystery is gone," Birdie said dramatically.

Tenner nodded, pretending to understand what she was talking about, as the server approached. "All set?" said the man.

Birdie looked at him quizzically.

"Finished?" the man said.

"Ah. Yes. Thank you."

"You're welcome." There was a hint of warmth in his voice now as he picked up the plates. Before he left, he reached into his apron and pulled out a slip of paper, then set it on the table upside down. "I can take that up for you whenever you're ready."

The two kids exchanged a questioning glance. "Do you have the money?" Birdie asked Tenner. What else could the man mean?

"Yeah. Sorry." Tenner reached for his backpack on the bench next to him. He rummaged through it and pulled out the money. Then he laid out each piece on the table in front of him.

The waiter's eyes widened. "Oh," he said at the sight of the bills.

Birdie saw his hawkish glance and reached across the table, gathering up all the money along with the receipt that the server had set down. "One moment, please," she said icily.

"Of c-c-course," said the server, who seemed strangely rattled now. Birdie wondered if maybe he'd never seen this much money before. "I need to check on something," the man said. "I'll be right back." He slipped away.

Birdie leaned across the table and whispered, "Don't show people the money."

And just like that, Birdie was scolding Tenner and things were back to normal. "Sorry," said Tenner. His face flushed. "You can hold it from now on if you want." He looked where the server had gone, but the man had disappeared.

Birdie studied the receipt. There were some abbreviations and numbers on it that made no sense, except for the words *brisket hash* and *egg 2*. At the very bottom there was a stack of numbers like a math problem with the answer being $17.46. She squinted at it. She remembered Dad teaching them about dollars and cents, but it hadn't seemed important at the time. What she could recall was that the dot separated the dollar part from the cents part. She didn't have any of the cents, only dollars. After an exasperated moment, she laid a twenty-dollar bill down on the receipt. "Maybe he'll give us change back."

In an instant the server appeared at their table again. Birdie tentatively held out the twenty and the receipt. "Do you bring the change back?"

"Well," said the man, eyes darting, "uh, first, I'm not sure where you got this money."

Birdie tensed. She kept her gaze steady, and when she didn't answer, he continued.

"I . . . had to check with my manager to see if we would accept it. I told her that you were children, and she seemed . . . sympathetic, but . . . she's . . . checking. There may be a, um, a problem." He looked increasingly uncomfortable. "Unless you have the correct local currency?"

Birdie stared, feeling like she was slipping underwater with terms she didn't grasp. Was he trying to scam them? "What's wrong with our money?" she asked.

"It's . . ." He seemed momentarily baffled. "Don't you know?"

"Know what?"

"It's . . ." His voice grew thin. "It's the currency from before."

"Before what?" asked Birdie. But she was reminded of what

the sign outside the Cordoba Museum had said about housing old currencies.

"Before President Fuerte changed it. Fourteen years ago?" The server glanced uneasily over his shoulder at the restaurant's entrance, and then turned the other way to look at an office. A woman appeared in the doorway, and she stood there with a phone to her ear, watching them. She wasn't smiling.

"Fourteen years ago?" Tenner asked. That was right after their parents left.

The server narrowed his eyes. "Are you from a different country?"

Both kids knew the answer to this one. "We live in the city," said Birdie as Tenner said, "We live up the street," both of them insisting a little too loudly.

"Then surely you must have . . . regular money?"

"Nope." Birdie shoved the twenty-dollar bill at him. "Do you want this or not?"

The man's eyes widened. "Ah . . ." He looked back at the woman. She gave him a subtle nod, but Tenner noticed it. He tuned in to see if he could hear what she was saying into the phone.

"It'll only take a moment," the server said, not looking at them. "My manager is checking with the authorities to, um, see if we can accept it."

Birdie's expression flickered, and a sense of dread stirred in the pit of her stomach. *Authorities?* She studied the server's face. His eyes were shifting like Troy Cordoba's when he'd told a lie. He looked away and tried to brush things off too easily, like Lucy Cordoba did whenever Troy was being a bully. Was he a criminal? If so, he was messing with the wrong kids. The two might not know much about culture or currency. But they knew about criminals.

Help, Birdie thought. She closed her eyes and thought it again. *Help!* What were they supposed to do?

Tenner's eyes widened as he listened to the manager's conversation from afar.

The server dabbed sweat off his brow. "I'm sorry for this inconvenience," he said. "It's just that my manager insists we wait." He stood close to the table, blocking Birdie in the booth so she couldn't get out, and sent a searing glance at the manager. The woman put her phone in her pocket and stared back at the man. What silent conversation were they having?

Tenner had a clue. He kicked Birdie under the table, then winced, knowing she'd be annoyed by it. But it couldn't be helped. "We'll go get the other money," he said smoothly. "I'm sorry—we found this money in our grandfather's old desk, and he said we could keep it. We thought we could still use it, but I guess not. I wish we'd brought the other kind. But we can go get it."

Birdie stared at him. What was he talking about? Outright lying like it came naturally. She'd never seen him do that before.

"You're staying with your grandfather? What is his name, please?"

Tenner inched to the edge of his bench. "Come on, Birdie. Papa's probably on his way to pick us up right now. We'll go get regular money from him."

"Okay," Birdie said. When Tenner hopped out of the booth, the waiter lunged at him and grabbed his hand where he'd rubbed it against the shark's scales. Tenner yelped in pain.

"Leave him alone!" Birdie slammed her fist into the waiter's stomach, and he let go of Tenner. The two started running for the exit. *HELP!* cried Birdie again.

Just then, two police officers rushed into the restaurant, blocking the door. Birdie and Tenner slid to a stop and whirled around, but the server and manager were coming at them from that direction. The police lunged at the kids and grabbed their shoulders, sending Tenner's sunglasses skidding across the floor. The officer holding Birdie turned her around. "What's this all about?"

BONES

Cabot, Brix, and Seven stared at the nearly complete skeleton and familiar-looking backpack before them. They'd come down the cliff to the rocks that lined the bay, and the rolling waves lapped at their feet. The bones were nestled inside the cove, laid out as if the person had been lounging there . . . or perhaps was moved to that spot by others. A few bits of thin, faded cloth remained trapped under the bones, decomposing in the harsh sun and salt water.

Cabot's eyes moved to the backpack. "Should I open it?"

The fresh spray of the waves hitting the rocks was a welcome coolant after their recent trek through the jungle and journey down the cliffside. The rocks spread ahead of them like a wide, uneven path along the bay shore, as far as they could see in the direction they needed to go. The mountain, which they were glad to avoid, shot up. But down here were the bones. Several of the ribs were cracked, and a few were broken in half. Part of the skull had crumbled away, as if it had been crushed. Brix spied a piece of frayed rope that had caught on a sharp piece of jutting rock above them. It dangled down near the skeleton. Clearly someone else had tried to come down this way . . . and failed.

Seven's heart thudded. Would the backpack reveal who this was? And if so, was he ready to know if it was one of his parents? He glanced at Brix. "You okay if we find out who this is? It could be anybody."

Brix's face changed, realizing that it could be his mother. "Uh . . ."

Cabot glanced at the skeleton again, then turned to Brix. "This is a tall person—see how much longer the femurs are than the one we saw earlier? Your mom is short like you. So I don't think this is her." She cringed. It could be her father.

Brix's shoulders relaxed. "Oh. Okay, yeah. Ready when you are."

"Yeah," said Seven. "Open it."

Cabot nodded, steeling herself for the worst. She knelt on the wet rock and yanked on the pack until it pulled free. "It feels empty," she said, holding it up. The mouth of the backpack flopped open. Cabot looked inside. "I don't see anything." She stuck her hand in and felt around. "Nothing." She lifted it and turned it upside down and shook it. "Empty."

"What about the front pocket?" said Brix.

Cabot turned the backpack around. That pocket was already open, too, and empty, like it had been ransacked. "Someone took everything," she said. She turned the backpack inside out, looking for a name tag or anything to identify who it belonged to. At the bottom of the main compartment, she spied a small pocket held shut with Velcro. She pressed it and felt something lumpy. "Hold on," she said. "Secret compartment." She pried the Velcro apart, then reached inside. Her eyes widened as she pulled out a tiny velvet pouch, about one inch square. Carefully she loosened the pouch strings, then poured the contents into her hand. They sparkled in the sun. "Diamonds," she whispered, then swiftly counted them. "Thirteen of them." She looked up.

Seven took in a sharp breath. "Thirteen diamonds?" The three looked at one another, then at the skeleton. "It's Troy Cordoba," Seven said. "Louis was right. He did have them all this time."

Cabot blew out a relieved breath. It seemed almost certain this skeleton was Troy. If any of the parents had to die, he was the best one to go.

Brix wasn't sure how to process it. How was a kid supposed to feel about the death of a parent who'd been a bully? Was it okay to feel bad? Because he felt terrible. "No wonder my dad moved the stash," said Brix after a while, glancing up at Cabot. "He was keeping it safe from Troy."

Cabot dropped her gaze. "Yeah." She still didn't like it. Her parents had been trustworthy, while Louis kept important information from them. It wasn't right. But she didn't feel like fighting about it.

Two dead. The three children survived something multiple parents hadn't, which seemed impossible.

A rogue wave doused their legs. The water receded. The bones, freshly sprayed, stayed tucked in their spot except for a few phalanges in a shallow divot in the rocks. They wobbled and rolled around in the pool of water. Cabot studied the location of the skeleton, then looked up at the top of the cliff. "The person couldn't have fallen into this protected spot. I think Troy—if it's really him—died in the fall and someone moved him here." She glanced over the water, wondering why they didn't bury him at sea. Maybe they intended to come back for his body but couldn't. Maybe because *they* needed the stash money, too, in order to hire a boat to use. Cabot couldn't stop her mind from churning over these unknown details. She wanted answers.

"Why would they leave the empty backpack, though?" Cabot asked.

"They were each carrying one already," said Seven. "Maybe they needed their hands free and divvied up his stuff. But they missed the secret compartment."

"What do I do with these?" Cabot asked, carefully pouring the diamonds back inside the pouch.

Seven shrugged. "I wonder if we can trade them for food in Estero. Birdie and Tenner took all the bills." *Tenner.* Now they had something else to tell the other two. How would Tenner feel about his dad being *dead*?

"I'll keep the pouch in my backpack." Cabot placed it inside carefully and showed the boys where it was. "In case you want to check on it."

After the next wave splashed their legs, Cabot fastened her backpack and stood up. "Let's keep going."

AN INCIDENT

As the police held tight to Birdie and Tenner, the restaurant server handed over the twenty-dollar bill. "We called you as soon as we saw it," the woman said to the officers. She seemed worried.

An officer took it. "We'll run the serial number. In the meantime, we're going to take these two with us."

Tenner kept his head down, his heart racing—his sunglasses were on the floor, out of reach. If he said he dropped them and asked for them back, would they find that suspicious? Would they look at his extra-large pupils and figure him out? He and Birdie exchanged a glance. What was happening? Why were the police doing this?

"Where are you taking us?" Birdie said, her voice trembling. She didn't like being held by a stranger.

"To the station for a few minutes," one of the officers said.

Birdie and Tenner had no idea what a station was. "Why?" asked Tenner. "We didn't do anything. We thought the money was fine."

"We want to ask you some questions." The authorities seemed calm. Maybe a little too calm. But Birdie and Tenner had no choice but to go with them. Tenner glanced back at the sunglasses, but he was too scared to ask someone to get them. Maybe Birdie was right, that no one would notice his eyes if he didn't bring attention to them. He squinted, trying to keep them half-closed.

The officers put them in the backseat of their car and belted them in, all of which was alarming—it was their first time in a vehicle. The driver started it up, and soon they were going dangerously fast over the roads and bumping around in their restraints. Birdie's face paled. The brisket hash and egg and all that water sloshed around in her stomach.

Tenner looked out the window as a blur of grass and road went by. He wondered if they could escape, and he even tried the door handle, but it wouldn't open.

There was a metal grid with tiny holes separating them from the officers in the front seat. Tenner listened to their low conversation. He'd been picking up more than Birdie, but he hadn't had a chance to tell her what he'd heard the manager say on the phone. He'd figured out she was talking to the police, but he didn't know what to do about it. Everything was scary here. Strange people, strange signs and symbols, and the money? Why would an entire country change their money system? According to the server, it happened right after their parents left. That's why their parents had the old kind.

Tenner had a sinking feeling about it all. He didn't know for sure, but it didn't seem right for authorities to take children to their station to talk.

Birdie let out a small burp, and then a larger one. In her mind she pleaded for help once more. Puerco sent a weak response of warmth and comfort, but that was all she was getting despite multiple silent calls. Where was the raven? Were there any other animals in Estero who could understand her? Her stomach kept sloshing, and her face felt like all the blood had drained from it. She broke out into a cold sweat, and excess saliva forced her to swallow again and again. When she glanced at Tenner, the buildings flew by his window at a dizzying rate. She clutched her stomach . . . then covered her mouth.

As the vehicle turned sharply and went up a circular driveway, Birdie could take no more. "I'm going to throw up!" she whispered between her fingers.

Tenner turned sharply and noticed how green Birdie looked. "Oh, no!" He petted her shoulder helplessly, then pulled back as she yanked at the door handle. But hers wouldn't open, either. As they drove up to the building, Birdie leaned forward and retched, spewing the contents of her stomach over the car floor. The officer in the passenger seat jumped out and pulled Birdie's door open, trying to get her to point the stream outside, but it wasn't happening.

When she finished, she sat up, horrified.

"Are you okay?" Tenner asked, wide-eyed and forgetting his

extra-large pupils for a moment. He wrinkled his nose. While the officers spoke sharply to each other outside the car, barking orders about getting towels and a shop vac, Birdie wiped her mouth on her sleeve. She nodded slowly. Then she daintily moved her splattered shoes out of the vomit area. Tenner helped her unbuckle her seat belt.

The two kids stepped out of the car and walked in a daze to the building. Birdie left a faint trail of vomit footprints behind.

Once inside, one of the police officers handed Birdie a small bucket to carry in case she had to throw up again. But she was pretty sure she was done.

Hopefully things would all get sorted out in a few minutes, Birdie thought, and they'd be on their way back to the beach—on foot this time. Maybe once they reached the sand, they'd keep going—walk into the sea and lie down on an orca and head home, and forget about Dad's last request.

In her weak state, Birdie hadn't noticed the shiny black raven landing on the roof as they walked into the police station. And Tenner's squinting eyes were on something else: the gold lettering on the door to the police station that read ESTERO POLICE DEPARTMENT & JAIL.

HAVING A BAD DAY

The two officers seemed nice enough, so that was a relief, but Tenner and Birdie remained cautious. Tenner kept averting his gaze, which he was sure made him look guilty, but he had to protect his supernaturalness at all costs. The male officer, whose gray hair and mustache were neatly trimmed and styled, brought the kids into a small, stale-smelling room and told them to sit at a table. "You want a soda? Maybe some ginger ale to calm your stomach?"

Neither of them knew what those things were. Tenner shook his head, but Birdie said yes—something to calm her stomach would be good, though she was feeling immensely better now that they weren't bouncing around with the world rushing by. The man went to the counter, opened a low metal door, and pulled out a can. He set it in front of Birdie and left.

The table had crumbs and stains on it, and a stack of papers with tiny words. Tenner sniffed, trying to identify the smells. Vomit still hung predominantly around Birdie, which was unfortunate for a companion with an especially good sense of smell. There was a bitter odor coming from a machine on the counter. The machine had a small orange light on it and a carafe containing dark brown liquid. It smelled burnt.

Tenner hoped a soda was something that smelled good. As he reached for the papers in the middle of the table, Birdie lifted the can and bobbled it. "It's freezing!" she exclaimed, then pressed it against Tenner's cheek. "Feel it."

"What the—stop that!" he said, sliding away. It was colder than the water from the stream back home.

Birdie pulled it away and examined the top of the can. Words were indented in the metal. "*Lift tab to open,*" she read aloud as she turned the can and noted the tab on top. Then she turned the can upside down to see if there was writing on that end. She could hear liquid sloshing around inside, kind of like her stomach had done earlier. She shook it near her ear. Then she set it on the table and pried up the tab.

The can exploded, spraying Birdie in the face. She yelled, and Tenner jumped and nearly overturned his chair.

"What the heck, Birdie?" Tenner exclaimed, using the papers to shield himself from the spray. "Can you please keep all of your liquids, like, over by you?"

"Sorry! I don't know what to do!" Ginger ale continued to froth out of the slit-sized opening she'd made in the can, and the liquid started spilling over the edge of the table. Birdie pushed the can away, leaving it spewing like a volcano in the center of the table while she wiped her eyes with her sleeve. She looked around helplessly. "I don't like soda."

"You are a complete mess," Tenner remarked. He moved to the counter and grabbed a towel, then started cleaning it up, but the towel was soon drenched and the liquid kept oozing out of the can. Tenner threw his hands in the air and gave up, then rescued the papers and scooted his chair away from stinky, sticky Birdie. He turned back to the paper he was reading, leaning over as he absorbed the small print. Birdie pushed her chair back as a new stream of bubbly liquid surged toward her.

A uniformed woman they hadn't seen before came in and stood for a moment, taking in the scene. "What happened here?" She hurried to a cupboard, grabbed a roll of paper towels, and tossed it to Birdie. Startled, Birdie caught it, then deduced that she was to use the roll to continue wiping up the mess. She did so, rubbing the entire roll over the table to great effect. The woman's lips parted in confusion.

Birdie set the stained roll on end and smoothed her shirt. Her fingers stuck to her parachute top, and she peeled them free. "Sorry about that," she said, feeling mildly faint again. She dropped into her chair and tried not to cry. "There's a lot going on today."

The woman's expression softened. "So I've heard."

Birdie glanced up. The woman had light brown skin and

short wavy brown hair, and she looked a little older than the moms Birdie knew. Her skin was wrinkled at her neck. She had extra-long eyelashes—but not the spider kind—and wore a burnt orange color on her lips. She took the can away and put it in the sink. "You want to try again?"

"No thank you," said Birdie. "Can we go soon?"

"Not quite yet." The officer closed the door and sat at the table. She cleared her throat and looked pointedly at Tenner. "Something interesting in that newspaper, young man?"

Tenner startled and sheepishly folded it, struggling a bit with the big, thin pages. "No. Sorry." He set it on the table and tried not to look at her.

The woman eyed the two. "I'm Commander Collazo. You're Birdie," she said, pointing to her. She must have overheard Tenner say it. "And you are?" She looked at Tenner.

"Um, Tenner."

"Siblings?"

"No." Tenner sat back, keeping his eyes narrowed, which was starting to make his face ache. All five kids had heard about what it was like to be interrogated by police. Somehow this room seemed the most familiar of any place they'd been thus far . . . though from the description Louis had given them, none of them could have imagined it was a room with kitchen items and soda and newspapers in it.

Birdie's eyes widened. Tenner had told the police earlier that they were staying with their grandfather. "Cousins," she said.

The commander nodded. "All right. And what's your address?"

Birdie blinked. "We don't have to tell you that."

The commander pulled out a notepad and pen from her shirt pocket and wrote something down. Birdie shifted uncomfortably. Tenner trained his eyes on her notepad but couldn't see what she was writing because she held it facing her. Without looking up, Commander Collazo asked, "Where did you get the contraband?"

Tenner frowned. "The what?"

"The illegal tender. The cash. The bucks. What do kids call money these days?"

"We call it money." Birdie glanced guiltily at her backpack as she remembered she had even more of it there.

"All right. Where'd you get it?"

Birdie looked at Tenner. He'd started that wacky story earlier—he may as well finish it.

Tenner shifted. "Our grandfather had it in his desk. We were helping him clean, and he said we could have it. We didn't know it wasn't real money."

The commander studied the two. "How old are you?"

"We're kids," Birdie said, and then lied. "Twelve." The lie came easily, which was a bit of a thrill.

"And have you ever seen this kind of money before?" The commander set her notebook facedown on the table and leaned forward on her elbows, scrutinizing the children's faces.

"Yes," said Tenner at the same time Birdie said, "No." This time they didn't exchange a glance. Birdie stared back at the woman. Her hands started to sweat.

"In books," Tenner explained weakly, keeping his eyes down.

The commander tapped her pen on the table for an agonizing moment. Then she put the notebook and pen into her pocket. "Okay. Well, now you know you can't use that money, and if you have any more, you should turn it over to me now."

Birdie glanced at her backpack. The server had seen all six of Tenner's bills—and they weren't any good here, so they might as well give them to the officer. She reached into her backpack and pulled out the other five, then laid them neatly on the table. But she left the ones from her father buried. She looked the woman in the eye. "That's all of it."

"Perfect," said the commander. "Now, if you give me your grandfather's phone number, I'll call and he can come pick you up."

"We're fine walking," Birdie said. "Papa is . . . not much of a driver. And I'm . . . not much of a . . . passenger."

The officer with the gray mustache from earlier opened the door and poked his head in. "Confirmed that the serial number doesn't match any of the stolen bills," he said.

"That's what I expected," said the commander. She handed him the rest. "These won't match the stolen ones, either."

The kids perked up. Stolen bills? But this money wasn't any good. Why would anyone steal it?

"But . . ." the man said hesitantly. "There's been another . . . incident."

The commander's face flickered. "Get the squad assembled for a briefing," she said to him. "Five minutes."

The man left, and the commander turned back to grab her notepad, then got up. "Okay. You're free to go. I'll smooth things over with the restaurant, but you might not want to go there again unless it's to pay your tab with real money." She went to the door, then called over her shoulder to Birdie, "You can clean yourself up in the bathroom on your way out."

"Thanks." Birdie stood, too, and once Commander Collazo was out of sight, Tenner grabbed the newspapers, quickly folded them, and slid them into his backpack. As they entered the hallway, a crowd of uniformed men and women walked together and went into a large room—probably for the briefing. Once the hall emptied of officers, Tenner peered both ways as if looking for something. But Birdie was too focused on her disgusting self to notice. She beelined for the bathroom with the triangle sign.

Instead of waiting for her, Tenner snuck down the hallway and peeked around a corner. Down the hall was a desk with a sign overhead that read ESTERO JAIL. Five or six chairs lined one side of the hallway, all empty. There was no one standing by the desk, so Tenner moved swiftly toward it, his senses buzzing, trying to detect anything that would tell him if Elena Golden was there. He could hear clanging noises and low voices. A faint smell of smoke and body odor grew stronger. And as he drew close, he could see a long hallway of cells with vertical bars, but there was a metal gate keeping anyone from entering the area without a key. Tenner kept going, hoping to get a look inside the nearest cells before whoever was supposed to be at the desk came back.

"Elena!" he shouted, running up to the gate. "Elena Golden! It's Tenner!"

"I'm here," said a man in falsetto voice. Others burst out laughing.

Tenner frowned. His superhearing detected distant footsteps behind him, and he glanced over his shoulder. A uniformed officer with a weapon was at the far end of the hallway, coming toward him. He turned back to the gate, desperate. "Elena Golden!"

"Hey, kid!" the officer shouted. She started to shuffle faster toward Tenner. "Kid—what do you think you're doing?"

Tenner pushed his face against the metal gate. "Elena! Are you in here?"

He waited an endless second as more voices jeered back at him. "I'm Elena. Get me out of here."

Anger and embarrassment welled up inside, and Tenner started to sweat. He turned abruptly and gave the officer a helpless shrug, keeping his eyes lowered. "My friend Elena said to meet her at the main exit. Where is it?"

"This is definitely not it," the officer said, sizing him up. "You don't want to go back there. Those people will eat you for lunch." She pointed down the hallway. "To the end, turn right, then past the bathrooms."

"Thanks," Tenner said. He hurried away, all the while listening to the chatter in the jail cells. There was definitely no one who sounded anything like Elena.

Inside the toilet room, Birdie splashed her face. She cleaned the dried vomit out of her hair and washed the sticky ginger ale off her arms, neck, and shirt. She sniffed herself carefully to see if she'd missed anything, then took off her sneakers and cleaned those, too. When she exited the bathroom, Tenner was jogging toward her down the empty hallway.

"Where did you come from?" Birdie asked.

"Tell you in a bit," Tenner said in a low voice.

They exited into the parking lot, and both let out a sigh of relief. Three ravens swooped around their heads and landed on the pavement. One was the raven from the beach last night. They each sent Birdie a warm greeting.

Birdie felt tears well up. *Finally.* "Hello," she murmured. She closed her eyes and let the feelings from the birds flood her. Feelings of strength. They'd heard her and responded. "Help is here," she said to Tenner.

"We're beyond help at this point," Tenner said. He glanced nervously over his shoulder. "Let's go."

Birdie ignored his snide comment and fished through her backpack for some berries she'd brought from home, then bent down to offer them. The birds crowded around to eat from her hand. Birdie looked them in the eyes. "Hello," she said to each. "Hello. Hello. I'm glad you're here. You have no idea."

Tenner glanced back again and saw the commander breeze past the window, then stop, back up, and look at them. Her eyes narrowed as she observed Birdie's unusual interaction with the ravens.

"Come on, Birdie," Tenner urged in a low voice. "I'm serious. Don't look back." He started walking.

Something in Tenner's tone told Birdie to follow his lead. She slipped the remaining berries inside her backpack and jogged to catch up. They started down the road to the seafront, with the ravens darting and circling overhead. Two of them flew off, but the one from the beach stayed with the children. The commander turned away from the window with a look of consternation on her face.

THE NEWSPAPER

When Birdie and Tenner were far enough from the police station to talk freely, Tenner told Birdie what he'd done. "Your mom isn't in the jail," he said.

"Oh," Birdie said, deflated. "I didn't even realize that the jail was in that building. Are you sure she wasn't there?"

"I called out her name a few times, and others repeated it . . ." He wrinkled his nose and decided not to tell her *how* the men had done it. "And I listened the whole time I was there. I remember her voice," he said. "I would have known it immediately."

"Maybe there are more jails," Birdie said uncertainly. "We'll search the map and start checking out all the marked places."

Tenner stopped on the side of the road to pull the newspapers out of his backpack. "But there's something else," he said. He showed a page to Birdie. "The commander called this a newspaper. It looks to me like some sort of group journal, like a whole pack of entries is written every day by lots of different people. Reports of events, business news, crimes, and stuff like that."

"Crimes?" Birdie raised an eyebrow at him, impressed.

He pointed to the date. "That's today, right? I also took the pages from yesterday." He hesitated, then confessed. "And . . . I grabbed a small bag of corn chips, too. Not sure what they are, but it was kind of a rush."

"You are a thief," Birdie said, slightly appalled by both of their actions today. She thought about how easy it had been to lie to the restaurant server and the police commander and to not hand over all the money. Her face flickered. Was that something her parents would have done?

"These papers are important," said Tenner. "Look—this is why I took them." He pointed to a line in large capital letters: *CORDOBA MUSEUM LOOTED OF OLD LOOT.* "Check out the reason why the president changed the currency."

"Wait a minute. What?" said Birdie, taking the newspaper. She scanned the article and stopped cold when she reached the last paragraph. *"Detectives speculate that a supernatural band of criminals have resurfaced after disappearing fifteen years ago. Estero residents may recall it was their large-scale thievery that prompted President Fuerte to change the national currency to keep them from spending their stolen money here. Unfortunately, this isn't the first sign of their resurgence. A few small heists in the past three years point to the criminals' uncanny abilities to do what ordinary people can't. Based on the history of these supernatural criminals, the great loot heist from the Cordoba Museum likely won't be their last."*

"See what I mean?" Tenner asked. "And the new supernatural-style heists started *three years ago.*"

Birdie looked up. "Holy expletive," she murmured. "This proves it. Some of our parents are *here*." The thought bolstered and terrified her at the same time.

Tenner nodded, then glanced around nervously as if Troy and Lucy might jump out of the bushes any second. "Now we need to figure out how to find your mom and give her that map so we can go back home. I don't want to run into *my* parents."

THAT AFTERNOON, BIRDIE and Tenner looked for a more private place at the beach to set up their camp, open the map without anyone noticing, and organize their plans to search for more jails. They found an old, unkempt picnic area near a cypress tree on the water's edge. The table's planks were weathered and peeling, and its hinges were rusty. But there was a fire pit nearby with some scraps of dry wood scattered about. They dropped their packs under the tree and sat with their backs against the trunk, reading the newspapers and nibbling on the corn chips Tenner had swiped.

There weren't any more stories about the Cordoba Museum or the old money that had been stolen, but there were all kinds of other entries. It was amazing to be reading new content for the first time since they'd learned to read. Some of it was boring, like the articles under the "Business" heading. But others gave them valuable clues into how things in Estero worked,

LISA McMANN

like one about different programs for kids that the library was hosting, which made it clear that the library was probably a safe, friendly place full of useful information. Perhaps, if there were more newspaper articles there about past heists, they might contain a clue to finding Birdie's mom.

When Tenner got to the "World" page, he scanned the headlines until he came across one that said *"Intracontinental Unrest: Are Supernaturals to Blame?"*

Birdie looked up sharply and leaned in. "Intracontinental?" she said, unsure of what that word meant.

Tenner read the short article aloud. *"A spate of high-stakes heists in several countries surrounding Estero in recent months has international officials laying blame on supernatural people. 'It's deeply troubling,' President Fuerte told Estero City News. 'I will be meeting with neighboring leaders to get to the bottom of this. Supernatural thieves must be stopped at all costs—domestically and internationally.' The president offered no plan on how they hoped to succeed."* He looked up. "Supernatural people in other countries are copying what our parents did?"

"Either that or it's our group getting around." Birdie reached for her ponytail and started braiding absently, deep in thought. "Stop them at all costs?"

"What does that mean for us?" Tenner pulled his fingers through the sand and tuned in to the tiny grains squeaking against each other. "I wish I'd asked for my sunglasses."

"I don't think the president's got his sights set on a couple

of kids," Birdie assured him. "And nobody at the police station noticed your eyes. You don't need the glasses."

Tenner sighed. "I know. I just . . . I guess I liked feeling like I did."

"Hmm." Birdie studied him with a funny look on her face. Then she realized he was serious, and her look softened. Tenner was always trying to get noticed, and it was sometimes annoying. But maybe he was only trying to feel special.

While Tenner continued reading newspapers, Birdie pulled out her father's journal. The pages were dog-eared and turning yellow, and some were scorched at the edges. She'd already read the first, extremely long entry—mostly about stuff she knew, like a recounting of how the criminals had brought supplies and tools to the peninsula ahead of their escape so they could build their tiny village.

The next entry was dated a few months before Birdie was born. It was titled *TUNNELS* and began with a drawing. Birdie studied it—a sketch of a dove etched into a brick post.

She read the page opposite the sketch.

Estero has two levels of tunnels. The upper tunnels are aboveground in the heart of the city and are known to most city residents. Their walls are painted by artists and pleasant to travel through. These upper tunnels weave through neighborhoods and businesses built closely together. One might come across an entrance to an upper

tunnel on any city street. Most are marked with a symbol to help visitors identify the correct door. The bird in the bricks that I sketched is outside the tunnel where Elena and I shared a tiny apartment after we graduated from the foster home. Living there was intended for short-term only while we found our footing as adults. That proved to be harder than expected, and we ended up staying.

It is considered trespassing to enter an upper tunnel after dark unless you live in that community or have been invited in. However, the tunnels do provide shelter from rain and shortcuts through the city, so people use them at times even after dark. Some tunnel watchers are more lenient than others.

There is another level of tunnels underground. These are virtually unknown to the average resident who hasn't studied the ancient history of Estero. The lower tunnels were built thousands of years ago and are said to have several secret entrances throughout the oldest part of the city. These tunnels were forgotten as time passed. Some scholars speculate that the lower tunnels were used by aristocrats to hoard wealth, and that treasure could still be hidden there . . . if only they could find the entrances.

After years of searching, I finally discovered an entrance to the lower tunnels not long before we left Estero for the hideout. Through it, I was able to explore and locate one other exit before our final heist and escape.

This is one of a few secrets I kept from the others due to the thirteen diamonds incident. I didn't want Troy and Lucy claiming this abandoned hiding space—and whatever treasures remain—for something nefarious. I had my own plans for the lower tunnels if we ever returned: making the space into a secret boarding school for supernatural children. One that would not only provide shelter, like the foster home did, but also the training to survive and thrive in a hostile world, which the foster home did not.

But now we're in this beautiful hideout. And my dear Elena is pregnant. Why would I bring our child to a place that hates us? We're safe here. This beach may be the last place I live. The lower tunnels may not see another visitor for a few more centuries.

"Oof." The second-to-last line hit Birdie hard. She studied the words, written when her father's hand was strong. At first Birdie thought it was risky for her father to have written about the lower tunnels if he didn't want Troy to find out—especially since Troy had X-ray vision and could potentially read the journals without even opening them. But Dad didn't say where the entrance was. And the bully probably didn't even know Louis kept a journal, so maybe Louis thought it was safe enough. Perhaps he felt it was important to record the information so he wouldn't forget it.

"Hmm?" said Tenner, looking up from his newspaper. His

shoulder-length hair curled more than usual in the humidity of the day.

"What?" Birdie looked sideways at him.

Tenner put the paper down. "You said 'oof.'"

"Oh. Right." Birdie told him about the two different types of tunnels, then showed him the last part her dad had written about making a school for supernatural kids. "Isn't that sweet?"

Tenner nodded slowly. "Turns out he started his school after all. On the beach. With five students. And taught them how to survive."

Birdie's eyes welled up. "Yes, he did."

After a moment, Birdie checked to make sure no one was nearby, then opened the flaming map. "Tomorrow we start searching these places one by one," she said, pointing out the buildings that were marked on the map.

"They can't all be jails, though, can they?" Tenner asked.

"Maybe supernatural jail isn't like an average police station jail," Birdie mused. All she knew was that if her dad had included these places on the map, they could be important to finding her mother.

THREADS OF DOUBT

Seven, Cabot, and Brix sped over the rocks that lined the inner curve of the bay—they'd all had plenty of practice doing that. They went as fast as they could during the remaining daylight hours and reached the end of the traversable rocks as darkness fell, which gave them a good reason to stop, eat, and sleep. "We made up for yesterday," Cabot reported. "Good job, everyone. We'll cross the bay in the morning."

The sky was shielded by fog. Seven lay on top of his parachute blanket, draped over a flat wet rock, and stared into the fog as it swirled around like giant ghosts. His mixed feelings about everything—his parents; Birdie's and Tenner's safety; exposing himself to ridicule, hatred, and harm—all swirled around with the fog. For a moment he wished that the sky would swallow him up so he didn't have to do this. Then Brix, Cabot, and Puerco inched their way over to him for warmth. He threw a protective arm around them.

Meanwhile the sun had set on the beach in Estero. Birdie gathered firewood and started a fire in the pit, thinking about the bird sketch and the tunnels. Tenner found a long stick to use as a spear and whittled the end into a sharp point. Then, after the other people left the beach, he went out to catch dinner.

Once the fish was roasted, they picked the flaky layers apart with their fingers and relaxed a little, listening to the sound of waves. The raven muttered to new friends in the trees. The fire crackled. For the first time that day, Birdie felt like she could relax.

Their light conversation trailed off, and each went to a quiet place in their mind. Thinking about Seven and Cabot and Brix and Puerco. Wondering which of their parents were here doing evil deeds again. Birdie couldn't imagine her mother stealing— not now, anyway. Tenner couldn't imagine his parents *not* leading the resurgence, and he believed they'd traded him for the rush of being a part of it. Perhaps the lure of fame or infamy or the addiction of thievery was stronger than the love Troy and Lucy had for their child. Or maybe they'd never loved him at all. Tenner tipped his head back and pressed his thumbs into the corners of his eyes. He was tired of returning to that same thought. But it wouldn't let him go.

The salty air made Birdie's lungs feel tight. She thought about the others. Missed them. She longed to talk with Seven about what they'd found out today. Wished he and the others were here so they could all go in search of Birdie's mother.

All those buildings and shops, and now tunnels . . . If they were going to succeed in tracking down Elena Golden, they could use more help. She touched Tenner's shoulder. "Part of me wants to go back to the hideout and insist the others come."

Tenner tried not to startle at her touch. Birdie hung all over Seven and Brix, but it wasn't something she normally did with him. "You know Seven won't do it." He was kind of okay with that.

"What if he knew his parents are probably here?"

"Maybe." Tenner sighed. "He talks like he doesn't want to see them ever again . . . kind of like me with my parents. But I think he's a little more conflicted over it than I am."

Birdie studied him, surprised again by Tenner's insight. He had good things to say when he wasn't tripping over himself. "I know it's not actually worth it to go home and get help. We're going to have to find my mom on our own. This city is big, though. I don't think it'll be too hard to steer clear of . . ." She stopped. "I mean, keep the stash out of the wrong hands." She glanced guiltily at Tenner.

Tenner let out a huff, and this time he couldn't stop his frustration from boiling over. "Will you please stop with that?" Time after time, Birdie and the others gave him that sidelong glance whenever talking about his terrible parents. "When you give me that look, it makes me feel worse, okay?"

Birdie leaned back, surprised. "Worse? I was trying to make you feel better. I'm, like, sorry your parents are . . . not great."

"They're *terrible*, Birdie! And I know that, okay? Better than anyone. It's okay to say it." Tenner leaned forward and gripped the sides of his head in frustration. "It makes me feel like I'm somehow . . . I don't know. Connected—no, *responsible* for the things they do. I don't care if you talk about my parents as criminals who are also terrible people, okay? I'm . . . I'm . . . divorcing myself from them. I *hate* them. I wish you would all stop . . . *pitying* me about it!"

Birdie blinked. She'd never seen Tenner impassioned like this. "I'm . . . sorry, Tenner."

Tenner blew out a breath. He knew he'd lost it. And that was the last thing he wanted to do—blow up. Like his father often had.

He was nothing like Troy. Nothing. He wished he could pretend his parents didn't exist. He scowled and looked at the sea, trying to calm down. Trying to be the person he'd told himself he had to be in order to keep the others liking him. He didn't want them to mistrust him like all the adults had been suspicious of his parents. "It's okay. I . . . Can we talk about something else? Let's look at the bleeping map."

Birdie nodded, wide-eyed. "Sure," she said quietly. But her mind was in a whirl. This was the first time she'd ever seen Tenner act . . . real. Like a regular person with emotions. "Thanks for telling me that." When Tenner shifted uncomfortably, Birdie hastily pulled out the map.

Tenner and Birdie sat shoulder to shoulder looking at it. Things were starting to make sense within the inset box. They confirmed that the Cordoba Museum had the initials *CM* near it, and the police station was marked *EPD&J*.

"Estero Police Department and Jail," Tenner pointed out. "We can cross that off the list."

"We should at least walk by Palacio de Magdalia tomorrow," said Birdie, pointing at the *PdM* initials. "It's a couple miles down the same street as the Cordoba."

Tenner agreed. As they started to figure out other identifying initials, Tenner looked out occasionally into the night along the shore, keeping watch. Keeping them safe. Searching for danger Birdie couldn't see. "Let's try not to end up at the police station tomorrow."

"My stomach churns every time you mention it." Birdie got up and spread out the parachute blanket. "We'll scout out the palace. And I think we should find the library and see if they have more newspapers. You were smart to read the ones on the police lunch table. We got a lot of information that way, and I would never have even noticed them."

Tenner nodded, appeased. He was feeling a lot better after his outburst. Birdie seemed to respect that he told her what was bothering him, which was surprising. He'd half expected her to brush it off or think he was whining or even yell back. It felt like something good was happening between them.

After an exhausting day in an unfamiliar place, with an overload of information and no answers about what to do next, the two lay down under the stars. As Birdie's breath evened out and she closed her eyes, she thought of the sketch of a dove on brick and wondered if that was a clue from her father, too. Her eyes popped open. A bird. On bricks.

Birdie and Brix.

OVER SEA AND LAND

I t was a cold, wet night on the rocks in the bay, and by the time the edge of the morning sky turned pink, the three travelers were eager to get started. Cabot turned slowly as she gazed anew at their path ahead, always calculating: Distances. Levels of difficulty. Odds of death or success. She barely saw the beauty of the boulders, the brightness of the silky green sea moss, the fingerlike coral reaching for them from below the surface.

"I thought we'd be able to see the other side of the bay," Seven said doubtfully. "Are you sure it's where you think it is?"

"I'm sure we're at the narrowest part of the bay right now," she said. "Once the fog lifts, we should have at least a partial view of the other side. But the curvature of the earth is a factor. I'm afraid we can't do anything about that." She turned north toward the path by land that they would be avoiding. "See how the bay widens again before it narrows into a point? That's why it would be much farther to travel to Estero if we went back up there." She nibbled on her lip, thinking. Looking at the pig.

"How much time will it save us to cross the bay here?" asked Seven.

"Probably two days," said Cabot. She turned to focus on the boys. "If we can swim at two miles per hour, we'll get across in a couple of hours. It should be a fairly easy climb up to land, and the rest of the journey over there is pretty flat. We could potentially arrive in Estero . . ." She calculated some more distances in her head. "By tomorrow night."

Brix bounced on the rock as he stared at the water. He could swim. It just wasn't his favorite thing to do. And to swim for two hours without stopping? He wasn't sure he could do that. But the thought of getting to Birdie and Tenner tomorrow night with the information they'd found . . . It could save them. And it would make Cabot feel better, too. Plus, maybe he'd get to see his mom after all.

"Brix, are you still okay with the swim?" asked Seven.

Brix felt his heartbeat quicken. "Uh . . ." His thoughts bounced around like his body. Climbing and walking felt safer, but getting there soon was winning in his mind. Even if it meant a long swim. "What if I can't swim that far?"

"Remember what your dad taught us," Seven said. "Flip on your back to rest. The salt water is buoyant. It doesn't want you to sink."

"And," said Cabot, "the best part about being this deep into the bay is that it's dead calm. Way easier than with ocean waves."

"Cabot and I will help if you need it," said Seven.

"We'll empty your backpack," Cabot said. "And—wait. I know what we can do." She knelt and opened her pack, pulling out her parachute sleeping tarp. She shook it out, lifted it, and let it float down as she brought all four corners together, trapping air inside. Then she tied it tight, making a small balloon. "This will help you float," she said. "We'll put it inside your backpack. Okay? Then your pack will be like Birdie's and Tenner's."

Brix nodded, relieved. "Yeah. That's pretty smart, Cabot."

"Thank you," said Cabot with a smirk. She might not have a supernatural ability, but she was the brains of the whole operation, and that was nothing to wave off. "Seven, you and I should do the same with the other tarps. Wrap the perishable stuff and clothes inside to keep them dry."

They rearranged their backpack items, repacked, and were left staring at Puerco. They couldn't put him inside a backpack under these conditions. "He can swim, too, can't he?" asked Seven.

"He loves the water," Brix confirmed, "but I don't think he can swim that far."

"I've been thinking about him," Cabot said. "We'll make him a hammock." She'd left a rope out of her backpack when repacking. Now she lifted it up and kept the two ends together, doubling it. From the folded end, she tied a series of loose knots, making a small, cube-shaped pig basket. "If Puerco gets tired, he can climb inside here. Seven and I can pull it between us through the water."

Soon all three kids were standing with puffed-up backpacks, and they maneuvered into the water. Seven held Puerco to his chest with one hand and pushed off the rocks backward, but the pig struggled to get loose and swam freely, his little snout above water. Seven flipped onto his stomach.

The water was shockingly brisk. They started out with a hard breaststroke. After a few minutes, Brix flipped over onto his back and started kicking. His balloon backpack forced his head out of the water in its urgency to float, which calmed him down a bit. He knew he could swim on his back for two hours. It was all that face-in-the-water stuff that he didn't like.

Seven kept an eye on the other two. Cabot was a strong swimmer, the best of the three. Seven was decent at it. He kept remembering how much time they were saving by going this route.

After a while, Puerco began to struggle. Cabot stretched out the rope hammock, and Puerco swam to it. He climbed in and placed his little front hooves on the top rope, while Seven and Cabot pulled it between them through the water, careful not to let it sink.

Every now and then, Cabot checked to see where they were on the journey and called out their progress. It was slow going, but the calm water helped. "We're halfway already," Cabot exclaimed.

"Everyone doing okay?" Seven called out.

"I'm good," said Cabot. She'd stayed in the lead.

"My legs are tired," said Brix. He'd been focusing on the sky. "But I'm doing okay."

"Good job, everybody," Seven said. His teeth were chattering. "Let's keep up the pace."

Finally the bay grew shallow and even calmer as they were protected from the wind by the rock wall. Seven could see the bottom. "We're nearly there," he called out. "In a minute we should be able to walk the rest of the way to the rocks."

When Seven could touch bottom, he picked up Puerco under one arm and grabbed Brix's hand with the other, hauling him along until Brix could touch, too. Finally they made it to a rocky ledge where they could rest for a bit.

They huddled together in the shade of a cliff, cold, wet, and exhausted, trying to warm up without the sun to help. Seven passed around some dried fish to help boost their energy, then stood up on shaky legs and surveyed the short, steep climb ahead of them. He assembled the grappling hook and rope as Brix, still shivering, changed into a set of mostly dry clothes.

"I can't feel my fingers," Brix said, flexing them.

Cabot rubbed them to help the blood flow. "We need your fingers here, buddy," she said. "Seven's going first, then me, and you're going to need to get up without a spotter down here. Sound okay?"

"Sure," said Brix. His teeth chattered.

Cabot had brought one sweatshirt—mostly blue with a spray

of orange flowers in the center. It had been her mother's, and she draped it around his shoulders. "Warm up!" she commanded, as if that would magically help.

Brix laughed. He slipped his head and arms through the holes and started hopping up and down, flapping the long sleeves like wings. Water squished out of his boots. Cabot made him take off his many layers of wet socks, then wrapped his feet in gauze from the first aid kit to help them fit into the large boots properly. She squeezed out the socks and bundled them up. They'd spread them out to dry tonight.

Soon Seven was flinging the grappling hook up and over the edge, trying to find something sturdy for it to grab on to. Finally it stuck fast. He tested it, swinging low in all directions. Then he started climbing with Puerco in tow. After several minutes, he reached the top and pulled himself over the edge. He freed Puerco to run around and peered down, checking the grappling hook to make sure it was secure. "It wasn't that hard, Cabot. You ready?"

Cabot took her sweatshirt back from Brix and stuffed it into her backpack. "Ready," she said, and Brix came over to stand beside her because he knew it made her less nervous. She shook out her hands and arms, trying to wake up her tired muscles, then grabbed on and climbed. She made it to the top, arms shaking from all the swimming, and Seven helped her to safety.

She and Seven leaned over the edge to watch as Brix latched

on. "My fingers are like ice," he said, sounding worried. Despite that, he worked his way up the wall. When he neared the top, Cabot reached over to grab his hand and help pull him up like Seven had done for her. But this time, when Brix took it, his grip slipped. His other hand loosened on the rope, and he started sliding.

As Brix realized what was happening, his eyes widened and his arms flailed, trying to grab the rope again. "Help!" he screamed, and finally caught his arm in the twist of the rope halfway down. The force of the jolt pulled his arm so hard that his shoulder dislocated. "Aaah!" he screamed, and dropped the rest of the way to the ground. When he hit the bottom, he bounced a couple times, like a coconut on hard-packed sand.

Cabot and Seven peered over the ledge in horror. "Are you okay?"

Brix rolled around, squealing in pain, gripping his shoulder.

"It looks like it's dislocated again!" Cabot called down. She reminded him what to do to put it back in place and got ready to go back down to help if he needed it.

After a moment Brix staggered over to the wall to brace himself. He lifted the dislocated arm with his other hand straight out in front of him and pulled. When that didn't work, he sat down and hugged his knees while leaning back, trying to pull the arm to make the joint pop. Just as Cabot was about to climb down, he pressed his dislocated shoulder against the rock. He gritted his teeth, then wrenched his body to the side. With a squelching pop, the shoulder moved back into place.

Brix let out a big sigh of relief. The pain swiftly dissipated thanks to his healing ability, and the rope burns on his hands and arms healed, too. Soon he was feeling better. "Okay," he said. "Let's try that again."

NO ENTRY

Tenner and Birdie stood outside the iron gates to Palacio de Magdalia, which happened to include the exact words of Seven Palacio's mother's name. The name coincidences were strange. What did they mean? Had Magdalia Palacio been named after this palace? The same question held for Tenner's parents—did they have some sort of connection to the Cordoba Museum?

Birdie felt certain that the sketch her father had drawn of a dove on bricks was the inspiration for her and Brix's names. Now she wondered when she'd find the Golden name plastered somewhere. On the firehouse, maybe, she thought wryly.

The palace took up an entire city block and was surrounded by a tall, thick black iron fence with guards stationed at gates that were centered on each of the four sides and at a little guard station alongside the main driveway into the property. The grand building shot up in the center with spires and turrets decorated with elaborate gold curlicues. And it had two sprawling, not-quite-as-tall wings spreading out to the right and left. The palace walls were studded with deep purple jewels that caught the sunlight, making it seem magical.

The raven had followed Birdie and Tenner, and it alighted on a giant rusty padlock that secured a gate. The bird poked its beak into the keyhole and pulled out a bug, then gobbled it down. Birdie reached out with her forefinger, and the bird let her pet its head.

"What do you think?" Birdie asked Tenner, indicating the palace.

"That we're never going to see inside," he said, glancing surreptitiously at the guards.

Birdie's face flickered. This was one of the places marked on the map, so Dad had thought it important enough to include. Though Birdie couldn't imagine why her mother would be in this palace—it belonged to the presidency, and the president hated them. "What would it take?"

"What do you mean?"

"To go in. I mean, like, if we were our parents. Secretly. Sneakily." She didn't expect Tenner to have an answer.

"What would it take?" Tenner thought for a long moment. "Darkness. You sending the bird in to give you information. Cabot figuring out the layout. Me keeping watch and listening for guards. Brix and Seven to scale up to the roof. Seven going in, full camo." He glanced at Birdie, a triumphant look on his face. "Hey . . . that almost sounds like it would work. The only thing we need is an inside person to let us in—I'm sure it's locked up tight."

"Maybe we should become criminals," Birdie said, half joking.

"We could start a school for wayward youth, like we're turning out to be," Tenner said with a laugh. "But you and I are nothing without the other three. Especially Seven. Even if you could convince him to come, getting him to go anywhere naked would be impossible."

"True. Also, I'm not sure the whole climbing-to-the-roof part would be necessary."

Tenner grinned. "Yeah, but it would be cool." He stepped closer to the iron gate and pressed his face between the bars to get a better view as foot traffic around them increased.

Behind them on the sidewalk, a person slowly walked backward holding a fan of papers in the air. "First palace tour of the day starts in ten minutes! Fifteen dollars at the door. Only thirteen if you come with me. Tickets!"

Birdie watched him. "Or we could take a tour."

"We don't have any money," said Tenner. "Speaking of that, why didn't you give up your dad's cash yesterday?"

Birdie shrugged. "It's worthless here, so why bother? It felt daring. But it also belonged to my dad."

Tenner nodded and hitched up his dad shorts. They'd

belonged to Troy, but he felt no attachment to them other than the fact that he'd been running out of clothes, and his options were chopping off the legs and making do or wearing the same parachute pants every day.

Birdie watched the tour make their way to a special entrance. She noted every barrier point, wondering how they each functioned, then realized she was thinking like a criminal. Maybe that was what it would take to find her mother. "You know what I want to do?"

"What?" Tenner turned. "Go to the museum?"

"No." Her eyes narrowed. She wanted to go there sometime, but not now.

"Right. Okay, what?"

"Learn more about the recent heists and see if there's anything new in today's newspaper. Let's find the library."

The raven flew down from the tree and sat on the sidewalk in front of them. It hopped a few steps.

Tenner scoffed. "You think the library is going to be free to go in when the museum and palace aren't?"

"We can find out," Birdie said. "There was something labeled *EPL* on the main street that goes to the beach. It was a little beyond where we walked—we wouldn't have passed it. Maybe the *L* stands for *library*." As soon as she said it, she received a warm feeling from the raven. She made eye contact with the bird. "You know what the library is?" she asked, incredulous.

"Intelligent creatures," Tenner reminded her. "Maybe the

people who work there are kind to birds, and that's how it knows."

They headed to the main street with the raven leading the way. It stopped on the sidewalk outside big doors near a trio of bird feeders. There were no guards or police officers here. No one standing and asking them for money or a ticket. Birdie glanced up and saw ESTERO PUBLIC LIBRARY in block letters. This was the place, but she approached with trepidation. What if this turned out as bad as the restaurant incident? But Dad had included it on the map. Maybe he thought this place would help them find Elena. "Okay, here we go," she murmured to Tenner, and pulled the door handle. It opened, and she went inside with Tenner right behind. The raven hopped over to a feeder and didn't come with them.

They stopped inside the entrance and took it all in. The place was filled with bookshelves and books, desks with computers. Paintings and statues and a long counter with more computers on it. The counter ahead of them had two people behind it, but a silver horizontal bar was blocking their path at waist height.

"Now what?" she whispered, turning to Tenner.

"I ... don't know."

A woman behind the counter noticed them.

Birdie glanced around uneasily. If this was like a gate to keep them out, where were the guards? Where was the person asking for a ticket or money?

"Can I help you?" The woman had dark brown skin and wore her black hair even shorter than Cabot did. Her orange sleeveless dress reminded Birdie of some of the clothes she'd seen in Bootsie's Boutique. "You're a few minutes early, but it's okay—you can come in."

Birdie felt even more confused. "But . . ."

The woman took a closer look and seemed confused, too. "Is the bar stuck?"

Birdie shrugged helplessly. "How do we get through?"

"Just . . . push on it. Did you try that?"

"Oh!" Birdie pushed on the bar, and it swung open with little effort. "Sorry—I should have thought of that. It looked . . . more solid."

The librarian raised an eyebrow and watched the kids walk through the turnstile. "First time here?"

"Could you tell?" Tenner said, and the woman laughed.

"Can I point you in the direction of whatever you're looking for?" She leaned across the counter in a casual, conversational way that made Birdie and Tenner feel comfortable. If she thought their clothes were strange, she didn't show it.

Birdie had planned this out on the way over. "We're studying the recent heists and the currency switch fourteen years ago. Are there books or, um, journals—"

"Newspapers," Tenner interjected smoothly.

"Yes, newspapers or anything about who is responsible and how it all happened?"

"Of course." The librarian studied them—not in a judgmental way, but with a hint of puzzlement on her face.

Birdie shifted uncomfortably and looked down at her parachute clothes. The librarian's expression smoothed immediately, and she came around the counter. She spoke as if nothing had troubled her and beckoned Birdie to follow. "Did you make this cute top?" she said. "It's very fashion-forward."

"I—yes," Birdie said, glancing up. She wasn't sure what "fashion-forward" meant, but it sounded like a compliment. "Thanks."

The librarian guided the kids along and lowered her voice. "As you probably know, the president is tight-lipped about the, ah, the types of people that are involved in the heists. As a result, not many journalists wrote about it in detail, for fear of retaliation from the government. But . . . whatever *was* written about it, we have." First she pointed out the local history section of books that pertained to the subject and let her finger stop on one of the bindings. She hooked it with her fingernail and pulled it out suggestively, half an inch, then left it.

"Let me show you the archives and periodicals," she said before they had a chance to inspect that book or any others. She led them to a room lined with racks of newspapers and magazines. A quilt with different-colored squares hung on the wall next to the window, which overlooked a grassy courtyard with a few leafy trees and a sculpture of a bench with an old person reading to a young person. In the center of the room was a black screen on a stand, with a keyboard on the table in front of it. "You can look things up on the computer," she said. "The physical periodicals only go back a year or so." She hesitated and studied them once more. "Summer school?"

"Pardon me?" Birdie said. She was overwhelmed as she looked at the computer. Her parents had talked about using them, but she certainly didn't know how it worked.

"Is this assignment for summer school?"

"Oh!" said Birdie, blinking hard. "No. Um, it's for our own personal information."

"We're curious about a lot of things," Tenner said. He was picking up on how to talk to people faster than Birdie. His ears tuning in to conversations had helped him adapt.

"Well, this is a place for curious people. Let me know if you have any trouble logging in. You have your user ID? If you've got one from a different Estero library, it'll work here, too."

"Oh! Sure do," said Birdie, having no idea what any of that meant.

The librarian tilted her head. "You do? Well. I'll leave you to it, then." She left them alone in the room.

Birdie and Tenner looked at each other and stifled their nervous laughter.

"How about you tackle that computer thing," Tenner said. "And I'll look through some recent newspapers."

Birdie made a wry face. "Perfect." She sat down in the chair and looked at the computer screen. It was black and lifeless. Then she studied the keyboard on the table and saw it was connected to the screen with a wire. "All the letters are in the wrong place," she said. "Do you think you're supposed to, I don't know, like, put them in alphabetical order to make the computer work?"

Tenner shrugged as he scanned front-page headlines of the hanging newspapers. "Try it."

Birdie tried to pick up the *A* key, but it was stuck. "Nope. They don't move."

"Maybe the president changed the order of the alphabet, too," said Tenner.

"That would be pointless."

"Like changing the currency?"

Birdie frowned, still studying the keyboard. "I think that did have a point—to keep our parents from spending stolen money here." She pressed a few letters, realizing they had a satisfying amount of give to them. The screen lit up with a scene of brown hills and blue sky. "Oh!" Birdie exclaimed. A narrow horizontal rectangle appeared, and a short vertical line blinked inside it. "Hmm." She typed the letter *A* into the box and saw the blinking line move. She typed a few more letters, but nothing else happened. Then she saw a key with the word *Enter* on it and pressed that. The rectangle shook its head.

Birdie's eyes widened. "I think it's alive," she whispered.

"Does it know who I am?" She found the letters of her name and typed them in.

Tenner, enraptured by headlines, pulled a dowel rod and held it under the ceiling light. "Birdie, listen to this: *'Cordoba Museum Break-In Brings Old Fears Back to Spotlight.'*"

GATHERING INFORMATION

Tenner brought the newspaper over to Birdie's table and sat down to read the article aloud. *"The recent break-in at Cordoba Museum and theft of millions of dollars of old currency—still useable in other parts of the world—brings back an eerie sense of unease. Many in Estero believed the fugitives to be dead in a helicopter crash fifteen years ago. But the recent heists are similar. Are the notorious supernatural criminals back, or is this a copycat group? Authorities admit footage from video surveillance cameras gives them little to go on, increasing their suspicion that the responsible parties have supernatural abilities. The Cordoba Museum heist was the largest in a string of thefts around the city. Estero Police Commander Collazo said, 'The thefts appear to be related, and fears of the supernatural criminals' return after a long hiatus are warranted.'"*

Tenner looked up. "Millions of dollars? Still useable in other parts of the world? Are they stealing it here to use somewhere else?"

Birdie pulled the paper to her and studied the article. "They're either expanding . . . or leaving." The lullaby Birdie's mother had sung for her randomly started playing in her head. Birdie couldn't imagine her mom becoming a part of this. Yet . . . she wasn't in jail, and so far they hadn't found another prison. Her heart twisted.

This was complicated. Birdie looked up sharply. "Don't you miss them at all? Not even a little? Are you pretending not to care?"

Tenner's face was puzzled. "Who are we talking about?"

"Your parents."

"Oh." He grimaced, then got up and went to the window. "Do *you* miss my parents, Birdie?"

"No. I mean . . ." She watched him watching the tree branches move outside.

"Neither do I. For all the same reasons you don't miss them. Your dad is the only one I'll ever think of as a parent. And Cabot's parents, too." He hesitated. "My parents . . . are exhausting. I constantly worried about making my dad mad, and that made me feel like my life was always on the verge of disaster. And my mom never stood up for me. I spent way more time with Greta Stone and your dad than them." A small, melancholy smile played on his lips. "I bet they were sick of me."

"No way," Birdie said, surprising herself by how much she meant it. "They loved you. We all do." She studied him. She'd known some of this about Tenner on a surface level, but she was just beginning to grasp that growing up in the hideout, even in such close quarters, had been a strikingly different experience for each kid. "I'm sorry your parents weren't good to you," she said, making sure not to sound pitying this time. She got lost in thought for a moment and then asked, "What if we accidentally find them while we're searching for my mom?"

Tenner snorted and turned back toward her. "That would be fine," he said bitterly. "Then I can send them to jail."

Birdie abandoned the computer and scoured the room for something to write on. She found a box full of mini pencils and took five—one for each of them. Souvenirs to bring home. Then she pushed some buttons on a strange machine in the hallway outside. It beeped at her, then a piece of white paper shot out. She looked underneath and found a stack of paper in a slot, and snagged a few more pieces. Then she peeked into a tiny closet and found a mop and bucket, cleaning supplies, and office supplies. She lifted a couple of cool-looking pens and some oval wire bendy things that looked useful—maybe she could use them in her sneakers where the laces had been.

"Hey, Bird," Tenner said as she was loading her backpack, preparing to leave. "Look at this." He spread out a newspaper, and the article he pointed to had a group of photos with it. "Pictures of our parents."

Birdie's lips parted. "Photos?" She rushed over.

"Yeah. From when they were younger. Three of their faces are X'd out." The article was recent, but the photo was dated fifteen years ago. It was a large collage of eight headshots, except one had a question mark instead of a face. Birdie's mother's and Cabot's parents' pictures each had a sheer gray X over them, so their faces could still be seen. Birdie and Tenner crowded over it. They ignored the tiny print in the caption below the picture and began to identify their parents' faces one by one until only the question mark remained. "That's Seven's dad," Tenner said. "They must not have been able to get a photo of him because of his invisibility."

"Can you imagine them trying to take it?" Birdie said, snickering. "Him going invisible as they're about to click."

"And trying again and again, and always just missing and getting mad about it," said Tenner, laughing, too.

"I wonder if Magdalia's photo is really her or if it's a projected image?"

"Hard to tell," said Tenner.

Birdie brushed her finger over her youthful-looking father's face. He'd had short, messy hair back then. Then she studied her mother through the gray X and imagined her two parents daring to jump out of a helicopter. She was suddenly glad her father had insisted on retelling the story regularly. It gave her courage to know how brave they'd been.

"Does it say why some of them have X's on their faces?" Birdie asked, going to the beginning of the article. Then a terrible thought struck her. "I hope it's not because they're dead." Could Cabot have been right all along?

Tenner skimmed it. "Oh!" he said. "This says to be on the

lookout for the criminals without the X's. They are still considered fugitives and thought to be operating the current crimes." He gave a sour laugh. "Somebody needs to tell them your dad is not exactly on the loose in Estero." He stopped and glanced at Birdie. "Sorry."

"No, it was funny," Birdie said, forcing a smile. But she was more concerned about the X's. She leaned in anxiously and scoured the report.

Tenner continued. "Some of the five have been spotted in Estero over the past three years, but they continue to elude police."

"What about the ones *with* the X's?" Birdie's heart pounded. She still couldn't find the answer.

Tenner's eyes widened as he landed on it. He glanced up. "Captured."

APPROACHING CIVILIZATION

Hey, Cabot," Seven said as they walked down the gently sloping ridge on the opposite side of the bay.

"Hmm." Cabot glanced his way, mildly annoyed to be disturbed from her thoughts. It was the only private place she had these past few days, and she liked it there.

"Help me remember the inset part of the map. Have you figured out any of the letters?"

Cabot frowned. She had the picture of the map burned into her memory, with all of its key initials and distances. "Well, there are several sets. *CM. PdM. EPD&J. GBB. EPL. CIS. ECH.*"

Cabot had a few clues about the city and what it was like, but she could only guess at what the letters stood for. "All of the *E*'s could stand for *Estero*. Maybe the *H* in ECH stands for *hospital*, like Estero Something Hospital. The *B* could be a bank. And the *M* . . . *museum*?" The latter two were places that the criminals had stolen things from long ago—Cabot had picked up that info when the parents had all talked together in the evenings. "That's all I've got."

"What do you think Birdie and Tenner are doing right now?" Brix asked.

Cabot frowned. "Helping your mom steal the stash?" she suggested sourly.

Seven sighed. He felt certain Louis hadn't meant for this to happen. But there was no convincing Cabot.

Cabot walked faster, keeping the boys moving at her pace—something she'd learned at a young age to get people to hurry up and do what she wanted them to do.

She could smell life happening around them. Cooking, which was making her stomach growl. But there was something bad souring the air, too, like the odor of the compost pile in the garden, only less natural. The sky above Estero had a thin grayish-brown fog hovering over it.

They could make excellent time now that the route was flat and free from obstructions. They'd pass the first village before the day was through, which got Cabot's heart racing with excitement. It would be much bigger than their little compound of cabins.

The boys lagged behind. It wasn't Brix's fault—he'd totally healed from his climbing incident. It was Seven, and Cabot understood why. The closer they got to civilization, the more Seven didn't want to be there.

As they approached the first village, with house roofs appearing in their line of sight, Seven blew out a nervous breath. Cabot heard it and turned abruptly. "Let's have some lunch," she said.

She felt bad for Seven. Before the boys could catch up, she started spreading her tarp on the short grass along the cliff.

They sat down. Brix leaned in, ready to pounce on whatever food there was.

"How is everyone?" Cabot asked them. She piled some food in the center of the tarp and answered her own question as Brix grabbed his share. "I'm doing well but sometimes feeling anxious because of everything we've been told about the civilized world hating us. And I'm worried that the first bones we found could be my mother's." She turned. "Brix?"

"I'm good," Brix said, munching on a slice of coconut. "Never better. All healed up." He rotated his shoulder to prove it.

"Good." Cabot looked at Seven. "And you?" she asked with a hint of gentleness that she usually saved for Brix.

Seven shifted on the tarp. "I'm not sure how to do this," he said, peeling an orange. To the others it looked as if the orange was peeling on its own.

"Physically enter society, you mean?" Cabot asked. "Or . . . mentally?"

"Both, but I meant physically. I guess I need something wrapped around my head. I brought a scarf . . ."

"Ah." Cabot nodded, understanding now. "If I were a stranger, I would be much more freaked out if I saw a person with no head than if I saw a person with a scarf completely wrapped around their head."

"Yeah." Seven set the orange down on the parachute blanket without eating it. "That's pretty much what it comes down to."

"You could take all your clothes off," Brix reminded him, eyeing the orange.

"Believe me, I'm tempted," said Seven. He saw Brix's look and split the orange, handing half to him. Then he opened his backpack and took out the scarf he'd brought for this purpose. It was warm and wooly with a gray plaid pattern, and had belonged to his mother.

"I've got a pair of my mom's sunglasses for you," Cabot told him. She searched through her bag and pulled them out. "She called them her big movie-star glasses. She always wore them on the beach. They'll cover your eyes, and then you only need to use the scarf over your nose, mouth, and hair. It'll be an illusion. With the glasses, people will naturally fill in the parts they can't see."

Seven took them. "Thanks, Cabot." He shoved her playfully. "You think of everything." He quickly started eating his half of the orange, realizing he'd be covering his mouth soon.

"That's pretty much all I do," said Cabot. She gave him a weak smile, because sometimes the constant thinking was exhausting. "I want you to feel as good as possible." She needed him, and she didn't want him to bail at the last second.

Once they had him covered in pants, boots, his dad's thin sweater, gloves, and the sunglasses and scarf around his head and face, Cabot checked for uncovered spots. "How do you feel?"

"Miserable," said Seven, muffled.

"You'll live, though," said Cabot. "Right? Can you breathe okay?"

Seven shrugged. "I guess." Then, as if he'd remembered who he was and what they were trying to accomplish, he nodded firmly. "Yes. I'll be fine."

"Chin up," Cabot said. "We're getting close. Let's keep moving." She turned to lead, and they started out at a jog.

THE JOURNAL

In the library's periodical room, Birdie sank into a chair. Dad was right! Her mother *had* been captured, and Cabot's parents, too. Thank goodness they were alive—Cabot would be surprised! But where were they? Surely Cabot's parents would have responded to Tenner yelling for Elena, especially since he'd said his name. Which meant they weren't in that jail, either.

There was nothing more in the story to tell them where to look. And they couldn't access newspapers older than a year ago to find out what happened, because those were somehow magically on the computer.

"There has to be another jail marked on my dad's map somewhere," Birdie said. "Or *someplace* they keep prisoners. I don't dare open the map in here, though—we could burn the place down with all these newspapers." She tried to imagine her dad with his sparking hands in this room, and the corners of her mouth ticked up. "Or get seen with it."

"We'll have to walk by *all* of the map markings to see if any of them are places that could hold prisoners," said Tenner. "I know it's a lot, but that's why we're here. I think I've got all the newspaper articles that could give us clues about where the captured ones were sent." He set the article with the pictures of the criminals aside with the other papers he wanted to keep. "I think we're making progress." He grinned.

Birdie grinned back. "Me too." She folded the papers carefully and put them in her backpack along with the other useful items she'd found.

With the room tidy, they emerged into the open area of the library. The librarian they'd seen hours before was nowhere in sight, and the place was bustling with patrons now. They watched as a dad and his two kids put stacks of books on the counter in front of a librarian and handed over a little white card. The librarian set each book on a pad, then piled them up as the kids watched excitedly.

"I guess that's what families are like in civilized places," Tenner said under his breath. The scene set a melancholy mood. What would it be like to grow up here with noncriminal, nonsupernatural parents? To go places without worrying that people will find out you have a special ability? Birdie thought her life could have been quite different with all of these opportunities in the city. But Tenner thought life would be more of the same: struggling to stay out of his dad's way—only with different scenery.

The father tucked the white card back into his wallet.

Birdie's face lit up. "*That's* the library card," she whispered.

Tenner pulled himself from his thoughts and tuned in to the family's conversation. He narrated to Birdie as the librarian made small talk and explained when to return the books. The dad and kids took the books without paying for them. Normal people would bring the books back, Birdie knew—that was how they were raised. Her expression flickered.

"Those kids are so excited," Tenner said wistfully. He couldn't take his eyes off the family as they walked to the exit.

Birdie glanced at Tenner, surprised by the longing in his voice. He was different here. Showing actual feelings, like when he'd raised his voice about the pitying glances he was tired of. And how he'd been impassioned when talking about his parents back there in the archives room.

Tenner watched the way things worked behind the desk. "Do you see the sign above the librarian? It says library cards are free, but you need an ID."

"What's that?"

"No idea. All I know is that we don't have one." Tenner paused. "Let's go find that history shelf."

The two went to the section the librarian had shown them. They sat down on the floor and pulled a few books out, scanning them for the interesting bits.

"This one says President Fuerte hated the supernatural criminals because they'd stolen money from the country,"

Birdie said, "so he changed the currency after they left. He didn't want them to come back and use the stolen money here. That's two sources saying the same thing."

"Mine is about the failed heist of the Stone Crown from his palace," said Tenner. "It says that the president added the gate and security guards after that. The crown can only be viewed from a distance on the palace tours."

Birdie frowned. "I wish we had real money so we could see the thing our parents tried to steal." She turned back to her book. *"After he changed the currency,"* she read, *"President Fuerte exchanged people's old money for new, and he put the old currency on display in the museum."*

"Yes, I get it now!" Tenner exclaimed, causing people nearby to frown at them. He lowered his voice. "It's because millions of dollars of the old currency were taken from the Cordoba Museum that we got hauled into the police station. We tried to use the kind of money that had recently been stolen."

Birdie blew out a breath. "It's all making sense."

"If your mom and Cabot's parents were captured," said Tenner as he closed his book, "that means the four who *weren't* captured are probably the ones doing all this. My parents and Seven's parents."

"Yeah," said Birdie. She started to draw her shoulders in and give Tenner the usual pitying glance, but she caught herself. And then an idea came to her. "Hey, Tenner, do you think it would be easier on you if we called them Troy and Lucy? Because they definitely weren't parents to you."

Tenner bristled. He set his book on the floor and studied Birdie's expression. She faced him, cross-legged and leaning forward earnestly with her elbows on her knees, between the stacks. Not pitying at all like in the past. He nodded. "That's a good idea. I like it." He hesitated, then added, "Thanks."

Birdie smiled and went back to her book. Tenner flipped through a few others and landed on the thin one that the librarian had pulled out. He lifted it up. *"Sometimes You're the Villain,"* he read. "By Evane S. Gribaldi." He flipped the book over and read the back cover.

A MEMOIR FROM A
DIFFERENT PERSPECTIVE

EVANE S. GRIBALDI (a nom de plume) was one of the notorious supernatural criminals who tormented Estero, then disappeared. Gribaldi describes the group as a misunderstood bunch of people who first met in a foster home for unwanted supernatural children. They grew up knowing the world despised them, and experienced many hardships as adults. Excluded from higher education and jobs, the group of eight stayed together . . . then turned to crime in order to survive.

Tenner looked up and connected his gaze with Birdie's. Neither knew what to say. This had been written by one of their parents. A mom or a dad. Or a Troy or a Lucy. Birdie checked the copyright date and discovered it had been published a year ago.

Birdie checked the people who were in their area browsing for books. "Turn around," she whispered, taking the book from him.

Tenner gave her a quizzical glance but did it.

Birdie opened his backpack and put the book inside. "We need this." She sealed the pack and stood up, glancing all around again. "Let's get out of here."

They slipped through the stacks and waited behind a display for a group to either come or go, so that if something happened because of them stealing a book, they'd be able to cause confusion and escape.

When a large group of high-spirited teenagers shoved through the door together, laughing and talking excitedly, Birdie watched them wistfully. But then she grabbed Tenner's sleeve and headed for the exit.

They pushed through the bar and made for the door just as the alarm went off. Birdie looked at Tenner and mouthed, "Run."

A WEALTH OF KNOWLEDGE

Tenner and Birdie pushed past the librarian in the orange dress who had helped them earlier, nearly knocking her lunch out of her hands. "Sorry!" Tenner called over his shoulder.

Birdie elbowed him. "Keep running!"

After recovering from the surprise, the librarian watched them run down the library steps and to the sidewalk. A raven flew after them.

Though the librarian didn't condone stealing, she knew that stolen books could be replaced—if indeed that was the reason the alarm had gone off. As others swarmed outside the building to see what had happened, the librarian closed her eyes. Instantly the alarm stopped. After a few seconds, the ones who'd come out seemed to no longer care about the incident, almost as if they'd forgotten why they'd exited the building. They went back inside.

The librarian opened her eyes, and a hint of a smile played at her lips. She was certain about these two now. She loved it when special people came in, especially children who were coming to realize their potential. Even if they couldn't be bothered to sign up for a stinking library card when they needed information. It wasn't that difficult.

But it was okay. She understood their reluctance to give out any information about themselves. Their very existence meant they were in danger. She'd snuck books out of this same library when she was their age. How else was anyone supposed to find out the truth about supernatural people? She'd have to keep an eye out for these new ones because they might not come back to the library again after such a narrow escape.

Inside, she set down her coffee and lunch and checked the resource room, noting the missing pages from several newspapers, and shook her head. She checked the computer and saw the word *birdie* in the username box, then cleared it. "Birdie," she said quietly. "Hmm." Something seemed not quite right there—the username wouldn't show up if the girl had gotten into her account.

Then she checked the history section, finding the books out of alphabetical order. With a sigh, she straightened them and went to the desk computer to order a new copy of the missing book. It was at least the fifth time she'd reordered *Sometimes You're the Villain*. It was the most stolen title in the library this year. President Fuerte might have banned supernatural people, but they were crawling back, coming out of hiding, and trying desperately to find a narrative for themselves in a bleak world.

And at least one of them secretly held a government job.

BIRDIE AND TENNER ran down an unfamiliar street, dodging people in their path and looking over their shoulders to see if anyone, other than the raven, was following. After half a mile with no one behind them, they slowed to a walk near a park. "That was close," Birdie said, breathing hard. "I'm surprised nobody came after us."

"They might be out looking." Tenner glanced around. "Where are we?" The park had a shady section with soft green grass. The two, sure that they weren't being followed, took off their shoes and sat down. They weren't used to wearing shoes all the time, but almost all the surfaces in Estero were hard and dirty. The grass was soft and felt good.

The park took up the space of a city block. Two of the streets around it were busy with traffic; the other two were side streets and less busy. There was a water fountain in the center. While Tenner filled their canteens, Birdie looked around, wondering if any of the map markings were nearby. The raven alighted on a branch above her head, then hopped down. Birdie gazed at it, sending warm feelings its way in hopes of strengthening their bond like she'd done with Puerco. Maybe it could help them somehow.

A wave of longing rushed through her. She missed her pig. She missed Brix and Seven. And Cabot, even though she'd snuck into their cabin. She missed the quiet sounds of the sea lapping the shore—the kind that didn't have honking, squealing, rumbling traffic behind them. The noise of vehicles and the acrid smell they made was off-putting enough that Birdie didn't want to spend much more time here. She couldn't wait to go home. There she wouldn't have to think about money or crossing streets or traffic pollution or people chasing her anymore. But she still had her father's wish to tend to and a new jail to find. *Where are you, Mom?*

Unlike communicative animals, Mom didn't send any warm feelings her way.

Tenner returned with the canteens, then turned sharply, looking in anticipation down the street. Soon a pair of horses with police riders clopped up the sidewalk. Tenner and Birdie gasped and stared at the beasts. Louis had sculpted a horse with wet sand once, after he'd told the children that police sometimes used horses in Estero. But his sculpture couldn't compare. These were black and shiny and strong, and their tails swished, and their noses were broad, and their eyes bulbous and beautiful. Birdie wanted to run up to them, but the officers on their backs had Tenner and Birdie rethinking that move.

Hello, horses! Birdie said to them. Both horses swung their heads and looked at Birdie. The near one whinnied to her. Birdie clutched her heart. *I'll be your friend!* she said back to it.

The police and horses moved on, out of sight. Birdie whirled and clutched Tenner's arm. "That was amazing! Can you imagine riding one of those?"

Tenner sniffed. "It's no orca."

As Birdie sipped the fresh water, she gazed at a building across the street. The faded sign on the pale yellow brick said SUNRISE FOSTER HOME. As she studied it, a girl about Birdie's age with elbow crutches appeared in front of the building. She had cute round-rimmed glasses and curly light brown hair that fell past her shoulders. The girl hadn't walked out the door or come from the street—she literally appeared out of nowhere, then glanced over her shoulder at the entrance to the building and started moving away from it with a pronounced limp, like her steps were too short.

Birdie blinked. "Did you see that girl *appear* in front of Sunrise Foster Home?" she asked Tenner.

The girl began walking faster, using her crutches to maneuver over the uneven parts of the sidewalk.

Tenner followed Birdie's gaze. "I can see her, yes," he said. "What do you mean, she *appeared*? Like, she's projecting from some other place? Or she teleported?" The kids might not have known what toast was, but they had a significant vocabulary of supernatural terms.

"Maybe I imagined it. Though one second the sidewalk was empty, and the next, she was there."

"Wishful thinking?" Tenner asked. "Looking for something

that seems familiar?" He trained his eye on the big picture window, trying to see inside.

Just then a man rushed from the building, making the door slam against the brick. "Get back here!" he called. "Lada!" He swore and punched the door in anger, then shook his fist in pain. "You're not allowed out!"

"Whoa," Tenner muttered. Images of his father flashed in his mind. "He seems ridiculously angry." Old childhood memories came rushing back: his father yelling at him for being a few minutes late for dinner, even though Birdie and Seven were late, too, and their parents had brushed it off. Chastising him for not being able to carry more firewood or for running away after being humiliated by him. Tenner's heart raced, and his face flushed as he worried about the girl.

"Go, Lada!" Birdie called softly in encouragement, though surely the girl couldn't hear.

Lada disappeared again. The man threw his hands in the air and went back inside the foster home.

"There!" Birdie said. "Did you see that? She disappeared!"

"I hope she teleported farther away from that guy," Tenner said. "But why would she do stuff like that in public if it's dangerous?"

"Maybe she can't control it yet." Birdie tapped her lips. "I wonder if there are any more supernatural kids inside."

"I don't see anyone else, but there's a glare on the window that's blocking my view." Tenner felt a weight on his shoulders.

"I hope she's . . . okay. Living there with *that* guy." He tried to bury the depressing thoughts by thinking about the two things that gave him the most comfort. Fishing—pure quiet bliss, away from everyone so he could express his emotions into the sea. And then, of course, eating the fish. "Hey, can we go back to the beach? I'm—"

"I know. I'm starving, too. But I'm not sure where we are. I got turned around after the library. And I want to go past a few more places on the map and maybe get a better look inside Sunrise." Birdie checked the privacy level of their space. There were others in the park. Families with small children. A young woman a few years older than Birdie stretching on a mat with her back to them. She wore tight black shorts and a black tank top—a little bit like Birdie's parachute outfit—and had little white bulbs in her ears. Birdie wondered if she lived nearby.

She moved out of sight of the people, then took out the map and unrolled it, trying her best to hide the explosion of flames. When they settled, she studied it, finding the park. There were initials on the map nearby, across the street. At first Birdie thought the letters, *CIS*, marked Sunrise Foster Home, but they didn't match up to the name. She looked farther up the block and saw another building but couldn't quite make out the small signage on it. "Can you read that?" she asked, pointing.

Tenner focused. "Cabot Industrial Services."

"Cabot?" Birdie exclaimed. "Another coincidence?"

This building had awnings to keep the sun out, and Tenner's eyes pierced through the windows. "It's dark in there. Abandoned, maybe."

"Could it be a jail?" Birdie raised an eyebrow. "Maybe it's in the back of the building where you can't see it." She got up. "Let's take a stroll across the street and check out a few things."

"We've already gotten into trouble once today," Tenner reminded her. "Besides, I don't want to go anywhere near that angry guy."

"Fine. I'll go. You stay here."

Tenner's mouth opened as if to protest, then closed. He sat back, knowing Birdie would do what she wanted regardless of his opinion. Birdie dropped her backpack next to him and went to the corner where the signals were, then crossed the street when she was sure no cars were going to run her down. She walked past Sunrise Foster Home and stopped to peer curiously through the window. The angry man sat at a desk, barking into a telephone next to a long, bare white wall. A few kids about Brix's age passed through the space and went into a room. They didn't seem supernatural, but then again, neither did Birdie. She glanced at the door. Did she dare go inside? She wiped the dusty window with her sleeve and looked inside again.

When the man noticed she was pressing her face against the window, he slammed down the phone and pounded on the glass. "Move along!" he shouted at her. "Or I'll call the police!"

Birdie gasped. She fled up the street toward Cabot Industrial

Services, then ducked into the alcove in the brick wall below the sign. She peeked out to make sure the man hadn't come after her and breathed a sigh of relief to find the sidewalk clear. Tenner had moved to the edge of the park and looked like he was ready to assist if she needed help. She waved and flashed a shaky grin to let him know she was okay.

She turned around and faced two doors. Etched into the brick next to the door on the left was a sheaf of wheat. Birdie sucked in a breath. Was this like the dove? One of the symbols that pointed out the entrance to a tunnel? She opened it and peered down a long hallway with rough walls lit by occasional sconces. Pretty meadow scenes were painted on the walls. It looked inviting. Maybe she'd check it out sometime with Tenner, but right now she was more interested in the Cabot property.

The other door had glass in the top half, which was cracked but not broken. Birdie peered in and saw another door inside, to the right. Straight ahead was a staircase leading up.

Birdie pushed the handle. When it didn't move, she pulled instead, and it swung toward her with a creak. "Never going to get that right," she muttered. She glanced back as the raven swooped and landed on the sidewalk behind her. Birdie signaled to Tenner that she was going in, and she held the door open to let the raven in, too.

The entrance area was small, and there was an old rug on the floor, suggesting the building wasn't entirely abandoned. She tried the door, but the handle wouldn't turn.

As she started up the staircase, the raven flew up and landed on the handrail at the top. Light streamed down through a small multicolored glass window straight ahead. When Birdie reached the landing, she found a wall of glass to the right, with a door in it. Birdie's heart pounded as she studied what was on the other side of the glass wall. There was a huge open room with different partitioned sections. It looked like something called a gym that they had passed on the main drag to the beach, with people sweating and running on machines that didn't go anywhere. It seemed pointless. But these machines stood empty.

This building smelled better than outside. It was almost familiar, like coconut, which made her feel hungry and homesick simultaneously. Birdie checked in with the raven and got a neutral response—nothing notable here, but also no immediate danger. She tried the glass door and found it locked. "Elena Golden!" she called out. "Are you here? Mom? Elena!"

There was no response. And clearly no prisoners here. The raven lost interest and flew down to wait by the door.

Eventually Birdie slipped back down the stairs, not noticing the woman who came to the window as she descended, pulling out her cell phone as she watched the girl go.

SUSPICIOUS ACTIONS

Birdie and Tenner went back to their secluded spot on the beach. While Tenner fished and cooked, Birdie searched the map for initials that had the letter *J* for *jail* or *P* for *prison* in them, but there weren't any more. Stymied, she picked up the book by Evane S. Gribaldi, trying to get a sense of which parent wrote it. Could there be a clue to the prisoners' whereabouts in here? The author didn't refer to the hideout but described their time at Sunrise Foster Home at length.

A chill passed through Birdie as she made the connection. "Sunrise Foster Home was the place our parents met," she exclaimed. "It's where they lived—the home my dad talked about."

"Now I wish I'd taken a better look," said Tenner.

"The park across the street from it," Birdie said, "where we saw the horses and got water, was where my dad took the photo of my mom that he kept in his wallet." Birdie had looked right into the place her parents had fallen in love! And the foster home was obviously still in business. "Oh, but listen to this," she added. "The author says Sunrise stopped allowing supernatural children around the same time the president changed the currency. And that things have only gotten worse in Estero for supernatural people since then, not better."

But if Sunrise no longer allowed supernatural children, what was up with the teleporting girl they'd seen?

At dinner, Tenner filled Birdie in on what he'd read. "I found something else in today's newspaper."

"About our parents?"

"Maybe," said Tenner. "About President Fuerte. He's been taking a lot of nighttime trips out of Estero lately, and nobody knows why. In the news today? An airport worker saw the president arrive at the jet hangar with a mysterious guest. One who disappeared into thin air before boarding."

"You mean like the teleporting girl?" Birdie asked, incredulous. "Lada?"

"Not Lada. A man." Tenner gave Birdie a hard look.

Birdie's eyes widened. "Martim Palacio?" Seven's dad could go invisible in an instant.

"The worker didn't identify him. But I thought it was interesting."

"It *definitely* is!" said Birdie. "Why would the president be hanging around with supernatural people if he hates them so much?"

Tenner shrugged and pulled out a piece of paper and a pencil.

"What are you doing?" Birdie asked.

"Starting a list of the initials on the map. We can cross off the places we've been to and focus on the rest."

While she and Tenner worked on the map, Birdie mulled over the president possibly being with Seven's dad. "Remember that article about international heists?"

Tenner nodded and didn't look up from his writing.

"It said that President Fuerte was meeting with leaders of other countries to stop the supernatural criminals. Do you think that's where he's going?

"And he's bringing Martim along . . . why?"

Birdie shook her head. "I don't know." When Tenner finished, she let the map roll up and extinguish. Then she turned. "The article you read—does it say which day the airport worker saw the disappearing man?"

Tenner fished the article from his pile and pointed out the date. "It was last week, right before we got here."

Birdie sucked in a breath and grabbed Tenner's wrist. "That's the day after the Cordoba Museum heist!"

"So?"

"So . . . if Martim was involved, he'd have the stolen money, right?"

"Okay . . . ?" Tenner's face was a puzzle. "I don't get what you're saying."

"The old currency isn't good here, so he'd want to go somewhere it would be worth something."

Tenner frowned. "I still don't see how the president fits into this, other than having a jet that can fly to places where the money is still good. They can't possibly be friends—the guy changed the currency of a country and shut down entry to supernatural children because of our parents. He hates them."

Birdie sighed, then slumped. Things weren't adding up. "I know. But there are a lot of very strange coincidences."

DRAWING NEARER

Ever since Birdie left, Cabot had been trying to figure out what to say when they found her. And while she thought Birdie would probably tell the truth once confronted, Cabot couldn't be completely sure about that. But she *was* sure they would find her. Despite the overwhelming size of the city, Cabot knew exactly how to locate her. Because Birdie had left her very intelligent pig behind.

By late afternoon they reached the outskirts of a small village—there was a cluster of rooftops in the distance. They stopped for a moment to spy on some field-workers through a long row of bushes. A vast garden with tall green plants stretched out as far as they could see. There was an enormous vehicle moving through the rows a few hundred yards away. Seven shifted uneasily. "Let's get past this village and look for a quiet place to camp for the night."

But with their food supplies running low, Cabot and Brix first wanted to sneak into the fields to see if they could gather something to eat. They slipped in between stalks taller than their heads and discovered each plant bore oblong cobs with soft brown tassels at one end. Inside were yellow kernels in rows. They smelled and tasted good, but the firm kernels sprayed juice when they bit into them. They took an armload and continued on.

At sunset they came to another farm—this one of gnarled trees. There was no one in sight. While Seven and Brix set up camp, Cabot culled the grounds, picking up sweet-smelling round red fruit. She took all she could carry back with her to share with the boys and packed the rest for the next day.

AT DAWN, WHILE Brix doled out breakfast, Cabot surveyed the grassy trail ahead. It was downward-sloping to sea level and looked to be an easy trek. From this height she could make out the skyline. "Less than twenty miles to go," she mused. They could get to Estero City by dark if Seven would stop dragging his feet. That was one of the things Cabot worried about—that Seven wouldn't actually go through with entering the city. And frankly, she didn't blame him. He could decide what he wanted to do according to his comfort level. But Cabot was going for it. And that might mean leaving Seven behind. He'd be okay.

Cabot hurried the boys along. With them trailing, Cabot was in her element, deep inside her thoughts. Calculating every-thing. Like, based on their approximate distance from the city center, and factoring in the curvature of the earth and their elevation versus the probable just-above-sea-level elevation of Estero City, the height of the tallest building had to be over a thousand feet. Cabot couldn't explain how to calculate such things. She just *knew* them. Her mind did it automatically.

Having a building of that height was astounding and seemed impossible at first, but Cabot's mind kept whirring, trying to come up with a way for humans to create structures much taller than themselves. "If they built something to climb on and set it up outside of the actual building . . ." she muttered. "And used ropes and pulleys . . . hmm."

As she navigated the footpaths, Cabot's anxiety and nervousness over confronting Birdie grew. Were they too late? Hopefully she and Tenner were still there. Cabot couldn't bear to think that Elena had the whole stash and Birdie and Tenner were on their way back to the hideout. In their haste to depart, Cabot hadn't thought to leave a note in case Tenner and Birdie went home before the three found them.

Despite her feelings about Birdie's underhanded move, Cabot's throat tightened. The two would be scared if they returned to find the beach empty. But she'd see the mess they'd left in the Goldens' cabin. She'd find the note from her father lying there. And she'd figure it out.

Of course Seven and Brix could be right that everything was innocent and that kind Elena Golden would certainly share the stash. But whenever Cabot started to feel like she'd made a hasty decision about Birdie's intentions, she remembered how the older girl had concealed Louis's shocking confession. If that wasn't underhanded, what was?

Seven was definitely right about one thing, though: Wherever the remaining criminals were, they had to be mad if they found that the stash was gone.

As much as Cabot wanted to confront Birdie on her lies of omission, she also wanted Birdie and Tenner to be safe so that once this escapade was over, they could go back home and return to normal.

But one question continued to plague Cabot's mind. What if her parents *were* alive? Would the kids stay long enough to find out?

SEARCHING FOR ELENA

We have a lot of places to visit today," Tenner said to Birdie over their fish breakfast under the cypress tree. "I've got the list. Let's hit as many as we can, and keep our eyes peeled for signs that might point to a jail. Your dad only knew the city from fifteen years ago. Maybe there's a new one somewhere." He paused. "You've got the cell phones, right?"

"For what?" said Birdie, licking her fingers. She was wearing one of her mom's short dresses today—red with white dots. It was way too puffy in the chest, but the length was nice, down to her knees, and she liked the way it swished.

"To get into the Cordoba Museum." Tenner had switched out of his dad shorts last night and was wearing his parachute pants and a cropped green T-shirt with holes in the armpits. He'd been wearing the T-shirt—his mom's—since she'd left it behind, and it was almost too tight in the shoulders now.

"You think there's a jail in there?" Birdie asked.

"No. But I want to see what's inside *my* museum while I have the chance."

Birdie laughed. "I still haven't found anything with the name Golden on it." She cleaned her hands in the ocean and dried them, then pulled the cell phones out of her backpack and handed one to Tenner. Then she took two little bendy metal things she'd taken from the library and unwound them, then strung one through the top two shoelace holes of each sneaker and twisted them tight.

With dead cell phones in their pockets, the two set out, zig-zagging through the city and stopping at the various places Louis had marked on the map. Tenner dialed up his sensory abilities as they went inside an eclectic coffee shop, listening to conversations in hopes of finding a clue. But when they went past the counter, the person working behind it turned on a machine that pierced the air like a wailing banshee.

"Aaah!" Tenner shrieked, his eardrums throbbing. He covered them as they made a hasty exit.

Next, they strode with fake confidence over the black-and-white marble floors of a fancy bank, past a long counter that had a row of men and women working behind it, all wearing gold bar name tags on their lapels. Birdie's wire-tied sneakers squeaked with every step, and the sound echoed through the cavernous space. They caught fleeting glimpses of the money that Estero used now being slid beneath glass panels to the people waiting on the other side. Fascinated, the two stopped near a waist-high silver pole with a swinging velvet rope attached to it to watch the people who waited in line. There weren't many bright-colored pieces of clothing in here. Almost everyone wore blue or black jackets with pants or skirts of the same color and white or blue button-down shirts. It was very different from the beach or the library. Clearly none of these people shopped at Bootsie's Boutique.

"Next?" said one of the bank employees, looking over her glasses at the two with mild disdain. "Please don't hang on the stanchions."

Birdie and Tenner turned and looked behind them, then realized the woman was talking to them. "Uh," Birdie said. She grabbed Tenner's arm. "No thank you!"

She bolted, dragging Tenner with her, but he got caught up in the velvet rope, knocking the metal stanchion over with a resounding clang. He fell, landing spread-eagle onto the marble floor. "Oof!" He scrambled to his feet and ran, too.

"Current jail count, zero," Birdie said when they were back on the street. "Personal injuries, two. We are losing this game."

After a short walk they found themselves standing in front of the Estero Community Hospital, where the infamous helicopter had awaited their parents' escape. Birdie was suddenly grateful her father had made them tell the story over and over. She could almost see them racing up the street and into the building. Her heart pounded as she imagined their climb to the rooftop, worrying if they'd make it before the police got them. Then taking off and flying over the sea.

"It *seems* kind of like a jail," Tenner said slowly, rubbing his sore elbows and looking up to the top of the flat-roofed, eight-story building. "Cabot's mom said people get admitted, and they're not allowed to go home until the doctor says it's okay."

"I don't think my mom would be here," said Birdie. "But we can take a look at where Greta worked. Then we can tell Cabot about it later."

"Maybe we can bring her a special souvenir," said Tenner.

"Yes, she'd like that," said Birdie. The absence from Cabot had softened most of Birdie's anger toward her for sneaking into their cabin. And she also knew the tables would turn when they went home. "If we bring her a gift, maybe she won't be too mad about the part of my dad's note I didn't tell them about."

Upon entering, they found the staircase and trudged all the way to the top floor so they could work their way down. They walked through doors that said LABOR AND DELIVERY and slipped into a hallway, pretending like they were supposed to be there. Muffled screams from a woman behind a closed door unsettled them, but they exchanged a wide-eyed glance and kept going. Birdie's sneakers squeaked past a desk that said NURSES' STATION above it, and the two averted their eyes as a nurse glanced their way. Eventually they came to a broad glass window and looked inside.

There were two rows of little raised beds on wheels, with newborn babies squirming or sleeping in them.

"Babies!" Tenner exclaimed. "They're tiny."

Birdie stared at the wrinkled things. She had only been three years old when Brix was born and didn't remember him like this. "Not cute."

"That one is screaming," Tenner said, pointing to one whose face was dark red from exertion. "Can't the nurses hear it?"

Birdie and Tenner searched anxiously behind the glass for a nurse to go to it. But the ones working back there seemed to be unconcerned. Tenner heard footsteps coming behind them and turned to find the nurse they'd passed coming their way. He nudged Birdie and cleared his throat.

"Can I help you?" the nurse said. She wasn't smiling. "Where are your wristbands?"

"We're just looking," Tenner said. Then he added weakly, "That one is screaming."

"Are you a sibling?" the nurse asked sharply. She peered around Tenner, trying to see Birdie's wrists.

"I am," Birdie said. Technically it was true. "Can you help my . . ." She glanced sidelong at the crying one. "Brother?"

The nurse narrowed her eyes.

"Sister?" Birdie said before she could stop herself.

The woman's expression darkened.

"We need to go," Tenner said, steering Birdie toward the exit. When they'd gone a few paces, out of reach of the nurse, they broke into a fast walk out of there.

They scoured the other floors, looking through windows and doors in the areas they weren't allowed and trying to avoid the nurses. They peeked into a room where noise was blaring and saw a screen hung from the wall in the corner. An old man was in the bed, fast asleep despite the racket.

As predicted, there weren't any jail cells inside the hospital. But in one hallway on the second floor, Tenner noticed a dispenser attached to the wall that held disposable vomit bags. He glanced around, then pulled one out of the bottom. Another one dropped down. He frowned, then took that one, too. When a third dropped, his eyes widened. He hesitated, tempted to keep taking them as long as they dropped but not wanting to be greedy. In the end he kept two: one for Cabot, and one in case Birdie ended up in the backseat of a police car again.

"This is where Greta Stone worked," Birdie whispered when they exited the stairwell into the emergency room. While Tenner pocketed some gauze and a blood pressure cuff for Cabot from a vacant triage station, Birdie wandered toward the desk, beyond which doctors and nurses were moving between small rooms that had curtains keeping the patients hidden from view. She stood on her tiptoes to watch them and teared up imagining Greta hard at work here. She wished Cabot could see it. She tried to memorize everything to tell her later.

A nurse appeared behind the desk. "Do you need something?"

Birdie started. Heart pounding, she blurted out, "Do you know Greta Stone? She's . . . a doctor."

The nurse frowned. "No. Are you sick? Or with someone who is?"

"I'm—we're fine. Thank you." She turned and found Tenner by the exit, zipping up his backpack.

"Time to go," he said, slinging the bag over his shoulder. The doors magically slid open, disappearing into the walls, then closed behind them as soon as they walked out. Tenner glanced back in amazement.

They turned in the direction of the museum and went past a white man leaning against the building, talking on a cell phone. He wore a black suit and shiny shoes, similar to people in the bank.

He watched the kids go. Then he followed them.

THE LINE FOR the museum was longer than the other day when they'd walked around the building. They waited their turn, feeling pleasantly invisible in the midst of a crowd. The look here was casual and colorful, and there were a lot more sneakers on people's feet.

Tenner gave up his habit of narrowing his eyes to hide his pupils. Birdie was right—people didn't seem to notice. He wasn't as special as he'd imagined himself to be, which was actually good here in Estero. Especially since squinting all the time gave him a headache.

When their turn came, they slid their phones open and flashed the blank screens at the attendant. The young man gave them a curious glance, then said, "It's free on Sundays."

Birdie nodded like she knew that and put the phone away. The two advanced inside.

"Now we know," Tenner said. "Did you see him do a double take when he saw our phones?"

"Yeah. A person in front of us was using their in line. It was a lot different from ours. More like those moving screens we've seen around the city. But this person was interacting with it—touching the screen with their fingertip and flicking a red-and-white ball at a weird-looking creature that hopped now and then. The ball went flying, and it—it, like, ate the creature . . ." She trailed off, not sure how to describe it.

"I don't get the appeal," Tenner said snootily as they followed a group to an enormous skeleton on display. "The people are tiny on the big screens. Imagine how small they must be on a phone."

"Except for those huge-faced ones."

Tenner snorted. "Where even *are* those people? Have you seen one on the streets? I haven't. Do you think their bodies are big, too, or only their heads?"

Birdie shrugged. She looked around at the vast room, feeling about as small as those sports players on the screen. "This is the biggest indoor space I have ever seen in my life," she said. "Look at that huge skeleton—what the heck is it?"

They went over to read about the dinosaur that had been discovered and unearthed outside of Estero City. Then they moved around to other rooms, checking out the different items. As they studied a glassed-in display of ancient artifacts like arrow-heads and knives and spiked weapons, Tenner tensed up. "Don't move," he whispered.

Birdie's eyes widened. "Why?"

Tenner was silent for a moment, then said, "Someone across the room is talking about us. Act natural."

Birdie gulped. "What are they saying?"

Tenner remained quiet for a moment. "A woman said, 'Hey, there are the two specials from the library I told you about.' The other person said, 'I saw them creeping around in the park when LaDuca was trying to chase me down.'" Tenner's eyes darted from patron to patron, trying to locate the ones speaking.

Birdie's heart thudded in her throat. Specials? Did she mean people with special abilities? How could anyone know? Had someone noticed Tenner's eyes after all? She and Tenner pretended to converse about the ancient artifacts while trying to get a glimpse behind them. "Let's go over here," Birdie said, leading him away. What did the people know about them?

As they moved to the next room, Birdie dared a lengthy glance back. "Oh," she said. Near the entry she saw the librarian who had helped them. And with her, in a wheelchair this time, was Lada, the girl who had appeared out of nowhere outside the Sunrise Foster Home.

A FAMILIAR FIGURE

K eep moving," Birdie muttered. "It's the librarian. I bet she knows that we stole that book."

As Birdie and Tenner searched for an exit to make their escape, Tenner's keen eye caught a movement on the upper floor where the offices were—a shadowy figure in a shimmering garment, followed by a whoosh of purple when the figure turned in the light. Then she was gone down a dark hallway. Tenner's sight adjusted, and he watched for a moment before she disappeared into a room. The woman's movements seemed familiar. Had she been watching them?

Tenner scanned the room, looking and listening for anyone else acting suspicious. When he made eye contact with the librarian, he panicked and rushed to catch up with Birdie, who was trucking through the open space. But the librarian and Lada didn't chase after them.

Wondering how to get to the upper level and figure out who the spying woman was, Tenner looked around for a staircase but didn't see one. As they reached the end of the vast hall, Tenner noticed a strange small room with a sliding door. He'd seen them at the hospital, too. The sign above it said ELEVATOR. Two people got in, and the door slid closed with no one moving it. There were buttons that lit up outside it.

He looked up at the second floor and saw another silver door like this one. The door opened, and the same people got out. "More magic," Tenner whispered. He kept moving, searching for Birdie and finding her long black hair flipping around as she jogged down a wide hallway. He darted after her. Finally she turned, saw he wasn't with her, and waited for him to catch up.

"We need to leave," she said. "What if the librarian called the police on us?"

"I have a vomit bag," he said, nervously going for the joke. But he was rattled. "I saw someone spying on us," he said in a low voice. "Tell you later." Maybe the woman was only gazing down at the crowd, but Tenner had a weird feeling about her.

"Here's the side exit," Birdie said, starting toward it.

Tenner followed.

Safe outside and with no one coming after them, Birdie and Tenner turned to go past another marked spot on the map. As they walked, Tenner explained what he'd seen. "There was a woman in the shadows on the upper floor of the main room," he said. "When I looked up, she slipped down a dark hallway, and by the time my night vision focused in, I could only see the outline of her body for a second before she went into a room."

Birdie seemed skeptical. "It could have been anybody. Like a worker or the owner or something."

"I know." Tenner hesitated. "But the way she walked felt . . . familiar."

Birdie stopped. "Familiar how? Like, parent-familiar? Or someone we've seen in Estero?"

Tenner pursed his lips, not quite sure. "I don't know," he said finally. "Maybe I'm imagining she was familiar because I want to find your mom so badly."

Birdie studied him. He sounded defeated. She slipped her arm through his as they walked, like she often did with Seven. "Cheer up," she said. "We've crossed a lot of places off our list today."

Tenner stiffened and glanced at Birdie's arm. Had she forgotten who she was with? "But we still haven't found your mom or anything that looks remotely like a jail. I feel like we're wasting our time." He relaxed as Birdie kept her arm linked with his.

"I wish we'd thought to look for a local map at the library— then maybe we could find out if there is another jail somewhere. I think . . . I might go ahead and ask a stranger."

"Like a police officer?"

"Sure," said Birdie, though she didn't feel quite that brave. "Or anyone who looks like they might know."

They stopped in the block where the initials *MdP* had appeared on the map. "Monasterio de Piedra," Birdie said, reading the sign.

"A monastery?" Tenner said, not sure what that meant.

"It's like a church, I think," Birdie guessed. At least it looked like one of the old churches in the C–D encyclopedia, with great rounded doors, huge metal latches, and bell towers. As they gazed at it, three bells clanged, each with a different note. When the song was over, two of the bell tones rang out harmoniously for several seconds, then faded. It felt like a moment of reprieve in this busy city. "That was beautiful," Birdie said. "We need to listen to more music." They didn't have any back home other than their voices.

Tenner frowned. Bombarded with plenty of noise all the time, he'd mostly tuned out the bells. "I wonder why your dad put this monastery on the map. It doesn't seem like any of these places point to where your mom might be." It was frustrating.

They circled the block, trying to get a good look over the wall that surrounded the property, but it was too high. As they walked, they noticed two doors that had tunnel marker etchings in the stone next to them. One, near the locked entrance to the church, depicted a sheaf of wheat—Birdie had seen that symbol next to the tunnel by Cabot Industrial Services, but that was a long way from here. She guessed that this tunnel was a shortcut to there. The other symbol they saw was a dog and a cat curled up together.

Birdie squinted at the sky. The sun was coming in white-hot in the midafternoon, and they were hungry and tired. They found a bench in the shade and finished off the rest of their breakfast fish. When a person in a uniform walked by, Birdie cleared her throat and called out, "Excuse me, please. Do you happen to know where the jail is?"

The woman stopped. Her uniform said PIZZA SUPREME across the front. She eyed the children quizzically. "You mean the police department?"

"No," said Tenner. "Is there a different jail around here?"

The woman seemed even more confused. "Why do you want to know about jails?"

"It's for summer school," Tenner said, recalling the term from the librarian. "A project."

"Oh!" The woman's face cleared. "There's the new penitentiary outside the city limits. Three or four miles straight up the main drag, right before you hit the freeway." She pointed.

"Penitentiary?" Tenner asked. "Is that a jail?"

"It's a prison. The worst offenders get transferred there from the police station." The woman glanced at her watch and continued walking. "I'm late for work. Good luck with your project."

A surge of hope flowed through Birdie like new life. "Thank you!" Not only had she successfully talked to another stranger without anyone getting injured or accused of a crime, but it had resulted in important information that could help them find her mom.

"Calling anything suspicious a 'school project' sure seems to be the way to go," Tenner noted.

Birdie and Tenner got up and started walking in the direction the woman had pointed out, with a new mission . . . and a new hope.

"What the heck is a freeway?" Birdie asked as they jogged across the street with the walking white stick person guiding them.

"Whatever it is, at least it's free," Tenner said.

Down the street, a black car roared to life and crawled along, staying a block behind them.

A SICK FEELING

While Birdie and Tenner walked to the penitentiary, Cabot, Seven, and Brix were closing in on the edge of the city. Another five miles would bring them into the heart of it. Cabot suggested they break for a snack while they could still sit in peace, for Seven's sake, but also for all of them. Going into a space like this was nerve-racking.

After they sat down, Seven looked around carefully to make sure no one was nearby, then unwrapped his scarf and let out a deep breath. His face became the sparkling bay behind him. A sailboat cut across his forehead.

"Do you want Brix and me to go into the city alone?" Cabot asked him. "We can come back for you tomorrow."

Seven's throat closed, not allowing him to speak. He shook his head. Without the scarf, the head shake wasn't noticeable.

But Cabot understood silence. Her face flickered with sympathy. She rested her hand on his forearm for a moment. The sentiment made Seven choke up even more. This was the hardest thing he'd ever done. Back home, when the changes to his camouflage began, they'd happened slowly, almost like he was fading away. His parents had already left, so he couldn't go to them with his fears. There were only Mr. Golden and Birdie and the rest of the kids. They'd been kind, but . . . this was hard.

Birdie had bucked him up time and time again. She'd stuck by him and had never said a single word about how strange he looked. She hadn't made jokes about it, and she'd listened to him when he'd shared how scared he was that he would disappear completely one day—not just his body, but his spirit. His soul—the part of him that wasn't physical.

It wasn't like anyone else he knew had ever gone through this. This . . . feeling like you're disappearing from existence. Maybe Seven was being dramatic. Considering his parents' abilities, it seemed right in line. But the fact that they weren't around to help him through this was unconscionable. That had made everything worse. Birdie had been there for him then. And he needed to be there for her now.

"I'm going into Estero City with you," Seven said, now that the lump in his throat had receded. He paused. "Besides, it'll be dark by the time we get there. That'll make it easier."

Cabot and Brix nodded as they finished eating the last of the stolen red fruit. Cabot put the seeds from each core with the other ones she'd saved. Seven put the scarf back on. Then they packed their things. The two younger children led the way. Steeling himself, Seven followed.

STRIKING OUT

Tenner and Birdie approached the sprawling penitentiary complex with trepidation. The flat-roofed, rectangular, gray building surrounded by an electric fence was vastly different from the centuries-old style of Old Town Estero. Nearby, a huge conglomeration of streets rose up and curled together in a four-leaf clover, with vehicles shooting up the curves and merging with other vehicles. The freeway.

They found the prison's visitors' entrance and went inside. They were stopped by guards and told to put their backpacks on a belt that moved. Bewildered, the two did what they were told and tried not to freak out when their backpacks disappeared inside the machine.

The guard waved them through a doorway similar to what they'd gone through at the library. And then they collected their backpacks on the other side and were free to roam a large waiting room. There were people filling the chairs, and two of those screens up near the ceiling, broadcasting a show about people guessing answers to questions in order to win money. Lights flashed on the screen and letters appeared, but there was no sound, so nothing made sense.

On the far side of the room was a glass window with the word REGISTRATION above it. Birdie and Tenner exchanged a glance. This place was much larger than the little jail at the police station. Birdie went up to the window. A bald man with light brown skin was sitting on the other side. He typed on a computer keyboard without looking at the letters. Birdie wished she could see the screen. After a moment, the man looked up. He had a single wisp of long hair that sort of floated above his head. "Last name and ID?"

Birdie blinked. There was that term again. "Um . . . Golden. And Cordoba."

The man snorted. "You own the museum or something, kid? I need your IDs."

"Ha," said Tenner weakly. "Um, we don't have our IDs."

The man stopped and stared. "You have an appointment?"

"Appointment?" said Birdie. She pressed her lips together. "We want to see Elena Golden."

"If you don't have an appointment or ID, you're not getting in. How old are you? Where's your adult?"

"My adult is in there," Birdie said, feeling flustered. "My dad died, and my mom is Elena Golden. And I need to tell her."

The man's eyes widened, but he turned back to his computer and typed something. "You don't have an appointment." He picked up a thin pad of paper and slid it under the window.

"Write your phone number here, and we can ask your ma to call you during her free time. Elena Golden . . . hmm. That name is familiar."

Birdie stiffened. Would he know she was one of the supernatural criminals? She stared at the pad of paper. "I don't have a phone number."

The man sighed like he'd run out of sympathy. A line had formed behind them.

Tenner leaned in. "How do we make an appointment?" he asked. "Can we wait in the chairs?"

"You got ID?"

Tenner closed his eyes. "Still no."

"You need an adult. And you need ID. You can make an appointment with me now, but I can't let you in unless you have those things." The man turned back to the computer and typed. "Wait, wait. She's not even here."

"She's not?" Birdie asked. Her face fell. "Where is she?"

"Transferred out three years ago."

"To where?" Tenner asked.

The man frowned as he studied the screen. "Government custody." He sneered. "*Ooh.* Is she one of the supernatural criminals?"

Birdie gulped and looked around to see if anyone else had heard the question. Several people turned to stare. She didn't answer.

The man leaned toward the glass and looked Birdie in the

eye. He scowled as if disgusted by her. "She's not here. Okay, kid? Sorry about your dad. But I can't help you." He looked beyond the children to the people in line behind them. "Next!"

Birdie and Tenner walked out of the penitentiary in dejected silence. Government custody? What was that? It sounded ominous and impossible.

The raven followed them. *Do you know where Elena Golden is?* Birdie asked. The raven landed on Birdie's shoulder for the first time, sensing her sadness. But it didn't have an answer.

Nearby, parked in a black car, the librarian and Lada watched the two. "She's got an animal ability," Lada said brightly. "I'm still not sure about the boy. I think he sensed we were talking about them in the museum—that's why they took off."

"Something's unusual about his eyes," said the librarian. "And he's always looking around. They're after information about the supernatural criminals. I was able to figure out which articles they stole once I replaced the copies of the newspapers. All of them were about the eight fugitives." She tapped her finger to her lips. "They look thirteen or so, wouldn't you say?"

"My age," Lada agreed. "How long since the criminals ran away?"

"About fifteen years."

"Do you think they could possibly be . . . related?"

The librarian nodded. "That's exactly what I think."

It was dark by the time Birdie and Tenner stopped to rest and refill their water in the park across from Sunrise Foster Home.

The black car pulled into a parking space nearby. Across the street, the man who'd followed them to the museum strolled down the sidewalk, still wearing his suit jacket. He had his hands in his pockets this time. He glanced their way, then slipped inside one of the doors under the CABOT INDUSTRIAL SERVICES sign.

Birdie and Tenner hadn't had lunch, and now it was past dinnertime. Birdie rummaged through her backpack for food, but all she had left were a few shriveled berries, which she split between herself and Tenner. She shared one of hers with the raven.

Then she organized the items in her backpack, adjusting the map to keep it from being crushed between the library book and her father's journal. None seemed useful anymore. Birdie's mother was not in any traditional jail. "Government custody" sounded too big and official for a couple of kids who had no idea how the world worked. After resting for a while, Birdie glanced at Tenner. Her lip quivered. "I think maybe we should just . . . go home."

Tenner leaned forward and put his elbows on his knees. This was her choice, and he didn't want to talk her into leaving without finding her mom, but he'd had enough, too. "We seem to have run out of ideas," he said carefully, and sat up. "You tried your best for your dad. Home sounds good, but we can keep looking if you want."

Birdie sighed and dropped her head into her hands. Tenner

rested his hand on her back and patted now and then. After a few minutes, she sat up, too. "Well," she said, "I don't want to travel across the bay at night—it's scary enough during the day."

"Plus we're famished," Tenner added.

"Yes. But before we head back to the beach, there's one more thing I want to check out."

"The tunnels?" Tenner guessed.

"Yep."

"Your dad wrote in his journal that it's not good to use them at night."

Birdie shrugged. "It's now or never. There's an entrance to one next to the Cabot Industries door."

Birdie showed Tenner the sheaf of wheat etched into the stone. She and Tenner slipped into the tunnel, which was lit by electric sconces. The first intricate paintings on the walls were of fields, but as they progressed down the hallway, the scenes became vineyards, with castles and mountains in the distance. After several yards, they picked up the pace, keeping an eye out for tunnel watchers who might not appreciate them being there.

They came upon a door in the wall. They opened it, finding themselves facing an unfamiliar street. Tenner's stomach growled loudly. "Let's turn around," he said. "And head to the beach."

Birdie agreed. It had been cool to see. But it was just a tunnel. They went back the way they came.

As they moved along, Tenner heard footsteps behind them.

"Someone's coming," he whispered close to Birdie's ear. He grabbed her hand, and they started to run.

"Stop!" a man's voice rang out. The sound of footsteps increased. And then the lights went out.

"Keep running!" Tenner whispered. "I'll guide you—hang on!"

Birdie held on to Tenner's hand and ran for her life through the blackness. Their footsteps pounded and echoed and blended in with the ones behind them. As they neared the exit, a flash of light blinded Birdie and Tenner, followed by moving shadows, and then it went dark again.

A few steps later, they ran straight into a group of people who yelled in surprise. The impact sent Birdie and Tenner flying backward to the ground.

As Tenner whirled around, trying to make out their pursuer in the dark, an animal squealed and landed squarely on Birdie's chest, knocking her flat.

PART THREE

THE CLASH

In the confusion, bodies tangled and tore apart. Fists and feet connected with faces and stomachs. Stifled screams of surprise led to shouts of pain. All Tenner could see was a person with something wrapped around their head plowing into him. Knocking him flat. Tenner threw the person off and scrambled up. He found Birdie's hand and yanked her past the attackers and outside, onto the sidewalk where Birdie could see. They ran wildly across the street to a park, not caring about the blinking street signs. Then they crouched behind some overgrown bushes to catch their breath.

"Who was that?" Birdie whispered, touching her bottom lip, which was bleeding and swelling up like a grape. "The tunnel watcher?"

"The person following us earlier was a man by himself. He could have been a tunnel watcher. I'm not sure why he would've turned the lights out, though." Tenner paused for breath and winced when he felt his side. He'd taken a hard kick to his lower ribs. "The group we bumped into were strangers coming into the tunnel, I guess."

"They had a pet," Birdie said. "It landed on me. For a second, I thought it was Puerco."

Tenner laughed. "The one who kicked me and knocked me down had his face all wrapped up like that mummy replica we saw in the museum. I just wanted to get out of there."

Birdie squinted through the shadows, her head suddenly full of communication from animals. "I'm hearing the raven and . . . and Puerco, who is coming through stronger than ever, for some reason," she said. Perhaps because she'd been thinking about him. Her communication with Puerco had been spotty for days, but he seemed ridiculously loud at the moment, dominating Birdie's thoughts. "Maybe he could feel I was in danger and that's why he's so insistent right now."

"Shh," said Tenner. "The tunnel door is opening." He peered around the bushes to get a better look, then gasped. "Bird, you're not going to believe this."

"What?"

A car horn blared.

"Geez!" muttered Tenner. "They ran in front of a car!"

"Who?" Birdie jumped up and parted the bushes. "Holy expletive! It's Cabot and Brix! And . . ." She faltered. Could that possibly be Seven?

She and Tenner ran out of their hiding place toward them and confirmed it was definitely Seven wrapped up in the scarf.

And there was Puerco, bounding toward her—he *had* been the animal that had landed on her in the confusion. The pig squealed and jumped into Birdie's arms.

"Seven?" Birdie said, stumbling backward and trying to control the excited pig. "Brix, and Cabot! How . . . ? You nearly got crushed by a car—you have to watch out for them, both directions. What are you doing here? I'm so happy to see you!" Blown away that Seven was here, she ran to him for a hug. He held her for a moment, then stiffened and stepped back.

Birdie, confused, looked him over from hiking boots to scarf to Greta's glam sunglasses. "What's going on?"

"What's going on with *you*?" Cabot said coolly.

Birdie turned slowly to face her with a sense of dread. "What do you mean? How did you get here?"

"We came by land," Brix told his sister. "It took us four days."

"That's impossible," said Tenner, narrowing his eyes.

"And yet," said Cabot, folding her arms over her chest, "here we are."

"How did you find us?" Birdie asked, overwhelmed. Confused. Something was wrong, but she couldn't seem to get the right words out to question them.

"Puerco led us to you." Cabot leaned in to study Birdie's face. "Are you sorry we came?"

"No, I'm . . . I'm excited to see you! But why are you acting so . . . hostile?"

A young couple with their arms entwined walked past them,

oblivious to the children. Seven ducked behind a tree and started breathing hard while Cabot and Brix watched the couple curiously. Then an older woman rushed past as if she were in a hurry.

"Did you find your mother?" Cabot asked in a quieter voice.

"No," Birdie said. Her face fell. She'd failed in her mission. "But I still don't get what's happening. Seven, you said you'd never come here. What changed your mind?"

Seven peered from behind the tree. "We found the note."

Birdie blinked. "Note?"

"The one from Dad," Brix said.

"My . . . private, personal note?" Birdie's stomach twisted.

"The one you hid inside the encyclopedia," said Cabot. *"Dear Birdie,"* she recited. *"Now that the end of my life is approaching, I have a confession to make. Fifteen years ago, right before your mother and I and the other adults were forced to leave Estero, I moved our hidden stash . . . without telling anyone. I've created a map that leads to it. When you are of age and feeling especially brave, I want you to go to Estero, find your mother, and give her the map. Please be careful. I love you, and I'm sorry . . . about everything. Dad."*

It sounded . . . really bad. Birdie was furious they'd read her note, but she had no right to accuse them of that now. They'd read it and they'd traveled all this way, worried over it. She didn't know what to say. She smoothed her hair back, trying to find words. "I can explain everything."

"You should have explained before you left," said Cabot.

"It was a hard journey," Brix interjected. "We got attacked by a mountain lion, and I had to swim for two hours."

"Oh, Brixy," Birdie said, opening her arms to him. He seemed the least angry with her and slid into her embrace. "I know I should have, Cabot . . . but it was complicated. I hope you all know my mother would share the money with your parents, right? That she wouldn't keep it for herself. That was *never* the plan, I promise."

Cabot and Seven exchanged a cool glance. Then Cabot turned back to Birdie. "It was sneaky of your dad to move the stash without telling anyone. It seemed like you could be doing something sneaky, too, by not telling us you were delivering this map to your mom. Why didn't you say so? Did you keep it from Tenner, too?"

Tenner stepped in. "Birdie told me as soon as we got here. And she said she should have told you. But she knew it sounded suspicious, and she didn't want to raise doubts about it." He paused and realized Cabot was actually listening to him, so he kept going. "She didn't want to tarnish her father's memory, especially right after his death. And she promised me she wouldn't give the map to Elena unless she agreed to split everything." He lowered his voice as another couple walked by, and beckoned the kids a few steps away from the sidewalk, closer to the tree where Seven was hiding. "It doesn't matter anyway. We didn't find her. We've been everywhere. The guard at the prison said she's in government custody. And . . . we can't get to her."

Birdie nodded emphatically and shot Tenner a grateful look. "We've run out of ideas. We were planning on coming home in the morning."

"With the stash?" Cabot said accusingly.

"With the—no!" Birdie said, alarmed. "We didn't even look for it. We just want to go home and have everything be normal again." She shook her head, overwhelmed. There was way too much to explain standing out here in the park with late-night pedestrians walking by. And maybe even the watcher who'd chased them. "By the way, did you see what happened to that person that was following us?" Birdie asked.

"After you left the tunnel," said Brix, "the lights turned on and we saw a man in black clothes run the other way. We didn't see his face."

Birdie exchanged a glance with Tenner, then looked nervously at Brix and Seven. "We should go somewhere private," she murmured. "It doesn't feel safe to be out here."

DELIVERING NEWS

Seven stayed behind the tree. "That's actually the other reason we came, Birdie," he said. "We learned about a safe place we can hide. Your dad—he wrote directions to the entrance of the lower tunnels in his last journal entry."

"You read his journals, too?" Birdie exclaimed. Heat rose in her cheeks. "Isn't anything private anymore?"

Seven stepped toward her with his gloved hand out. "Listen. After what you did, we had to figure some things out. Besides, it was opened to that page and lying on the floor after Brix used a piece of paper to write the note to your mom."

"Oh," said Birdie, focusing on his sunglasses and wishing she could see his pupils. "Okay. Go on."

Seven dropped his hand and glanced around nervously. He lowered his voice even more. "Your dad wrote that the other criminals don't know about the lower tunnels. And we'd be safe down there."

Dad's first journal, which Birdie had brought with her, had given her details about the lower tunnels, but not the entrance location he'd found. This was important news—or it would have been if they'd decided to continue the search for Elena.

She faltered, curious about the tunnels but not seeing the point of exploring them if they were going home in the morning. And at this moment she was faint with hunger. She and Tenner had been away from their camp since morning and had trudged countless miles with only a few berries to eat. "I love that you discovered that, Seven," Birdie said carefully. "And that you came to give us that information. But Tenner and I haven't eaten all day. We can go to our safe place at the beach, catch fish, and cook out, like always. And then go home in the morning."

Cabot frowned. They would have to talk about that. But she and Brix and Seven were out of food too, and there wouldn't be anything to eat in an ancient tunnel. "If you think your beach spot is safe for Seven and Brix," she said, "I say we go there. It's been a long few days for us, too."

"Our camp is deserted at night," Tenner assured them. "Wait'll you see the toilet rooms."

Birdie and Cabot walked together, speaking quietly as they came to an understanding about Birdie's mistakes and intentions. Seven walked right behind them, then Tenner and Brix, who sandwiched Seven in, making him less noticeable from any street or pedestrian traffic. Brix bounced along, trying to look more like a goofy, excited kid than a supernatural one.

Soon Tenner and Birdie were showing them their little

beach campsite. While Birdie started the fire and showed the newcomers to the restrooms, Tenner caught enough fish to feed the hungry group. Then they gathered around and ate, almost like old times.

But now that they were all together and fed, Seven, Cabot, and Brix had some news to share before they went to sleep. And it wasn't the good kind.

Seven left his extra coverings off. His face and hands were divots of brown wet sand, and he wore foam from the shoreline like a snowy white cap. He turned toward Birdie and Tenner. "There's something important we need to tell you."

Birdie looked up quizzically at his serious tone. She had some things to tell them, too. "What is it?"

Cabot shifted, nodding slightly at Seven, and he continued. "We found two sets of human bones along the journey. One in the jungle. And one on the rocks along the bay."

"Bones?" said Tenner. He glanced at Birdie, and she reached out to touch his sleeve, her heart thudding. The waves whooshed gently behind them, and the fire popped and crackled.

Seven cleared his throat and continued. "The one on the rocks had a backpack next to it—one of our parents' backpacks. And . . . it had the missing thirteen diamonds hidden inside."

Birdie gasped.

Tenner's jaw slacked, and he felt the blood drain from his face. "My dad?"

"We don't know for sure," Seven said carefully.

"The bones indicated a tall person," said Cabot. "That could be your dad, or your mom, or Seven's dad, or my dad."

"But the backpack . . ." said Tenner, tight-lipped. All the sights, the sounds, the smells that pounded him every day went silent for a moment as the truth slapped him in the face. "I think we all know who stole the diamonds." He dropped his head as conflicting emotions battled in his mind and lungs. He huffed as something thick and harsh crept up his esophagus, threatening to choke him. Then a huge, ugly sob burst out.

Birdie leaned over to comfort him. "Oh, Tenner," she said. "I'm so sorry."

"I don't know why I'm crying," Tenner sobbed. He buried his face in his hands as his back shuddered. "I hate him!"

"But you didn't want him to die," Cabot said quietly. "It's okay."

Tenner cried for a while. The others went to hug him and help him through it and cry with him. After a while his tears ran out. He wiped his eyes and blew his nose with some toilet paper from the restroom. Then he looked at Cabot. "What about the other bones?"

Cabot's mouth slacked, and tears sprang to her eyes. "Oh, ah, yeah." She blew out a breath. "My best guess is that it's my mother."

A CHANGE OF PLANS

Tenner and Birdie exchanged an alarmed glance. A log shifted in the campfire, and a spray of embers whirled through the air and settled. "Cabot, no," Birdie said. "That can't be."

Cabot shut her eyes. "I appreciate you trying to be nice, but it makes sense. It's what I've always thought. And I'm dealing with it." She pinched the bridge of her nose.

"No," Tenner said quickly. "Birdie's right. It literally can't be, because your mom made it to Estero."

Cabot opened her eyes and stared a hole through him. "What?"

"There's a lot to tell you," Birdie said apologetically. "But your mom made it here. We have proof. She and your father were captured along with my mother three years ago."

"My father, too?" Cabot said softly. Her shiny eyes flickered, reflecting the flames. "They're both here? Are you sure?"

Birdie nodded. "I'm sure those bones you found aren't them," she clarified. "We don't know what happened since then."

Tenner was already digging into his backpack for the article. "Here." He handed Cabot the clipping with their parents' photos and explained the X'd-out faces. Cabot, hands trembling, squinted to read it by firelight while Seven and Brix leaned in to read bits and pieces, too.

After a moment, Cabot looked up. "Wow," she said, a dazed expression on her face. She handed the article back to Tenner. "I don't know what to think. I was sure . . . I was sure Mom was dead because I knew she would have figured out how to break out of jail and come home to me if she were alive."

"Maybe there were too many guards and police," Tenner said gently. "We've definitely seen our fair share of them, haven't we, Bird?" He smiled at her. They had a lot of stories to tell.

"More than our fair share," Birdie said, smiling back.

Brix yawned. "Can we go to sleep now and talk more in the morning?"

"Good idea," said Seven, standing up to stretch, then limping over to his backpack to get his blanket.

"I'm bushed, too," Birdie said. "Let's get some rest, and I'll make sure we're up early so we can decide what to do." She glanced at Cabot, wondering what the girl was thinking now that she knew her parents were here somewhere. Would she want to stay? If so, would they all stay?

But Cabot was silent, lost in her thoughts. Calculating every scenario. She would let the rest of them know what she was doing in the morning . . . and they could make their own choices from there.

They lay down in a row in the sand with their parachute blankets. Puerco plopped down near one end where Birdie put her parachute blanket, and soon he was snorting gently in his sleep. Once Birdie settled down next to Seven, she slung her arm over him and closed her eyes. "I missed you," she said.

Seven's eyes fluttered, then closed again. He'd missed her, too. He touched the back of her hand, and they fell asleep under the stars to the lull of soft, rolling waves.

Before sunrise, Birdie shook Tenner awake to catch breakfast. The city would be waking up soon, too, and they needed to decide if they were going to go home—and if so, how. Or if they should go to the lower tunnels and hide. The others soon woke to the delicious smell of fish roasting on the fire and heavy thoughts on their minds.

Seven swiftly adjusted his wrappings as the janitor appeared at the top of the beach and rolled his yellow bucket into the restroom to clean. The kids' moods ranged from tentative to mildly anxious. What were they going to do? As the sky brightened, they packed their backpacks—they for sure weren't staying here.

But as they gathered to eat and decide, a noise coming toward them down the walkway made Tenner look up sharply. "Uh-oh. Birdie, guess who?" The librarian was coming toward them with Lada, the teleporting girl, beside her.

Birdie turned and gasped, and the others whirled around, too. Seven dove behind the cypress tree. There was nowhere to go but in the sea.

"Birdie!" the librarian called. Her dress today was neon green with small white flowers. Lada wore a long-sleeve white shirt with cuffed blue shorts. "That's your name, isn't it?"

Birdie froze. "I . . ." She ran to her backpack and opened the main compartment. "I have your book. I'm sorry. Please don't call the police."

"What's happening?" Brix whispered. Cabot stared, trying to figure it out. Seven stayed behind the tree, trying not to hyperventilate.

"She knows we're supernatural," Tenner said under his breath to Cabot, Seven, and Brix. But he didn't know if that was a good or a bad thing.

The librarian's face was stern, but it looked like she was trying not to smile. "Thank you," she said, taking it and slipping it into a tote bag that hung from her shoulder. "The library appreciates it. That's not why we wanted to talk to you, though." She glanced at the ones she didn't know and spied Seven peering around the tree trunk with a scarf on his head. "Are there more of you? Or just the five?"

Birdie frowned. "We don't have to answer that."

Lada lifted her chin. "We know who you are," she said. "You're the children of the supernatural criminals, and we want to help you." She paused, seeing their shocked looks, which gave her the confirmation she was hoping for. When no one denied her assertion, she continued. "And, Birdie?"

"Yes?" Birdie said in a near whisper.

"I know where your mother is."

DREAM TEAM

Lada gazed at the sea of astonished and fearful expressions—and one scarf and glasses—and waited while they collected their wits. Now that she'd looked up the notorious criminals online, she'd seen that Birdie strongly resembled her mother. And the blond child with the buzz cut was unmistakably related to Jack Stone. The one with the scarf, hiding in the shadows? It seemed possible that he'd be the product of the invisible one. But she was unsure about the bouncing one and the boy with the unusual eyes.

Birdie found her voice first. "You know where my mother is? Tell me—where is she?"

"Where is she?" Brix echoed, bouncing up to Birdie's side.

Lada's crutches dangled from her forearms. Her body was stiff, but her legs moved continuously and her knees bumped each other. She seemed focused on balancing. Still, she didn't put her crutches down. "She's being held captive in the president's palace dungeon. She's been there for three years."

Cabot shoved forward between Brix and Birdie. "Is anyone else down there with her?"

Lada's lips parted at the earnest look on her face. "Unfortunately, no."

Cabot's expression flickered, then she dropped her gaze. She wanted to ask if Lada knew Greta and Jack Stone. If she'd seen them or knew where they were. But these were complete strangers. How was she supposed to trust them? She held back . . . for now.

The group started talking at once until the librarian raised her hand to quiet them. "One at a time, and keep your voices down," she said. "We don't want the janitor paying attention to us."

"How do I get my mother out of there?" Birdie asked. After the long, emotional day yesterday, she'd been about to give up. She held on to Brix's shoulders, and her heart pounded. They knew where Mom was!

"Yes—tell us, *please*," said Tenner. Seven stayed behind the tree.

Lada glanced over her shoulder at the librarian, then returned to face forward. "If we all work together, we may have the chance to get her out tonight," she told them in a low voice. "The president will be traveling this evening. He'll be gone for hours."

Tenner was puzzled. "You mean we should take a palace tour and slip away from the group?"

"Mm, not exactly," Lada said. She turned again to the librarian, who pulled a long tube of rolled-up blue-and-white paper out of the bag on her shoulder. "Does anyone know how to read architectural blueprints?"

Cabot's eyes widened. Silently she reached for the roll.

"Oh." Seven cleared his throat. He swallowed hard, then slowly stepped out from behind the tree. "I get it." He nodded as Birdie turned to look at him. "She means we're breaking in."

"Breaking in?" said Brix in a loud whisper. "To the *palace*? He didn't even know what a palace looked like, but it sounded big.

"That's right," Lada said.

"Whoa," said Cabot. She peeked at the blueprints, anxious to study them.

"We've got all day to plan, before the palace staff retires for the evening. Long enough to learn what all of you can do. There's no time to waste—the president's people already know two of you are in town."

"They do?" Birdie said. Fear filled her chest.

"Men in suits have been tailing you," said the librarian. "Lada and I have, too. We need to make our move before the president's goons make theirs—and their move is to take you out before you cause any trouble. So . . . that means now."

Phrases like "take you out" weren't exactly what the five hideaway children were used to hearing about themselves. It was unsettling to know Birdie and Tenner had been followed. Maybe the tunnel watcher wasn't a tunnel watcher after all.

The librarian's black car, parked along the street outside the taco shop, had room for Lada and the three who hadn't had the experience of riding in one before. It would be safer for Seven and Brix to travel that way, too. Birdie was more than happy to walk, since she'd just eaten and she wanted a moment to check in with Tenner alone. The other three climbed in and examined the seat belts and window controls. Cabot leaned forward and studied the steering wheel and control panel, and dipped her head to see the pedals on the floor. Their faces were pressed against the windows as the librarian took off.

"We're going to find my mother!" Birdie exclaimed as she and Tenner walked the familiar route into the city. A thrill rose up inside her, and she gave herself a delighted hug. "I can't believe it. Imagine if we'd left before the librarian and Lada found us."

"I'm really excited to see her," Tenner said, shifting his backpack straps, but his energy seemed lower than usual. "It's great to finally know where she is after all we've been through."

Birdie thought he was probably thinking about Troy. "Did you get any sleep?"

"A little," he said, and flashed a melancholy smile.

"I wish things didn't have to be this hard." Birdie reached around and patted his backpack awkwardly, as if it were part of his body, which made the two tired kids laugh and exchange a side hug instead.

"It's going to take some getting used to," Tenner said. "I spent a long time staying out of Troy's way, and now I don't have to worry about that anymore. You'd think I'd be thrilled, but my heart feels . . . twisty."

Birdie nodded. "Tell me if you want to talk about it. Anytime." She didn't throw any pitying glances his way.

Birdie kept an eye out all around for men in black suits, like the librarian had warned her to do. But it was still early, and the streets and pedestrian traffic were barely starting to pick up, mostly with joggers and dog walkers. They made it to the library without incident.

The librarian met them out front and led them to an entrance at the back of the building, which had cement stairs leading down and ending at a solid metal door. Soon they found themselves inside the basement of the library. It was a big office with no windows and books piled everywhere. A large coffee mug sat on a desk next to a computer. Seven, Brix, and Cabot waited near the desk, looking around, while Lada cleared books from a long rectangular table nearby. Cabot gripped the roll of blueprints while she paged through a book on the top of a stack, then moved over to examine the computer.

"How was your car ride?" Birdie asked as she let Puerco out to sniff around.

"Amazing," Seven said. "A lot smoother than I thought it would be."

"It was *fast*," Brix said, and Cabot nodded, though she seemed more excited about the computer.

"I have a lot of questions for you," Lada said with a pleasant laugh. On the short ride over, they'd explained that they'd never been in a car before, which was hard to imagine. Now she couldn't stop taking them in—their clothing, their hairstyles, their wonderment at seeing the city. Lada wanted to know more, like where they'd been all these years. It was blowing her mind to finally be meeting other kids like her. But they had more important things to attend to first. Hopefully there would be time to chat later.

Tenner grinned and looked at Birdie to see if she wanted to tell the story of *their* ride, but Birdie had turned to the librarian for further instructions.

The librarian went to the desk and sat down. She started typing at the computer. Cabot leaned over her shoulder. She was drawn to the woman—was it the super-short hair that made her feel like they had something in common? Or the mystery of the computer that intrigued her? Or knowing she worked with books that made her feel safe? Her eyes moved from the librarian's fingers to the screen, trying to figure out how it worked.

Lada called the five over to the table she'd cleared. Cabot reluctantly left the librarian and brought the blueprints with her. At Lada's request, she spread them out, quickly identifying each floor of the palace and putting the pages in order.

"The librarian is working today," Lada said. "Down here for a while, then upstairs with the patrons. So I'll be talking you through everything. Any questions before I start getting your info?"

"Have you been inside the palace?" Cabot asked Lada.

"Only on the tour," Lada said. She pulled a chair out and sat down, setting her crutches on the floor beside her. Her wheelchair was folded and leaning against the wall nearby. "I've taken it a few times, but the guides don't show you the dungeon or the servants' quarters or even all the relics the president has been hoarding."

"Hoarding?" asked Tenner. He and Birdie pulled up bucket chairs across from Cabot and Lada, staying a few feet back from the table so Cabot could move around it if she needed to. "How does he get to do that?"

"He says he's keeping them safe." Lada rolled her eyes.

"How do you know our mother is in the dungeon?" Brix asked.

"We have connections," the librarian said from the desk. She stopped typing and turned to face them. "What you don't know, you can't tell. We'll leave it at that for now."

"What does that mean?" Brix asked.

"It means if you get captured," said Seven, sitting on the corner of a different table and leaving all his gear on, "you can't give away the name of the person who helped you because you don't know what it is."

Lada glanced at Seven and nodded, trying not to study his unusual garb too closely. She knew what it was like to be stared at. "That's right."

As Cabot memorized the blueprints, Lada pulled out a cell phone and held it loosely above the table. "You've all met The Librarian. That is her preferred name. Her ability is to make people near her forget their recent memories. Somewhere along the way, she also picked up the ability to silence nonhuman-generated noises, like fire alarms, door alarms, drone buzzing, and stuff like that. It's something to do with a similar frequency level to the memory thing—I don't know."

"More of a trick to impress people than anything else," The Librarian said from her desk. "But that's why no one came running after you at the library." She glanced smugly at Birdie.

"What is she referring to?" Seven asked.

"That book I stole," Birdie mumbled. "We set off the library's alarm." The others reacted with surprise, but Lada moved swiftly to taking notes on their abilities. She lifted her phone and touched the screen with her thumb. The five all leaned closer, trying to get a glimpse of what she was doing—even Cabot took a moment to examine it. The phone screen turned yellow and had several horizontal stripes going all the way down, like a piece of journal paper. A picture of a keyboard slid up. She typed the letters *B-r-i* and then halted and looked at the youngest. "You said Brix with an *x*, right?"

"Yup."

"Okay. And what's your supernatural ability? Something to do with bouncing, I know. Can you describe everything to me?"

Brix took a bouncy step back, jumped, and twisted in the air. "I can climb, run fast, and heal quickly if I get hurt. And jump from high places. If I fall, I bounce and get back up." He jumped up on the table, shaking it, and hopped down, showing her the way he landed.

"Wow," said Lada. "That's handy." She typed on her phone for a moment, then turned to Birdie. "How about you?"

"I—first, how did you know my name earlier?" said Birdie. "Did Tenner say it at the library?"

"You typed it into the computer username box," The Librarian said without looking up from her computer.

"Ooh," said Birdie. She glanced at the back of The Librarian's close-cropped head. The woman was slightly intimidating with her occasional participation in the conversation.

The Librarian picked up her phone and started punching it with her thumbs.

Birdie turned back to Lada. "I can communicate with many different animals," she said. "Ravens, octopuses, pigs. And Puerco, my pig, is very well trained and can follow commands." She reached down and scratched the pig behind the ears. "I've also ridden on whales and dolphins."

"That's how Birdie and I got here," Tenner explained. Then added, "Not all at the same time. They went in shifts. First the gray whale, then the dolphins, and then the orca."

Lada's jaw slacked, and she stopped typing. "That's how

you . . ." She shook her head and wrote that down. Then her gaze returned to Birdie. "We saw you interact with a raven yesterday. Do you think it will do what you ask it to?"

"It showed us the way to the library," Birdie said, "so I suppose so."

"Okay, great." She finished up her notes, then scanned the room and landed on Tenner. "You're next."

"I've got heightened senses, and I can hold my breath for, like, a half hour." He pointed to his eyes. Then he added almost apologetically, "And I've got extra-large pupils. For seeing in the dark and long distances. You probably can't tell."

"Impressive," said Lada, leaning forward and checking them out up close. "Are they actually activated right now?"

"They're *always* activated," Tenner said, pleased to be asked. "See how they're slightly oval?"

"Yes, The Librarian told me she noticed that the other day," said Lada.

"She did?" Tenner sat up and flashed Birdie a triumphant look. "She noticed my eyes?"

"For sure." Lada finished her notes, then turned to Seven like she wasn't quite sure what to say. "So . . . Seven. Do you want to take that scarf off? It's pretty warm down here. And you're in a safe place."

Seven swallowed hard. "I mean . . ."

Birdie hopped out of her chair and went over to stand nearby for support. "You don't have to."

"No, she's right. I'm roasting." Seven reached up, removed his sunglasses, and set them on the table. Then he slowly unwound the scarf to uncover his face. "I'm a camo boy," he said, his voice cracking.

"Camouflage," said Lada, her face lighting up. "That's perfect." She smiled encouragingly and tried not to stare at the way his face blended with the stacks of books behind him. "Such a great ability. You can be anywhere in the world and be safe." She sighed. "Does it feel nice not to have that worry?"

Seven blinked. "I haven't experienced that," he said lightly. "But where we came from, I didn't have to think about it much."

"Oh." Lada bit her lip. Bits and pieces of their past were trickling in and starting to build a backstory, but she knew there had to be more. "Would you mind moving from side to side?"

Seven teetered on the table a few times.

"I can't even detect an outline," Lada said. "Wow." She glanced at The Librarian, but the woman was talking on the phone. "I feel like we've hit the jackpot." She turned to Cabot, who was poring over the final page of the blueprints—the dungeon prison area—then faced the others again. "I don't want to interrupt Cabot," she said in a low voice. "What is her ability?"

Cabot looked up sharply before anyone could answer for her. "I don't have one," she said, trying to sound like she didn't care. "I'm just smart." She turned back to the pages as a slight tension filled the room.

"Well then," said Lada, smoothing her sleeves and picking a

piece of lint off her shoulder. "It's down to me. When my ability to teleport developed at age ten, my caretakers at Sunrise didn't know what to do. They aren't allowed to accept supernatural people anymore, and a bunch of the ones who were there when Fuerte changed the rule got banished. But I was young then—I don't remember it. At least they didn't banish me," she said with a laugh that sounded hollow. Her laughter died, and she let her phone fall into her lap. "They'd probably like to now, though. Anyway, I can teleport short distances—sometimes when I don't mean to, which is an adventure. It drives the headmaster bananas." The five laughed. They'd heard the funny-sounding word *banana* before, even if they'd never eaten one. Lada grinned, and it seemed real this time. "I've been the lone supernatural kid in Estero all this time, as far as I know. Everyone else is either gone or in hiding. But then you showed up. With our combined abilities, I think we make a pretty competent team. A dream team, really," she said with a hitch in her voice. "You have no idea how much it means to me to have you here."

CATCHING UP

For lunch, The Librarian used her computer to order food to be delivered, a concept that seemed impossible to Seven and Brix. Cabot didn't weigh in—she was playing with Lada's cell phone and learning the keyboard.

Tenner and Birdie could imagine food delivery after their experiences. If servers could bring it to your table, couldn't they go a little farther?

Soon the children were eating pizza for the first time. Puerco squeezed in next to Birdie to sniff the new food, then reared back and snorted, as if the smell offended him.

"It's probably the sausage," Lada said. "It's . . . you know." She glanced sideways at the pig.

Birdie's eyes widened as she studied her slice. She picked off the sausage pieces and lined them up inside the pizza box. That left mushroom slices, which all the kids were familiar with. She dug in. The flavors made her taste buds explode. "So chewy," she said, taking another bite. "What's this called?"

"Pizza!" said Lada. Her smile was huge, and her warm laugh filled the room. "This is hilarious," she told them.

"Maybe they would like to try some chocolate," The Librarian said.

"Have you ever tasted chocolate?" Lada asked.

The five kids shook their heads. "Not that we know of," Birdie added. It was fun to watch Lada act delighted by such little things. Lada fetched five individually wrapped pieces from a jar on The Librarian's desk and passed them out, then watched with glee as the kids' faces lit up.

"This is pretty tasty," Seven admitted.

"It makes my face ache in a good way," Cabot said.

After lunch, Birdie and Tenner shared the story of what happened at the restaurant with the old money, their eventful ride to the police station, and their time spent roaming the city.

"That reminds me," Tenner said. "We got Cabot a gift." They'd actually gotten everyone a gift—the mini pencils. But they weren't about to admit that to The Librarian, so Birdie left those at the bottom of her backpack.

Cabot looked up from Lada's cell phone. "You got something for *me*?" She set down the phone gently on the table. Her pink lips parted in surprise as Tenner pulled out one of the vomit bags and the blood pressure cuff. He slid them across the table. "We got them from the hospital where your mom worked."

Cabot's expression softened. "Thank you," she said, examining them. "What are they?"

"You lifted a blood pressure cuff from the hospital?" Lada asked. Her expression switched between horror and admiration.

Tenner's face burned. "I feel a little bit bad about it," he said quietly. "I probably should have stuck with just the vomit bag."

"I asked an emergency room nurse if she knew Greta Stone," Birdie said, then shook her head. "She didn't."

"That was nice of you to ask," Cabot said. She turned to Lada, feeling more and more trusting of these strangers now. "You don't happen to know where my parents are, do you? Jack and Greta Stone? The newspaper said they were captured with Elena."

"Uh . . ." Lada averted her eyes. "Librarian?"

The Librarian swiveled around in her chair. "Right." She crossed her legs and leaned forward. "Cabot, I'm afraid your parents are working with the president."

Cabot's face paled. "What?"

"They stayed in the palace dungeon for a few days with Elena, but then they gave in to the president's offer. Elena refused . . . and continues to refuse."

Two spots of pink returned to Cabot's cheeks. She stood abruptly, upsetting her chair. "That's . . . impossible. They wouldn't do that."

The Librarian dropped her chin, and her stern face softened. "I'm sorry, Cabot. But that's exactly what they're doing."

The silent group watched The Librarian.

"The good news," said the woman, sitting up, "is that if we

are successful tonight in breaking Elena out of there, she might have more information on what's going on with these international heists. That would help us."

Cabot gripped the table edge in shock. Her parents were working with the president? The guy who hated them? What had happened to make them do such a thing?

Seven went to set Cabot's chair upright and give the girl some support. "What's this deal you're talking about?"

Cabot sank down and covered her face with her hands.

"I'll explain what I know," said The Librarian. Her cell phone rang, and she glanced at it, then put a finger in the air while she answered it. "What did you come up with?" she said softly. She listened for a long moment. "Eleven o'clock. Ten for the pickup. Got it." She swiped the screen and set the phone down, then continued as if nothing had happened.

"What we've figured out so far," she continued smoothly, "is that several of your parents returned to the area three years ago. Three were captured: Elena, Jack, and Greta. Others have been sighted around Estero—we strongly suspect Martim is here, working in partnership with the president."

"Intentionally?" asked Birdie. Sure, they'd been seen together in the airline hangar, but to imagine the supernaturals willingly working with the president seemed impossible.

"But the president hates supernatural people," Seven said. He folded his arms over his chest, unsurprised to hear his dad was involved. "Or at least he used to."

"He changed the whole currency because of them," Tenner added.

"True. But when they returned, he took an unusual step that the general public still knows nothing about. Instead of trying to run them out again, he came to them with a deal. And now they are making late-night trips to other countries and stealing their precious artifacts. And who knows what else."

Cabot lifted her head. "If the general public doesn't know about it, how do you?"

"Sources," The Librarian said. She shrugged. The children were starting to realize that The Librarian had a lot of secrets.

"So they are the ones doing the heists in other countries?" Birdie asked. "The news article we read said supernatural people from those other countries were doing it." She quickly told the others about the article Tenner had found about heists happening around the continent. And how President Fuerte vowed to help stop supernatural criminals worldwide.

"Yeah," Tenner chimed in. "Are you saying that the president's late-night trips aren't only to meet with other world leaders to discuss how to stop the heists?"

"I'm glad you're at least reading the articles you ripped out of my newspapers," The Librarian said. "I'm saying President Fuerte is *responsible* for the heists—at least partially. And things are ramping up."

Birdie and Tenner exchanged a glance as Seven, Cabot, and Brix absorbed the information.

"We're hoping Elena will know more," Lada said to Birdie and Brix. "What the president and your other parents are doing here and elsewhere . . . well, it's putting *us* in even more danger. The thefts could affect the stability of other countries as well as Estero, and that will make nonsupernatural people hate us even more."

Tenner ran his hands over his tangled hair, then brought it together at the back of his neck, but he had nothing to tie it with. He was surprised by how little guilt he felt on behalf of his parents. If Troy were alive, he'd certainly be working to steal from anyone he could. But he was dead. Which gave Tenner a sense of relief. Then again, his mom, Lucy, could be playing a huge role. But he felt detached from her . . . Maybe it was the numbness of the shocking news about Troy that had him not feeling guilty for once.

The Librarian was called to work upstairs, so throughout the afternoon and into the evening, Lada and the five went over the plan. Lada met with each of the five individually to discuss their roles in the rescue. She spent an extra-long time with Seven. Some of them dozed, since they would be up late and hadn't slept well for days.

Lada pulled up instructional videos on the computer to teach them how to make defensive and offensive moves, in case they had to fight. "Now, this is interesting," Birdie said, watching the screen.

"No giant-headed people," Tenner said. The others watched

wide-eyed, firing questions at Lada about how the videos were made and how it was possible to see them like this. "Do you know these people?" Brix asked. They'd never seen a video before, only snapshots and pictures in books.

Lada directed Brix to practice bouncing off tables and chairs so he could get used to moving inside, with a ceiling and walls, and using those things to his advantage, versus outdoors, where he'd had free rein and wide-open spaces.

Tenner and Seven shared more about their lives with Lada while Birdie went outside with Puerco to locate her raven friend and communicate with the two of them about what would be happening soon.

When the library closed, The Librarian returned to the basement office.

"Meet me on the street out front at ten forty-five p.m.," she told them. Then she disappeared into the night.

At the appointed time, the six children plus Puerco were piled in the back of a giant, bulletproof SUV, with The Librarian at the wheel and the front passenger seat empty except for a few supplies. Seven loaded Lada's wheelchair in the back. The raven didn't want to enter the vehicle, and Birdie didn't blame it. If she could have walked, she would have.

"We're going to get my mom!" Brix said from the middle of the rear seat. The others erupted in excitement.

Seven ruffled Brix's hair. "This is going to be great, Brixy," he murmured, pulling the younger boy in for a hug. He knew this break-in would be hard, but the prize was huge. What would it be like to have Elena back? Would they all return to the hideout together? They'd have to get the stash first . . . and figure all of that out. Knowing Martim was working for the president, Seven didn't exactly want his dad getting any part of it. But what about Cabot's parents? They were worth finding and talking to. He shifted uncomfortably. How long would he wear this scarf on his face?

After they started moving, Tenner opened his backpack and pulled out the other vomit bag. He handed it to Birdie. "In case we have another incident." Birdie's face was already turning green, despite The Librarian's careful driving, and she took the bag without comment and slumped against the car window. She tried to focus on staying in touch with the raven to keep her mind off the impending gurgles.

"Let's focus on the task," said The Librarian. She drummed her fingers on the steering wheel, showing her first signs of nerves. "Lada?" Without taking her eyes off the road, she picked up a small box off the seat and handed it back to the girl. "I've got my earpiece already."

"Thank you," said Lada, taking it. Then she opened it and handed out identical small containers with hinged lids. As she did so, she continued talking. "The Librarian will get us inside the gate and to the parking entrance on the back side of the palace. You with me on that location, blueprint girl?"

Cabot was messing with her seat belt shoulder strap, pulling slowly, then yanking it. She let go and accepted her container. "I'm with you. Parking garage entrance. Built in 1958. Most recent addition to the structure." She opened the hinged lid and peered inside.

"Good. You'll stay in the vehicle with The Librarian until we need you. Everyone, we'll communicate with these devices. Have a look, put it in your ear, and flip the tiny switch to turn it on. There's a microphone attached. Let's do a test."

The kids were mystified by the terminology but did what they were told. Soon they were testing out the microphone and hearing others in their ears. Tenner didn't need his for hearing, but he'd want it for speaking so others could hear him.

Once they had that figured out, Lada continued. "I'll teleport to inside the palace and let the rest of you in. Then the raven and Tenner can go ahead as lookouts, and the rest of the plan gets enacted as we went over." She glanced at Birdie, who was hanging on to the armrest and clutching her vomit bag. "Are you okay?"

Birdie gave a weak thumbs-up, and Lada continued. "The staff should all be in their sleeping quarters for the night, since the president is gone. We'll sneak in with Cabot guiding us and head down to the dungeon . . . which is nothing like what you've read in fairy tales. It's more like a science lab, I'm told. There's a guard down there. He's got the keys to the jail cell." She took a deep breath and blew it out. "I'm nervous."

Tenner noticed her hands shaking. "We've got this," he said. "One guard? How hard can it be?"

"Hopefully your mom can still fight," Lada said.

"Still?" said Brix. "My mom can fight?"

Birdie groaned from her spot by the window as The Librarian turned the vehicle into the long palace driveway.

"Everybody unbuckle and get down on the floor," The Librarian said over her shoulder. "We're approaching the guard station. Don't make a sound."

Birdie's stomach sloshed and gurgled as she moved. She looked up in a panic and saw Tenner. "It's happening," she mouthed.

As they pulled up to the guard window, Birdie pressed the bag to her face, trying to hold in the vomit. But it wouldn't stay down. As The Librarian showed her credentials to the guard, Tenner threw his body over Birdie to help muffle the retching sound, and Birdie threw up as quietly as she could.

BREAKING IN

uckily the guard didn't hear her. Birdie swiftly twisted the vomit bag closed, and everyone else politely pretended not to have noticed. Soon, a gate opened and they were pulling around the west wing of the palace, into the parking garage beneath. Birdie sat up, feeling a lot better.

"The palace was originally built without the east and west wings," Cabot whispered from the floor of the backseat, in case anyone else was interested. "Those were added a hundred and fifty years ago. Then they dug under the west wing for the parking garage. There's room for twelve vehicles down here."

"Who needs twelve vehicles?" Brix asked, incredulous. If he lived here, he wouldn't want any . . . though they *were* convenient for getting places fast. But if they made Birdie lose her lunch, was it worth it? His body buzzed with excitement as he looked around. Mom was so close!

The gate slid closed behind them, and The Librarian parked the vehicle. "Earpieces in and turned on," she instructed. "You all know your stations. Lada, I'm proud of you. Let's do this."

Lada made her way slowly out of the vehicle, and Seven handed the girl her crutches.

"Head to that door in one minute," Lada told them, pointing to it. "I'm going in." Then she and her crutches disappeared.

Birdie glanced at Seven, trying to find his eyes. "You holding up okay?" she murmured.

"I think I'm in shock," Seven said. "You?" He indicated the vomit bag.

"Fine now," said Birdie. "I'll find a place to toss this inside."

"No," said The Librarian. "DNA. Give it to me."

"Oh." Bewildered, Birdie handed her the closed bag of vomit.

"Time for you four to move," The Librarian said. She touched her earpiece, listening, and the others did the same.

"I'm in. Heading for the door. The alarm light is blinking red, so there will be a noise when I open the door," whispered Lada.

"I'll take care of it," The Librarian said. "Stay on plan."

Birdie with the raven, Tenner, Brix, and Seven piled out of the SUV and moved swiftly between empty vehicles toward the door. Puerco stretched and put his front hooves on the window of the backseat, trying to see where Birdie was going and letting out a squeal.

"Come 'ere, pig," Cabot said, and slid over to comfort Puerco and keep him quiet.

There was barely a blip of an alarm before the noise was silenced, and soon Lada was waving them inside.

Cabot closed her eyes to focus on the blueprints. She guided them using her microphone to the correct staircase. "Two huge rooms to get through," she said softly. "Kitchen first, then dining room." She couldn't imagine having a home this enormous. Two of their cabins back home would fit inside the palace's vast dining room. The president must have a big family or a lot of friends. How many fish would it take to feed all the people that could fit in that space?

Birdie sent the raven ahead to warn them of any servants or guards wandering around. They crept through the palace's enormous kitchen, around a long countertop and past a glass cabinet, and through double doors into the lavish dining room. The table had twenty chairs around it and huge vases of flowers down the middle. Brix's jaw dropped, but Birdie kept reminding him to stay quiet.

Lada led them past tall pillars and extravagant tapestries, two enormous sideboards, and a glass case holding dishes. They exited through another set of double doors into a hall.

The raven came flying back, warning Birdie of a creature coming toward them.

"Something nonhuman is coming," Birdie whispered.

"I can hear a jangling sound, like a chain," Tenner reported.

"It's probably one of the Rottweilers," Lada said. "Birdie, tell it to go lie down."

Birdie didn't know what a Rottweiler was, but she sent it a message, hoping it was communicative. It sent a warm greeting in return, and Birdie told it to lie down.

"Sorry—I forgot to tell you about them," Lada whispered. "I don't think they'll bite, especially if they vibe with Birdie."

Brix and Seven looked at one another. "Bite?" Seven whispered. He didn't need another animal bite.

After a moment, Tenner reported that the jangling had quieted, then stopped. Lada let out a relieved breath.

"Once you're through the dining room," Cabot whispered through their earpieces, "look for the grand hall, but don't go down it. The door you need will be off to one side."

They continued as instructed, seeing huge glass cases down the grand hall, something like the museum might have. Lada reported their location, and Cabot guided them to the door that led to the dungeon. Birdie tried it—pushing *and* pulling—and found it locked. Lada pulled a sharp metal file from a slot in one of her elbow crutches.

"Whoa, cool," Birdie said, eyeing the crutches to see if there were any other features like that built in.

"The Librarian spent a whole paycheck upgrading my crutches and adding special features," Lada whispered. "They've got all kinds of tools built in. She's stern sometimes, but she's the best." She slipped the file into the lock.

"You know I can hear you, right?" The Librarian said from the SUV.

Everyone snickered as Lada wriggled the file patiently, then twisted. They heard a click. Lada pulled out the file, then nodded to Birdie to try the handle again. The door opened.

Lada replaced the file and started down the stairs. Tenner stationed himself at the top of the stairs as lookout while the rest went down halfway to get a look at the place. There were lab stations and desks and exercise machines, and screens attached to the ceiling showing different rooms, whether in this palace or somewhere else, they weren't sure.

They couldn't see Elena from their location, but the guard had his back to them at one of the desks. Birdie's pulse pounded. Her mom was down here somewhere.

Birdie sent the raven to the bottom to assess the guard situation. After a minute she reported, "Two humans down there." She gulped.

"The guard and your mom," Lada whispered. "Good. That's what we expected."

Lada touched Brix's shoulder. "Wait here until Seven makes it to the cell door. Then rush in and distract the guard, draw him away from the cell if you can, and rip the key card from around his neck. Toss it to the cell area, and Seven will get it. Remember what I told you—stay low or bounce high. Knock him off balance. Use the walls. Kick him . . . wherever it'll hurt."

It sounded frightening. But Brix would do anything to free his mom. He nodded.

Then Lada turned to Seven. "You ready?"

Seven shook his head. "I'll never be ready for this," he whispered. He started unbuttoning his shirt.

"Give him some privacy," Birdie ordered, turning her back.

The others did, too. Birdie could hear Seven's breath coming in short bursts. "You've got this, Seven," she whispered.

Seven was sweating . . . then chilled. Even though the others couldn't see anything, it meant a lot to him that they turned around. He dropped his clothes on the stairs. "Here goes nothing," he said. "Descending." Lada turned back to watch his progress, but she couldn't detect his movements. Once in a while she caught sight of his earpiece moving through the air when he turned the right way. They waited, eyes on the guard to see if he noticed anything. The guard didn't move.

"I . . ." Seven whispered, and then he choked up. "I see her. She's asleep. Twenty paces to the cell."

Birdie sucked in a breath. Her eyes pricked with tears. When Seven whispered that he'd reached the cell, Birdie touched Brix's shoulder. The boy leaped down the stairs and over to the guard, whose back was still to him as he typed on a computer. As the guard turned at the sound, Brix grabbed the lanyard from the man's neck and bounced up to pull it free.

"Hey!" the guard yelled, swiping around his head. He jumped out of his chair, sending it crashing to the floor.

The noise roused Elena Golden from her cot. She moved swiftly to the bars to see what was happening, and gasped.

Brix saw his mom and waved excitedly, but she seemed bewildered. He hopped up onto the guard's desk and bounded quickly across desktops toward the cell with the guard in hot pursuit. Brix tossed the key card in the direction of Seven. Then he rushed past the guard the other way, grabbing the man's cap as he went. Lada directed the boys from the steps and got ready to make her move.

Seven picked up the key card. He stared at the strange lock, unsure where to insert it.

"Slide it down into the slot," Lada directed, "then pull it out gently."

Seven slid the card in the cell door, then yanked it out. But it didn't open. "It's still locked!" Seven said, panic in his voice.

"Try again," Lada directed. "Slower. Tell Elena you're there so she knows what we need her to do."

"Elena," Seven said, "it's Seven Palacio right outside the door. I'm camouflaged. We're here to get you out. Why won't this key work?"

"Seven!" Elena whispered, moving toward his voice. "Is that . . . Brix?" She sounded flustered, then stared at the boy who was being chased by the guard. Brix was much bigger than when she'd last seen him, and bouncing around like he had springs on his feet.

"Yes," said Seven. "We're all here. Do you understand this lock?"

"It needs the guard's thumbprint," she said, trying to stay quiet. "You'll have to take the guard down and press his thumb to the pad when you use the key."

"Yikes," Lada said. She and Birdie exchanged a glance. "Bring in the backup," Lada said. "Let's go." She disappeared and teleported to the top of a lab table near Brix.

Birdie ran down the stairs. She closed her eyes to concentrate, commanding all the animals who could hear her to come down to the dungeon and attack the guard. "Tenner, make way!" she said in her earpiece.

As the thunder of galloping Rottweilers was heard overhead and the raven swooped in and jetted for the guard, Birdie whispered into her earpiece, "Send in the pig."

MAN VS. BEAST

The Librarian, Cabot, and Puerco abandoned the vehicle and slipped inside. Cabot set the pig on the floor.

"Staff on the move!" Tenner yelped into his microphone. He could hear beds creaking and feet hitting the floor in various rooms nearby, and three Rottweilers pounding through the palace from different directions.

Puerco shot through the kitchen and dining room and came squealing around the corner, knocking over a precious vase with a loud crash. Tenner opened the door wide and flattened himself against the wall to get out of the way, and the dogs and pig barreled down the stairs to the dungeon. All of them headed for the guard, who was trying to get Brix off his back.

Brix, covering the guard's eyes, heard the animal army coming down the stairs. He leaped to a workstation, drawing the guard farther away from the cell, closer to Lada stationed on a table, and keeping him turned so he wouldn't see the animals coming. He danced and hopped from one spot to the next, staying out of reach as he kicked over computers and sent lab machines crashing to the ground. The man ran. Lada, with lips pursed as she focused on balancing, stuck out one of her crutches and caught him in the chest, knocking him backward. The force of the impact knocked Lada backward, and she went down to her butt on the table. The crutch went flying.

The raven dive-bombed. The guard shrieked. Birdie lunged at the man from behind, punching the backs of his knees like in the video, then grabbed him around the ankles to trip him. The dogs knocked him down, and Puerco jumped at the man's face, kicking his glasses off and sending them skidding under a desk.

"Go down and help the others," The Librarian said to Tenner and Cabot. "I'll handle the staff." Tenner and Cabot went downstairs as employees emerged from their rooms to see what was making the ruckus. As each one came out, The Librarian cleared their recent memories and used her suggestive powers to convince them to return to bed.

By the time Cabot and Tenner reached the dungeon lab, the place had been destroyed. Lada rolled to her stomach on the desk, wincing with butt pain. Setting her remaining crutch aside, she slid carefully off the edge until her feet reached the floor, then used that crutch to get the one that had gone flying. Her limp was tentative, as if she was testing her balance after falling. She gritted her teeth and willed her body forward to collect it, then moved as quickly as she could toward the cell.

Birdie took possession of the guard's phone and radio equipment, then took a ring of keys from his belt, too. The guard lay on the floor unconscious and surrounded by growling, squealing, cawing animals. Tenner, who'd heard all about how they needed the guard's thumbprint, rushed over to help Brix. Seven, invisible, joined them, and helped drag him to the cell.

"Holy coconuts," Cabot muttered from the bottom step. "What happened down here?"

"Lada clotheslined him," Birdie said, running up to her. "The animals attacked. I knocked him down. He hit his head on the floor and zonked out." She whirled around to see the cell. "Mom!" she cried. She ran to the bars and reached in, taking her mother's hands. "We're going to get you out of here."

"Birdie! I'm . . ." Elena gazed at her daughter, tears streaming down her face. "I can't believe you're all here."

"Coming through, Birdie!" Tenner said as he, Seven, and Brix brought the man to the cell and sat him up against the bars, next to the lock. Birdie let go and backed away from the bars as Lada reached them.

"Hurry, before he wakes up," Seven said. "How do we do this?"

Lada instructed Brix to press the man's thumb against the pad while Seven put the key card in and removed it slowly. After a couple of tries, Seven finally mastered the smooth key card slide. Finally the lock blinked green and the door slid open.

"Mom!" Birdie cried again, and ran in to embrace her. Brix followed and jumped into his mother's arms, making her stagger backward with a joyous laugh. "We did it!"

Elena Golden hugged and kissed her children. "How did you find me?" Her voice broke. Birdie hauled Brix off Elena and guided them out of the cell.

"It's a long story," Brix said.

"We have to get out of here," Lada said as gently as she could while urging them toward the stairs. She felt bad that she had to break up the reunion, but they weren't safe yet. "Let's take this to the SUV."

Tenner and Seven dragged the guard inside the cell, then slid the door closed until the lock clicked. Tenner pocketed the key card so the guard couldn't let himself out. Then Seven bounded up the stairs ahead of everyone to get his clothes and hastily put his pants on.

"I'll check the garage for guards and meet you at the vehicle," Lada said. She teleported out of there. The rest of the group went up the stairs with Elena and maneuvered back through the palace the way they'd come, with The Librarian waving them past as she continued handling the staff.

Cabot led the way back to the SUV. The Librarian made one last pass through the palace, ensuring all the employees who had awakened had their memories wiped and were back in their rooms. She disposed of the broken vase, locked the door to the dungeon, and turned the alarm system back on.

They piled into the SUV and stayed low as The Librarian, cool and collected as ever, waved to the guards inside the station.

The gate closed behind them, and she continued over the speed bumps to the street.

Finally they could sit up. "We did it!" Lada shouted, pumping her fists in the air. The others cheered, and The Librarian wore a satisfied smile as she drove. When they were safely far from the palace, she pulled over and invited Birdie to crawl over the seat and sit in the front. "That might help with the car-sickness," she said.

Lada explained a few things to Elena about the events that led to her rescue. But Birdie turned around in her seat and caught Brix's eye. They exchanged a troubled glance. "Wait until we get to where we're going," Birdie whispered to him, and he nodded. The news they had for their mother weighed heavily on Birdie's heart. She turned a brave face toward her mom and drank her in. She had gray at her temples now, and new wrinkles Birdie didn't remember. Her skin was pasty from lack of sunshine, but she was the most beautiful sight Birdie had seen in a long time. "I can't believe you're here," she said, eyes shining. "We almost gave up. But Lada and The Librarian made it happen."

The Librarian drove into a dingy parking garage beneath a tall apartment building. She let everybody out by the elevator and gave Lada a key. "Go into my flat and stay there. Don't let anyone in except me. I've got to return the SUV before the police realize it's gone."

Seven's eyes widened behind his sunglasses as he checked

that his scarf was in place. "Shall I take the wheelchair in?" he asked Lada, pausing at the vehicle's rear door.

"I think I'll use it now," Lada said. "Do you mind giving me a hand? My muscles are taxed and overstimulated. Sometimes they have a mind of their own." Seven retrieved it, and Lada showed him how to properly unfold it, lock the wheels, and place the seat cushion. She stowed her crutches in a bag that hung between the handles, then maneuvered into the wheelchair and asked Seven if he would wheel her to the entrance.

Once inside the building, Lada guided everyone into the elevator. She typed a numeric code, and the door closed. Brix, Birdie, and Elena clung together as the elevator zoomed up. Tenner explained what he knew about elevators to Cabot and Seven as the first-timers cringed and gripped the handrails. Finally the door slid open. Lada cautioned the others to wait as she rolled forward and peered out.

"Stay close," she said, and ventured into the vacant hallway. They passed a few doors and stopped. Lada inserted the key and opened the door, then went inside and invited the others to follow.

Birdie half expected the place to be grand and lush—she could picture the cool librarian with her brightly colored dresses living in luxury. But the place was almost bare—only a scratched wooden table with three chairs, a sofa that had seen better days, and stacks of books lining the walls beneath the window ledges.

Lada pointed out the bathroom and kitchen to the guests. "Please make yourselves at home." After everyone took a few moments to refresh themselves and return to the living spaces, Birdie and Brix sat down with their mother between them on the sofa. Lada moved into the room, and the others took the chairs from around the table and brought them over. Seven gave Birdie's shoulder a squeeze as he went past. He knew what was coming. She flashed him a grateful look.

"There's something sad we have to tell you," Birdie said to her mom.

Elena leaned back into the sofa, her expression turning immediately serious. "Is it something about . . . Louis? I've been wondering why he's not with you. And afraid to ask."

Birdie nodded. With a shaking hand, she opened her backpack and pulled out the map, unsure of how to explain everything to her mother.

But Brix couldn't hold it in any longer. "Dad died," he said. And then he burst into tears and buried his face in his mother's shoulder.

"What?" Elena whispered. "How?" She held Brix as her eyes desperately sought her elder child's, looking for confirmation.

"He got sick a few months ago," Birdie said, "and it got worse fast. A lot of coughing. Trouble breathing." Her throat threatened to close, but she pushed through it. "He died . . . not long ago." Had it only been last week? A million things had happened since then.

Tears poured down Elena's face, and she leaned forward, covering her eyes with her hands and sobbing.

Birdie stared at her mother, reliving the death through her. She clutched her shirt as if she could reach her heart through it to hold it together. When her mother's sobs subsided, she went on. "Dad's last request was for me to find you and give you this map." She held it out. "He confessed in a letter to me that he secretly moved the stash before you all went to the hideout. And he wanted to make sure you—and the other parents," she added, glancing at Cabot, "could find it."

Lada wheeled into the kitchen to get a box of tissues, then returned and handed it to Elena.

"I didn't expect this," Elena said, taking a few and blowing her nose.

"He also wanted me to tell you that . . ." Birdie's voice broke. She sniffed hard, took a tissue, and went on. "That he took care of us the best he could."

"It's true," Tenner said fervently. "He did."

Seven nodded. He removed his sunglasses and folded them in his lap. "We loved him."

"He taught us how to live on our own," Cabot said. Her eyes shone. She got up and perched next to Brix, on the arm of the sofa. "Without him, I don't think we could have made it."

Lada sniffed. She removed her glasses and wiped her eyes. As Elena Golden absorbed the shock, Cabot, Seven, and Brix exchanged a glance. The sad news wasn't over.

They filled her in on the discovery of Troy's death.

Elena Golden dried her eyes and went to Tenner. "How devastating," she said. He opened his arms for a hug, and she held him tight, patting his back as he cried and clung to her. "We've all been through so much," she said. "I don't know how you kids have done everything you did. You are all very brave."

Then they told her about the other bones they'd found, and how Cabot had thought the other set had belonged to her mother, but the newspapers and The Librarian had said otherwise.

Elena turned to Cabot. "Your parents made it to Estero with me. Those bones belong to someone else."

Cabot pressed her lips together and looked at the floor. "The Librarian told me my parents are working for the president."

Elena grimaced. "Oh, dear child," she said. "I'm sorry. I'll tell you everything I know."

Just then The Librarian returned. Lada quickly filled her in on the deaths, and The Librarian expressed her sincere condolences.

Cabot hovered near Elena, anxious for news, for any clue about what happened to her parents. Were they still in Estero?

Elena had a story to tell.

MORE NEWS

After a quick break, Elena returned to her spot on the sofa with Birdie, Brix, and Cabot on the arm. She launched into what had happened since they last saw her. "Jack, Greta, and I were captured in the village outside of Estero as we were picking up supplies. When we went to pay, we discovered our cash was no longer legal, and people in the store seized us."

Birdie and Tenner nodded emphatically.

Elena went on. "I think we would have been fine if Fuerte hadn't changed the currency. He definitely got us with that one. The three of us were taken into police custody and brought to the Estero PD and jail overnight. Then we were transferred to the penitentiary. A few days later, the three of us were inexplicably taken to the Palacio de Magdalia in handcuffs and ankle chains. We didn't know what was happening.

"Then the president showed up, and his guards took over and sent the police away. Fuerte offered to set us free. Obviously it wasn't out of the goodness of his heart—he went on to say we'd have to wear a tracking device so we couldn't leave the country unless we were with him. In exchange for our freedom, we'd help him . . ." She took a breath and blew it out through pursed lips. "We'd help him steal precious artifacts from other countries and meet other supernatural people along the way."

The Librarian, making tea in the kitchen behind them, paused in her pouring. "Meet other supernatural people?" she asked, glancing over. "For what purpose?"

"He wouldn't say," said Elena. "But we thought it was an odd thing to say for someone who'd been against supernatural people his whole life. He went on to tell us he would let us keep a share of the money, and we could move about the city as we pleased whenever we weren't out on a mission with him.

"It was tempting, but I was resolved not to steal again. Not to work with the man who'd helped make our lives miserable. He was slimy, and I was certain he was going to profit off our work. I couldn't do it."

The Librarian brought her a cup of tea, and she took a sip. "Fuerte kept Jack, Greta, and me in the palace dungeon and just . . . wore us down. I thought the three of us were solid in our plan to hold out. But one day I woke up and Jack and Greta were gone."

She paused and glanced worriedly at Cabot. "If your parents took the deal, I wouldn't blame them. Maybe they wanted to earn enough money to escape with. Not even your mother would ever have been able to work in a hospital again—not anywhere.

She was a wanted criminal. So I . . . I don't blame them for giving in to the pressure if that's what happened."

Cabot closed her eyes. Shame and embarrassment and anger and sadness all rolled up into a ball in her throat. "You'd think they would have made enough by now to come back if that was the plan," she said. Nothing about it seemed right.

"It could be the ankle tethers that have kept them from going home to you," Elena said gently. "Plus, none of us would *ever* lead Fuerte to where our children were hiding—not even Troy was that heartless. I know Greta and Jack were sick with worry about you when we were captured."

"I don't get it," Cabot said. The glob in her throat wouldn't go away. She felt terrible that she'd believed in her parents so stoically all this time. Clearly Cabot wasn't their only priority. And no matter how smart she was, she had never calculated *this* result.

The Librarian sat down in the chair Cabot had vacated. "Do you know who else is working with the president?"

Elena shook her head. "I haven't heard anything since the Stones left the palace prison. The guards kept quiet and stuck to their computers and texting, and rarely engaged with me except to bring me meals, no matter how hard I tried. They wouldn't give me a newspaper, and they kept their screens pointed away and muted—the ones on their desks, and the ones attached to the ceiling."

"Mom," said Birdie, leaning earnestly toward her, "did you

know that Troy and Lucy and Seven's parents all went to look for you, Jack, and Greta when you didn't come back?"

"I had no idea until you kids told me about the bones and the backpack you found," Elena said. "Our paths never crossed. I haven't seen them or heard a word about them. How do you know so much about it?"

Tenner looked up. His eyes were still red-rimmed from crying. "I read a lot of articles," he said.

"I can attest to that," The Librarian said with a wry grin.

"Sorry," said Tenner sheepishly. "Anyway, one of them said that someone at the airport saw a person with the president on one of his late-night trips. The man disappeared into thin air—like, he went invisible. Birdie and I wondered if it was Martim." He flashed a pitying glance at Seven, and then realized he'd just done what he'd told Birdie to stop doing. His expression changed into a small smile.

"I wouldn't be surprised if it was him," Seven said dully. He'd unwrapped the scarf from his face by now, and it hung around his neck. His face blended with a plant in the corner behind him. He hadn't wavered on this opinion since he'd first heard about it last night. He wished they could go home and deal with all of these new losses and hurts there. In private. He glanced at Cabot. Her face was distraught. The girl was as tough as nails . . . but he could tell she wasn't satisfied with what she'd been told about her parents.

It was getting late, but The Librarian circled back on

something. "It's curious how Fuerte suggested you would meet other supernatural people. That's new information to me. Is he coercing them, too? There's been a range of heists across the continent, and countries are suffering economically because of the thefts. The newspapers are just starting to report the story here in Estero—I think Fuerte may have tried to keep it quiet."

She hesitated and glanced around the room. "Lada and I have been working together . . . alone . . . to uncover what's going on. Then Tenner and Birdie showed up in my library, and I noticed Tenner's eyes." She leaned forward earnestly. "There's no way Lada and I could fight the president and his group of supers on our own. Just like we couldn't have rescued Elena without your help. And I look around this room tonight with a tiny bit of hope as I count eight of us."

Birdie slid her hand into her mother's. What was The Librarian saying?

The woman smoothed her dress as she thought about how to phrase her next statement, then she looked up. "That's why we need your help to stop President Fuerte and whoever his team is. And then once we've stopped them, enact change—here and everywhere."

She paused, then plowed forward. "Supernatural people need to be respected members of society. They need jobs. They shouldn't be punished for their gifts—they should be valued. I think it's possible! But Lada and I can't do it alone." She turned her appeal on Elena. "You understand what I'm saying, don't you? You've lived through this."

Elena closed her eyes and sighed. "I once thought the same way," she said. "But nothing changed before we left Estero, and it hasn't changed since. I'm not convinced we can make a difference." She shifted on the sofa, then shook her head. "I want to go back to our hideout. Take care of my children. Mourn my husband. And be there for these kids." She turned to face The Librarian. "I'm sorry. I understand your desire to make things better. But I don't think we can help you. It seems like an impossible task."

The Librarian sat rigid on her chair, but her face softened. "Yet I feel we have no choice. This goes beyond my own desire to live a secret, quiet life undercover. I can't ignore the unrest President Fuerte is causing here for people like us. What will become of us if we don't do something now, before it's too late?"

Birdie looked at Cabot, who'd been mostly staring at the floor all this time. Tenner wore a hardened expression. Brix slumped into the sofa next to his mother, exhausted and not quite understanding what was going on, but feeling The Librarian's plea deep inside him, making him want to do anything for her because she'd brought his mom back to him.

Elena closed her eyes. "I don't know what else to say."

Lada dropped her gaze. Then she looked up. "Then at least give us your stash," she said brazenly. "Money will help us figure out how to do it on our own, and we're broke. Every extra cent

The Librarian has goes into this fight." She swallowed hard. "I'm thirteen years old, and I have a lot of life in front of me. I'm not going to give up and live in fear." She lifted her chin defiantly. "Please. I'm begging. You don't need the money if you're going back to your hideout."

Elena and The Librarian looked at the girl. Then Cabot slipped off the sofa arm and went to fetch her backpack. "I'm staying," she announced. "I'm going to find my parents and knock some sense into them. I know I don't have any supernatural ability, but I can help you in my own way." She knelt between Lada's wheelchair and The Librarian's chair, and opened her backpack, then fished the pouch of diamonds out. "Finders keepers," she said lightly, daring anyone to stop her. "This will help." She handed the pouch to The Librarian. "It's a bag of diamonds."

Lada and The Librarian exchanged a shocked glance. "Thank you, Cabot," Lada said. "That helps a *lot*."

Brix stared at Cabot. She was very brave. He wanted to stay with her. But he couldn't leave his mother—not now. He looked at Birdie, pleading with his eyes for her to step up. But Birdie wanted to be with their mother. To get to know her again. She reached into her backpack for her dad's cash. "It's not much, but it'll help if you leave the country," she said, handing the old currency over to Lada.

"I don't have anything to give you," Tenner said, "but I'm

staying, too." He slid his chair next to The Librarian. "If my mother is working with *them*, I want to stop her."

Seven muttered an oath under his breath. He of all people didn't want to be here. His life was in the most danger. But his father was one of the bad guys. Didn't he have an obligation to try to stop him? "Okay," he said with a pained sigh. "I'm staying, too."

"What?" said Birdie, incredulous. "Seven?" Life at the hideout would be horrible with half of them not there. And her heart was splitting. She wanted to be with her mother, but she also wanted her mother to be here and willing to help.

Lada's face brightened even more.

Birdie tried to catch Seven's eye, but his face turned to the floor—he knew what she was doing. She didn't want to be anywhere without him again—or Tenner, she realized. The two of them had learned to appreciate each other in a new way, and they'd made a great team on this journey.

"Hang on a second," Birdie said, trying to figure out how to convince her mother to stay. "Mom, we have to at least be here long enough to find the stash and divvy it up. But not to the parents, who are all on the wrong side of things. To the kids, so they can fight for justice. Okay?" The last words she uttered felt like daggers. Would Birdie be okay with the others fighting for justice without her? "And," she added, "don't rule anything out."

"Come on, Mom," Brix said. "We're all tired like you. And we've been through a lot."

"You haven't been through prison for three years," Elena said wearily. "And a fugitive before that. And shunned since I was ten years old." She shook her head. "How exactly would you have me see the world, kids?"

Birdie turned on the sofa and looked at her mother. "You should see it through your children's eyes," she said softly. "With hope."

There was silence in the room. Birdie and Brix held their breath. Elena Golden looked from one hideaway child to the next around the room. Then she let out a long sigh and covered her eyes, then let her hands drop into her lap. "All right. You got me, kid. I can't argue with that."

"So we'll find the stash and *stay*?" asked Brix. He hopped off the sofa and bounced.

"It's looking that way," said Elena.

The room erupted. Everyone was staying, and they'd have money to go after the bad guys, too.

"Game on!" cried Lada, fists pumping the air. She and The Librarian slapped hands. For once, things were going their way.

When the cheering died down, Elena held out her hand to Birdie. "Now let me have a look at this map so I can figure out where the stash is."

"Watch out," Brix warned. "It's got a fire charm!"

"Of course it does," said Elena, a melancholy smile playing at her lips. She held it away from her face and opened it carefully. When the flames died down, she studied it with a nostalgic look on her face. She'd been in Estero since her capture, but she hadn't been out of custody. She'd barely glimpsed the city she'd once known by heart. It was sweet to see the markings on the map, and she realized immediately that most of them were the special places she and Louis used to visit together—the coffee shop that had the best chai. The museum they'd looted. The bank they'd robbed. The hospital where they'd made their big escape. Louis had left her a final gift with this map as well as the secret to the stash's location.

But then her eyes landed on the fiery bag of gold that marked the new hiding place, and her demeanor changed. She let out a long, helpless laugh, and then her head fell back on the sofa cushion. "Louis Golden, you dirty dog," she muttered, tossing the map in the air in disgust. It rolled up and extinguished before it landed. "You hid the stash *there*?" She looked up at the others gathered around, then laughed again. "I think I'm going to need a little help."

Birdie, Seven, Tenner, Cabot, and Brix exchanged a knowing look. "Good thing Louis prepared us for just about anything," Seven said quietly. They could almost see his smile.

ACKNOWLEDGMENTS

HUGE THANKS TO my superhero team: Ari Lewin, Elise LeMassena, Jennifer Klonsky, all the copyeditors, proofreaders, marketers, publicity pros, sales team, tech team, artists and designers, education and library pros, audiobook makers, and the GAOAT (Greatest Agent Of All Time), Michael Bourret. I'm so grateful to all for the amazing suggestions and help you gave me when we were putting this book together.

I'm also grateful for my niece, Lily, who helped me brainstorm the pitch for this book during the early days of Covid-19, and for my nephew, Jack, who gave me the idea to have Cabot strive for ambidexterity in all things because he did it himself. I miss you and love you and hope to see you both soon.

A special thank-you to Stacy McNeely, who came into my life as a teen when I was a young bookseller . . . and then became my employee a few years later when I was the bookstore manager. I'm so grateful for your wisdom and help in writing the character of Lada, who looks uncannily like you did when you were thirteen and coming into my bookstore looking for Sweet

Valley High books. (Sorry—I had to tell the world.) I'm so glad we stayed friends!

And big thanks to my husband, Matt McMann, who read and edited the drafts of this book at least three times. (He's telling me from across the room that it was *four* times, so.) I'm really sorry, my dear buddy, and I can't wait for *your* books to come out, which I promise to read four times each! That's right, y'all, keep an eye out—they'll be on the shelf next to mine starting in 2023. ☺

I want to thank all the parents, teachers, librarians, and booksellers who continue to strive to find just the right books for kids that will whet their appetites for reading. I can't tell you how many times kids write to me to say someone like you put a book into their hands and they fell in love. You are powerful, and you use your powers for good. And you readers—well, you're my favorite. You keep me going . . . but if you follow me on social media (@lisa_mcmann), you already know that. Thank you for your unwavering support of me and my books. You're the best.

I can't wait for you to read book two.

LISA McMANN is the *New York Times* and *USA Today* bestselling author of dozens of books, including The Unwanteds series, the Wake trilogy, and her most recent novel, *Clarice the Brave*. She is married to fellow writer Matt McMann, and they have two adult children—their son is artist Kilian McMann and their daughter is actor Kennedy McMann. Lisa spends most of her time in Arizona, California, and Vancouver, British Columbia, and loves to cook, read, and watch reality TV.